Something to declare

Guy Anders

Copyright © 2024 Guy Anders

All rights reserved. No part of this book may be reproduced or used in any manner without written permission of the copyright owner except for the use of quotations in a book review. For more information, address: guyanders.com

First paperback edition July 2024

www.guyanders.com

Prologue

Somewhere outside Moscow – 1965
The car bumped over the rough ground jerking him back to consciousness. He strained to open his eyes that were now bruised and swollen, but he couldn't see anything. The car lurched again over the uneven ground and his body hit something hard in the confined space, he felt a stabbing pain in his abdomen like a red-hot poker. Cracked rib? He had pain all over his body, but the pain in his right knee from one of the `many baseball bat strikes was the most acute. He was sure his left leg was also broken. He started to drift into unconsciousness again, but abruptly the car stopped, bringing him back. He had little doubt he was going to die, he just hoped it would be quick.

The boot lid popped open, the fresh air a relief but the brief sight he had of the starry night sky was blocked now by two of his assailants. He screamed in pain as they dragged him roughly upright and propped against the back of the car in between their strong arms. If they let him go he would not have been able to stand unaided, such was the damage they had previously inflicted. They were at the cement works where he had a job as a cement truck driver. His dread increased.

'Look at me Grigory,' a voice commanded.

He lifted his head slowly and painfully; through his swollen eyes he was now facing the man who had started all this torment. He knew who he was of course – the teenage son of his previous employer.

'It wasn't my fault,' he pleaded. 'He just stepped out in front of me, I didn't see him until it was too late.'

He was almost sobbing now, but he could see his words were having no effect on his attacker who just stood there mockingly.

'My father was crippled because you ran him over, and you are to blame Grigory,' he said. 'Can you imagine what it was like for a man like him to be disabled. He couldn't bear it and that is why after three weeks he ended it and shot himself. Now you are going to suffer like him. You will know what it is like to be a cripple. But don't worry, you won't have to stay crippled for as long as he did.'

One

September 1990

It was a brown Vauxhall Cavalier with British plates, male driver and male passenger. As it passed through the car hall entrance doors and headed for Will's bay, he felt a familiar tingle in the back of his neck. A distance of twenty yards. Ten seconds to reach his position.

Will had been on shift since 3pm and the cars had been non-stop for an hour. Mainly British holiday-makers and day-trippers, with a few foreign cars thrown in for variety. It was going to be a busy Saturday. He had already stopped a few that were of mild interest, but after a brief chat had sent them on their way. He was patient. He knew from experience which vehicles would be worth a closer inspection, but nothing so far had moved him.

Ten seconds is a long time to maintain interest. A long time to make an assessment you would think. But Will generally made his assessment in under two. This wasn't bragging, it was just the nature of his world. Every day he saw every type of behaviour. Sometimes he noticed obvious signs – a nervous look, avoiding eye-contact, over-confidence. All normal behaviour perhaps as people passed through Customs. Other times he just had a hunch. So what was it about the Vauxhall Cavalier that had stirred him?

Friends and family often asked Will what made him stop particular passengers. He found it hard to explain. He didn't subscribe to the theory that this was some sort of sixth sense, he just put it down to years of people-watching experience. With hundreds of passengers passing by him daily, a pulse seemed to trigger in his brain if what he was seeing was 'out of kilter'.

In this case, he decided, it was the mismatch between the car and the passengers. The driver and passenger simply did not suit the car. They were both in their mid-twenties, casually dressed and driving a new Vauxhall Cavalier. A look at their passports identified them as Michael Wright and John Reynolds, both from Liverpool. He could imagine these two in a sporty Ford Escort or VW Golf, but a car like a Vauxhall Cavalier? Too boring and middle-class. He knew that this apparent logic was 'poo-pooed' by his friends and family, but he was often right.

One day whilst at the supermarket car park with his girlfriend, Alison, he got her to try to guess the cars that certain shoppers were heading for.

'See that old lady dragging her shopping basket,' he pointed to a lady in her seventies. She was slowly walking towards a group of six cars. 'Which car do you think belongs to her?'

Alison looked at the potential targets. There were a two Ford Escorts, a rusty Land Rover, a BMW, a new looking Nissan Micra, and an old slightly dented Renault 5.

'I don't think she would drive a BMW or a Land Rover,' she said, 'and I can't imagine her in a Ford Escort, so it is either the Micra or the Renault. She doesn't look like she could afford a new car, so I am guessing the Renault 5.'

'That's a good process of deduction,' he commended, 'let's see if you are right.'

'As a Policewoman I hope I have developed a few deductive skills,' she replied with a hint of sarcasm.

They sat there waiting in anticipation and then Alison let out a whoop. The old lady had stopped behind the Renault and lifted the boot.

This was perhaps an easy illustration of the powers of observation, but Alison was impressed, nonetheless.

Michael and John said that the car did not belong to them and was hired, so Will had been right about them not being suited to the car. However, he also knew that hire cars were commonly used by smugglers, possibly to make them appear smarter in appearance or avoid their own car seized if their drug smuggling attempt failed. Whatever the reason, having now stopped them, he just had 'that feeling'. He knew that these two were hiding something.

Finding watches rather than drugs made him feel cheated. Five very expensive looking watches were concealed in a sports sock behind the car radio. Although he didn't know for sure the value of the watches, it was clear that quite a bit of tax had been avoided. This required a formal investigation and interviews with Michael and John. However, the unusual feature of these watches were the Swiss price tags on each one. It quickly became clear that they were stolen.

Michael and John both denied knowing about the watches of course. Even denied travelling to Switzerland. The fact that they were stolen was immaterial. Customs did not have the remit to investigate theft, but did have the remit to investigate avoidance of revenue.

It wasn't the first time for Will that a good concealment had not got the expected result. Sometimes the concealments were sophisticated, but empty. Other times the passengers had hidden things that did not have tax on them. He got excited once when he found lots of packages of a brown powder, only to discover it was coffee. Apparently the passenger thought it was illegal.

But he was required to follow-up on the watches and now he had the drag of an investigation that didn't motivate him. And more importantly, taking him off the floor where he could be hunting for more interesting results.

However, after a few months he did perk up a bit. The watches were a make called 'Vacheron', each with a unique serial number. He discovered that they were worth over £30,000 which meant tax evaded of about £5000. A call to Interpol confirmed they had been reported stolen. The location of the theft was from a display case in a hotel in Lucerne.

Despite the lads insisting that they had only visited France, evidence against them was growing. Will had found two rolls of film in their luggage. When the films were developed, several pictures showed scenes of what appeared to be Switzerland. This was enough for the solicitor to proceed the prosecution case and for Will to gain the rare opportunity of a trip to Switzerland.

Two

It was just after 11am when his flight was called and Will made his way up the steps of the SwissAir Airbus 320 jet, and settled into his allocated seat near the front on the plane. Will had only ever flown before on holidays, so it was strange for him to be sharing the plane with just businessmen. The plane was only two-thirds full, but at least half of the passengers were dressed in long black coats and sporting long beards. The snippets of conversation Will overheard suggested they were from London's Jewish jeweller community. Will was seated in a comfortable window seat. The seat next to him was vacant. *That's good he thought, I don't really want to chat with a stranger right now. I have a lot on my mind, and I am far from comfortable.*

As the Airbus taxied towards the runway Will considered the official task before him.

All fairly straightforward. He had to collect some witness statements from the police who investigated the theft; then work with the Swiss police to see if he could locate the places in the photos that showed Michael and John enjoying the sunshine in what looked like Switzerland. The photographs from the films he had had developed seemed to suggest that Michael and John had spent time at some lido's, probably in Zurich. They had denied ever going to Switzerland, or knowing anything about the watches, so it was up to Will to prove that they had been there, to show they had lied. He already possessed some circumstantial evidence; Michael had a Swiss franc note in his pocket when he was searched, despite being adamant he had only been to Paris. But it would be great to have some actual proof that would put them somewhere close to the scene of the crime. He remembered with a smile the interview with Michael and the typical Liverpool dry humour of this guy.

'Why have you got a Swiss Franc note in your pocket if you have only been to France,' Will had asked.

Quick as a flash Michael had responded, 'Well, I went to the Bureau de Change in Paris. I asked for francs and they gave me these!'

But his official task was the easy bit.

As the Airbus accelerated hard down the runway he got that mild flutter in his stomach as it lifted-off. He watched the ground get smaller through the porthole before it was quickly engulfed by cloud. He sat back and closed his eyes. In his head he re-ran the events from yesterday. The conversation that changed everything.

The Assistant Collector, Mr Smythe, had summoned Will to his office. He had been in charge of Eastern Docks in Dover for a couple of years and was based in Burlington House, the main Dover Customs building, rather than at the docks. Will had met him a couple of times, once when he had carried out an inspection at the docks, and once when he had opened the Drugs Identification course he had attended last year. Mr

Smythe was quite pompous and didn't seem to understand much about drug trafficking, or what the Officers did. But he always took the time to greet the Officers and pass the time of day with them. To Will's knowledge he had not caused the Senior Officers at the docks any grief. Will had heard that his last role was as Head of a VAT Office in Surrey, so no surprise perhaps that the uniform Customs Officer role appeared a little alien to him. Will assessed he was heading for retirement, so maybe he did not want to rock the boat too much with a pension looming?

Will had no idea why he had been summoned. It was a bit like being called to see the Headmaster, but he couldn't think of anything he had done wrong, so he was fairly chilled.

Mr Smythe introduced Will to a 'sharp-dressed man' in his early forties who didn't give a name. He simply advised that he was a Government Security Officer.

Will shook his hand. It was cool, smooth and firm. *Someone who knows what he wants and always gets it.*

With pleasantries out of the way they all sat. Mr Smythe got swiftly to the point.

'We have a job for you whilst you are in Switzerland' he said. 'I have agreed with, er, other parties, that you will work for, er, other parties, to assist them in the task.'

This was not exactly filling him with confidence, but he didn't show any reaction yet. *Let's see what he has to say.*

In the event, he didn't say anything, it was 'sharp-dressed man' who spoke next. He stood up, straightened his tie and checked the crease of his tailored trousers. *A ladies man for sure.*

He walked towards the window, before swivelling around like an actor about to deliver his first important lines.

'We have a live operation in progress in Lucerne,' he announced. 'For a variety of reasons that you don't need to know about, your expertise is needed to assist in, shall we say, moving this operation to the next stage.'

Will couldn't help but react to hearing this and leaned forward in his seat slightly to make sure he didn't miss the next words. He had to catch himself before his mouth dropped open in surprise. This was serious stuff, even without any detail yet. He was chuffed to be asked to help, but he was far from feeling comfortable. Whatever this was it was big, way outside of Will's comfort zone.

'What I am about to tell you' he had said, 'must not be shared with anyone else, not your colleagues, not your boss, not your girlfriend, nobody. I mean nobody!' He was staring hard at Will and Will stared intently back, holding the stare. After a few seconds sharp-dressed man seemed satisfied that he had got the message across. He relaxed and sat back down into his chair. Will stayed sat bolt upright, but now the staring game had finished, he relaxed slightly. It was then that he noticed that Mr Smythe had silently left the room. Clearly he came into the category of 'nobody' as well.

Sharp-dressed man continued 'We are tracking a major organised crime gang involved in, amongst other things, arms smuggling.'

'Who is we?' Will interrupted.

Sharp-dressed man sighed a little, as if he was being asked to explain patiently to a child why they couldn't play in the road.

'You don't need to know that, at least not right now. But let us just say that I represent an organisation that has our countries' security at its heart.'

Will noticed that he spoke as well as he dressed. You don't get a plum voice like that from being educated at the local secondary school, he thought, like him and most people he knew. No, this guy was a high-flyer, possibly Eton, almost certainly Oxford or Cambridge. He was 'no slouch', as one of Will's old bosses used to say. If he were to guess he would have said MI6, but at this point it didn't really matter – what mattered was what he wanted from him.

'What we want from you is to meet with one of the gang and gain their confidence,' he said.

Will could not stop his jaw dropping this time.

Sharp dressed man ignored Will's reaction and continued. 'His name is Elias Michaels, and he is one of the gangs transport organisers, a small fish in the scheme of things. He lives and works in Lucerne and runs a legitimate transport business, but many of his loads are now funded by the criminal gang. We believe the loads contain illicit goods – namely arms and ammunition.'

Three

'Would you like tea or coffee?' the stewardess said with a smile, shaking Will's thoughts back to the present.

'Coffee please.' He smiled back, although his smile felt as false as hers.

The flight was less than two hours and landed on schedule at just after 2pm Swiss time. He collected his black holdall from the carousel and headed for the Green Channel.

He followed the signs towards the train station – thankfully signs were in English as well as Swiss. Speakers announcing flight information echoed around the vast high ceiling. He didn't understand most words, but suspected it would still be unintelligible even if they were English. Some things were the same the world over, he thought.

The flood of arriving passengers dispersed in a variety of different directions, some heading the same way as Will. The Jewish jewellers seemed to know where they were going as they drifted off towards a host of waiting taxis, or towards persons holding up hand-written name boards.

He spotted the train ticket desk near a newspaper stand and headed over to purchase a single ticket to Lucerne. The English-speaking clerk directed him to the correct platform and advised him what time the train would leave. 'The journey will be one hour and two minutes,' the clerk said in perfect English, 'and the train will leave in sixteen minutes.' Will smiled to himself at the exactitudes.

The train to Lucerne was very clean, about half full of tourists, and very roomy and comfortable. Will took his seat opposite a middle-aged couple who were studying a guidebook. They were talking to each other in what appeared to Will to be German. He had heard plenty of German speakers during his time in the Customs halls, but this sounded slightly different, perhaps it was the accent. Swiss he guessed. They nodded at him as he sat down, but then continued with their travel plans. Will wasn't in the mood to socialise. Instead he opened his briefcase and grabbed the sheet of paper that held details of his arrangements for meeting his police contact, Jan. He had already memorised the arrangements, so knew Jan would be meeting him at Lucerne station.

He didn't want to make further eye-contact with his fellow travellers. As an only child he had grown up seeking friends so had no problem striking-up a conversation with strangers. In normal circumstances he would have tried to engage with them, but this was not normal circumstances. If he engaged in conversation, what would he say? Would he mention that he was a British Customs Officer? Or would he say he was a Freight Forwarder on business? Or pretend to be a tourist, or someone else? Every situation he was about to face on this mission might require a different approach, a different story. He needed to be constantly ready to adapt and tell lies convincingly. *Was he up to this?*

He was distracted from these thoughts by the train announcement in Swiss. He guessed the train was about to leave. He was fascinated to note that, as the second-hand on the big station clock clicked to the top, the train gave a mild lurch as it started to move off. *Like clockwork.*

In a few short minutes the city had been left behind as the train smoothly gathered speed on its way to Lucerne. The scenery was stunning. They sped along the edge of a lake and Will could see snow-capped mountains in the distance. He noticed the middle-aged couple were equally captivated by the view.

To avoid any chance of conversation he pulled a slim file from his briefcase and re-read the notes that sharp-dressed man had provided. They were marked 'Confidential'; he had been left in no doubt what would happen if he mis-placed them. It had been explained very clearly to him what his role was, and why he had been chosen for this mission. The file gave him the background and details.

Elias Michaels had been dealing with a Freight Forwarder in Dover, a man called George Reeves. He was ensuring that the paperwork for the lorries was perfect, even if the loads were not. This had ensured the lowest possible risk of the lorry being considered as suspicious and being pulled out for a search by Customs. The Customs Freight team had a risk system in place to help detect illicit loads. This system profiled certain goods from certain countries. No doubt George had worked out which loads would be very unlikely to be searched as a result. For example, loads from Switzerland tended to be low risk. It wasn't fool proof as there were always random checks, but so far George had managed to make it work. The other key factor was making sure the paperwork was accurate, as any mistakes would result in greater scrutiny. And if the load did get searched, it was also about hiding the contraband effectively.

A big problem for the criminal gang was that this particular Freight Forwarder was now doing time 'at her majesty's pleasure' for something completely different. Apparently he had got into an argument with his neighbour. Following an alcohol fuelled night in the pub he had decided to teach his neighbour a lesson and set fire to his neighbours car. Unfortunately, the fire got out of control, nearly burning his neighbours house down. Ironically it also severely damaged his own. He would be out of action for a couple of years, so Elias was keen to find a replacement Freight Forwarder. For the purposes of the meeting Will was to be that replacement. Somehow they had convinced Elias that he could be trusted. The reason they had chosen Will for this job was now clear – in a previous role as a Customs Officer he had worked in Import and Export Freight. He understood the paperwork and how Freight Forwarders worked, at least broadly.

'As far as Elias is concerned you are Bill Mitchell from Brighthouse Forwarders Limited' sharp dressed man had said. 'You come recommended by George Reeves, so Elias will have no reason not to trust you. We gave him an incentive to vouch for you,' he said.

He said 'incentive' with emphasis, and Will could imagine that they had done some sort of deal with him to reduce his sentence in prison.

Sharp dressed man continued. 'You only have to reassure Elias that you can arrange the correct paperwork and assist the clearance without risk of search by Customs.'

Would it really be as easy as he was painting it?

'Don't worry, you will be in and out in no time,' he had said as if reading his thoughts, 'All you need to do is find out the date and time of the shipment – plus, of course, the lorry registration number. Everything you need to know is in this file.'

At the time he accepted this task it had seemed fairly easy; a quick meeting with Elias to get the lorry details, then leave so he could pass the information on to the Swiss contact that had been arranged. But now as the train was only a few minutes from Lucerne station he felt a sense of panic. There were a hundred things that could go wrong. The gravity of the task was overwhelming him. He was worried that he would seriously mess up. Strangely, the thought of meeting with Elias did not bother him much. Elias was a criminal for sure, but by all accounts not a nasty one. He had met some nasty types in his time (and put a few behind bars), so he wasn't fazed by this. Elias was only there to give him information after all, so it should be easy. But his worry was seated in his concern that he might mess it up. Some important people had put trust in him.

The other thing that bothered him was the trust that someone else had in him – Alison. He should have told her.

With his black holdall and briefcase in hand Will disembarked the train and headed towards the exit. Jan was waiting for him on the concourse as he passed through the ticket barrier. Jan was easy to spot as he held up a cardboard sheet with Will's name scrawled across it. He was the Police Detective who had been assigned as his liaison officer whilst in Lucerne. Jan was in his early thirties like Will, but looked a lot fitter. He had a kind clean-shaven face and a pleasant smile. He was casually dressed in jeans and a check-shirt under a herringbone jacket.

They shook hands. 'Pleased to meet you Mr. Mortimer, I am Jan. I hope you had a pleasant trip.' His English was perfect, with a trace of a Germanic accent. 'Sorry that I didn't drive to Zurich to collect you, but the trains are far quicker and more efficient.'

'No problem, and call me Will,' he said, nodding in agreement that the trains were indeed very efficient. 'The journey was very straightforward, thanks.'

He took Will's bag and placed it into the boot of his very sporty-looking Audi. Will held onto the briefcase.

'I'll take you to your hotel and let you book in to rest from your journey. We have plenty of time so I propose that we don't work today. We can start refreshed tomorrow when you'll meet with the detectives who investigated the robbery. If you have no plans this evening I would like to invite you to my apartment to have dinner with me and my wife. She is looking forward to meeting a British Customs Officer and I too would love to hear about your work.'

'That's very kind of you Jan, I would love to come,' he said enthusiastically – anything to take his mind off the tasks in hand, he thought.

The journey from the railway station to the Hotel Romantique, was only five minutes' drive. The views were magnificent. The city sat on both sides of a wide river which shimmered in the bright sun. Small motorboats cruised up and down, burbling motors leaving small wakes behind them.

The hotel was in the centre of the old town and overlooked a square. The buildings in the vicinity could be described as quaint or even fairy-tale, thought Will. He was reminded of an illustrated book he had once read as a young child, something to do with a little Swiss girl. He couldn't remember the name of the book, but he recalled the Swiss scenery and the colourful houses like these.

'What a beautiful city,' Will remarked to Jan.

'Thanks, yes we love it here. We sometimes forget how lucky we are to have such a great place to live.' He opened the Audi's boot and handed Will his holdall. 'I'll collect you this evening at 6.30,'

The hotel was gorgeous. The reception area had high vaulted ceilings, there was dark wood veneer everywhere. Classical paintings adorned all the walls giving the air of a stately home. He had not stayed in many hotels so did not have much to compare, but this was far in excess of anything he had seen before or could have afforded. The allowances for overseas travel were quite generous and the hotel cost £80 per night. This was a far cry from his first ever trip away from home for work when he was only eighteen.

Mrs Turners B&B in Southend was £3 per night which was all his subsistence could afford fifteen years earlier. He was there for two weeks on his Assistant Officer Preventive course and had some great memories of that time. The course had been great, he had learned a lot. But the best memories were of getting drunk with his colleagues and dropping into bed in the early hours. He even managed to pull the barmaid in one of the pubs they frequented, he remembered with a happy sigh.

Part of that course was about maintaining integrity as a public servant; the trainers words of wisdom came back to him, 'When you are dealing with the public, just remember, you are now working for the Queen!'

The room was enormous, with a giant double bed and a bathroom bigger than his lounge at home.

'Thank you Your Majesty for paying for my lovely Swiss room,' he said to himself. He grinned at his reflection in the ornate bathroom mirror - the first real smile he had had for two days. Alison would love this, he thought. He immediately felt guilty. She knew where he was, of course, but he felt guilty for keeping secrets.

Will had met Alison at Dover Police station, when he was charging a 'client' he had arrested, who had smuggled a small amount of cannabis.

The shabbily dressed twenty-year old, carrying a dirty green canvas rucksack, had been on a solo trip to Amsterdam. He had returned with five of grams of cannabis resin hidden in his underpants. Will had stopped him off the early morning ferry from Ostend, Belgium and had immediately noticed some telltale signs that he might be a user. Apart from a slightly glazed look about him, the young man was not a lot different than the other passengers at this time of day. Most had travelled on the scheduled Eurostar bus from Amsterdam to Ostend then the four hour ferry trip overnight to Dover.

But this passenger seemed just a bit more nervous than others so Will stopped him. In his rucksack amongst the dirty laundry was a leaflet for a Coffee-Shop in Amsterdam announcing in English the availability of cannabis cake and cannabis tea – Will had seen many of these in his career. Although he had never been to Amsterdam himself, he was very aware of the liberal drug culture there. This leaflet coupled with some extra-large rizla papers, often used for hand-rolling cannabis cigarettes, was enough to get authority for a strip-search.

Will wasn't looking for a drug-user, this wasn't his motivation. He wanted the smuggler who was carrying larger amounts of drugs. But occasionally a drugs user would get involved in smuggling, so he felt he no choice now to search thoroughly just in case.

When Will booked the young man in at Dover Police station he got chatting with the good-looking WPC who was doing all the paperwork and they simply clicked. That was four months ago, and their relationship grew to the point that Alison spent most of her time staying at Will's house. She still kept her own flat on the other side of Dover to Will's place, but they were now virtually living together. However, neither of them anticipated that the relationship would become serious. They both had history. Neither was keen to commit, at least not yet. Alison had suffered a break-up of a long-term relationship a year previous. Will had suffered something much worse.

Six years ago, Will had been engaged. Although the date for the wedding was set nearly twelve months ahead, his fiancée, Rachel, was planning everything with military precision. Will was more than happy for her to take the lead. He supported and encouraged her in all the right places and agreed with most of her suggestions. Truth be known he would have been quite content with eloping rather than all the fuss, but he loved her dearly and she wanted the big day. If she wanted all the 'bells and confetti' then who was he to argue, when he saw the excitement and joy in her face.

But then his world came crashing down. There was no more joy of excitement for her. Or for him.

When the policeman and policewoman appeared on his doorstep at just before midnight, he knew. He also knew that his life would never be the same again.

He had changed much since her death. Right and wrong remained very clear to him, but he had become painfully aware that sometimes the system simply didn't provide justice to wrongdoers. If the system couldn't provide justice, then he decided it was up to him. Over the last six years he had done some things that needed to be done, some that he wasn't proud of. He had become tougher, maybe meaner, but his moral compass had guided him. Bad people needed to be dealt with and if the law couldn't then he might.

However, one thing hadn't changed. He was loyal to those he cared about. He didn't lie to those important to him. He hadn't lost his principles. So keeping a secret from the woman he was very fond of was wrong to him. Regardless of Clive's warning, he resolved he would tell Alison about this trip when he got home.

It was 4pm in his plush hotel room, so he had a couple of hours to spare. He decided to take out the file and re-read the details for the umpteenth time - he could not afford to get anything wrong. Maybe he would get to meet his contact before the evening with Jan and his wife? He could do with some more information, and not a small amount of reassurance.

Four

Mikhail shuffled his ample frame into the chair behind his large antique desk and pulled out a Cuban cigar from the ornate gold case that was placed within easy reach. The cigar case had been a present from his recently departed Uncle Nico. Nico had been like a father to him over the years and had taught him everything about the business with the expectation that one day, Mikhail would take over. That day had come sooner than either of them had expected; the accident, was simply that – an accident.

Mikhail studied the cigar from all angles, like it was a fine antique, before snipping one end off with a silver cigar cutter and lighting the other end with a gold lighter. He took a gentle draw on the cigar and blew out a satisfying plume of aromatic smoke, whilst staring into space. He recalled that fateful day six months ago.

He was shaken from his reverie as Sergei strode into the room and dropped down onto the leather sofa. Sergei was forty years old, five years younger than him. He was also much slimmer and had Slavic good looks. Sergei was his friend and second in command, but it grated a little on Mikhail that he didn't show him a bit more respect. He might have to start being a bit stricter. So far Sergei had not shown any disrespect to Mikhail in front of the men, so he let it go – for now.

'How are things Sergei,' he asked tiredly. 'Has Elias solved our little problem?'

Sergei stretched himself back into the sofa and rested his head on the back of his hands – the standard 'alpha-male' pose. 'No problem, Mikhail, Elias has found a replacement and he will be briefing him tomorrow. The shipment is still good to go, so don't worry.'

'But I do worry Sergei,' Mikhail said with emphasis. 'This shipment is our guarantee that we can deliver, and it will not go down well with the Irish if we do not. Don't get me wrong, Sergei, I am not worried about the Irish, they do not scare me, I have eaten bigger fish for breakfast. But they could tarnish our reputation, and that is not good for business.'

'You worry too much Mikhail, we can trust Elias won't let us down.'

Mikhail pushed himself to a standing position and strode slowly over to Sergei. He loomed above his friend and bent his head down so that he was inches from his face.

He lowered his voice to almost a whisper so that Sergei had to lean his ear towards Mikhail to hear properly 'Do you know what that little shit did last week? He had the cheek to ask for more money. And do you know what I said?'

Sergei looked Mikhail in the eye and felt a bead of sweat run down his neck. He had known Mikhail a lot of years – he was in Mikhail's gang as kids growing up in Moscow. Sergei knew that when Mikhail got serious it was not the time to protest or interrupt. He also knew that the question was rhetorical and waited patiently for Mikhail to continue, not daring at that point to break eye contact.

'You have a choice my friend, I said to him. You can take the generous cash I give you, my friend, I said. Or you can no longer be my friend.'

Sergei knew only too well what this meant, and he had no doubt Elias also had understood.

Satisfied that Sergei had got the message Mikhail stood up straight and strolled back to his desk, calmer now.

'What do we know about the replacement?' Mikhail enquired.

Sergei sat up a bit, no longer relaxed, but satisfied that Mikhail had calmed.

'Elias says he was recommended by George, the previous Freight Forwarder. According to him, he knows how to get past Customs without checks. George knows this guy from way back apparently and says we are in safe hands.'

'Yes, George,' he pondered thoughtfully, 'Elias hired him, didn't he, because he had had good dealings with him in the past?' Sergei nodded. 'But let me ask you this my friend,' continued Mikhail, 'Why have we been so successful in business? And what was the one thing Nico always drilled into us? Do not trust anyone!' Mikhail spat the last words as single syllables to let his words sink in before continuing.

'I think it might be a good idea for you to meet with this new guy and make your own assessment, yes?'

Sergei did not think this was necessary, but he knew better than to argue. 'OK, Mikhail, good idea. I will meet with this guy and make sure he can be trusted and understands his job.'

After Sergei had left, Mikhail stood for a while and stared out of the window at the lake. The house had been Uncle Nico's property and stood on the banks of Lake Balaton in Hungary. The family had a lot of business interests in Hungary, particularly the prostitution business, and it seemed logical for Mikhail to relocate here. It was nicer than his house on the outskirts of Saint Petersburg and with everything going on in Russia at the moment, he felt better being out of the country. He could keep a better check on his business interests here. Prostitution was one of his favourite business interests, he decided. The prostitutes were better looking and more accommodating than in his home country; especially the imported Romanian girls that made up the bulk of them. He still had some competition from the Arabs, but the prostitution business was now mainly in his hands. Give it another couple of years and the Arabs would be sent packing, but for now they had a business arrangement that suited them both - Mikhail provided the girls and they provided him with a lot of rich Arab customers. Uncle Nico had built up a good business in Hungary and it was a shame he had met his end here, but for Mikhail this was an opportunity to make his Uncle proud. He would take the business to a new level. He had already muscled in on the Latvians and taken over their arms deals with the Irish, which could only enhance his reputation and make him even more rich and powerful.

He poured himself a healthy measure of Brandy (vodka was for peasants he thought) and toasted his departed relative. '*Vechnaya pamyat* Uncle Nico,' he said raising his glass in the air, 'You will always be remembered, and I will make you proud.'

***

The forest was still and mostly quiet as Janos lay resting. A few birds singing and the rustle in the undergrowth of small animals were the only sounds. It was not his fault that the Mercedes had hit the tree, it had been travelling too fast on that country road and not his fault that his ancient Trabant has decided to stutter to a halt on that blind bend. The driver of the Mercedes had done well to avoid the Trabant as he rounded the bend, but lost control and hit the tree instead. The driver and single passenger were probably dead from the crash, but no one had the chance to find out as the car quickly caught fire and bodies became part of the twisted charred remains. Janos had said that it all happened so quickly and there was nothing he could have done, and they probably believed him, but someone had to take the blame. This was family and there had to be retribution.

Janos lay resting in the forest – five-feet under the forest floor.

Five

Jan was very 'Swiss' and arrived at exactly 6.30pm at the front of the hotel. Will had done the decent thing, and had purchased a bottle of wine from a nearby shop. He knew next to nothing about wine, but the label looked good, and it wasn't the cheapest so he hoped it would go down well.

'I hope you're rested from your journey, my wife Zoe and I are looking forward to our evening,' Jan said, as Will climbed into his Audi.

'Yes, thanks,' Will replied. 'I'm looking forward to it too.'

'I have an apology to make,' Jan said, looking a little embarrassed. 'I have to go back to the office for about an hour to deal with a small issue, so if you do not mind I will take you to our apartment and leave you in Zoe's capable hands and you can talk with her whilst she prepares dinner.'

'That's no problem Jan, I fully understand. Our jobs are very similar in this respect, as my girlfriend Alison would tell you if she were here. She is also in the police.' From the short ride to his hotel earlier, Will had learnt from Jan that they had no children, and that Zoe worked in a government role. But that was about it at this stage.

They arrived at Jan's apartment in just five minutes. It was in a very nice suburb (if that is what they call it in Switzerland, he thought). They were greeted at the front of the building by Zoe. She was tall, slim and as fit as Jan, but was more studious looking in her wire-rimmed glasses and tied back blond hair.

Will stepped out of the Audi and headed over to Zoe and they shook hands. 'Pleased to meet you,' he said.

She responded in perfect English and ushered him into the block as she waved Jan goodbye. She apologised on Jan's behalf for her husband running off. 'Whilst he is away you can tell me all about the English Customs,' she said enthusiastically.

The lift was quick and silent, and they got out on the second floor. The apartment was spacious, the decor luxurious. Will's house was furnished to what he could afford. He had a couple of nice pieces of furniture, but most had come flat packed from MFI. This was a massive contrast with everything looking expensive; he guessed much of it was handmade. Will gave Zoe the bottle of wine he was clutching, already feeling that it would be well below their standard, but she seemed very grateful.

'You must have known, this is one of my favourites,' she said.

He wasn't sure if she was telling the truth, but instantly felt better.

'Would you open it for me, and we can have a drink whilst I work on dinner.'

She led them into a very well-appointed kitchen and handed him the corkscrew from the drawer, whilst she fussed with the saucepans on the stove. Whatever she was cooking smelled delicious.

'I'm cooking a Swiss favourite, Zurcher geschnetzeltes, it's made with veal and calve-kidneys and some wine, mushrooms and cream. I do hope you like it.'

'It smells wonderful.' Will eased the cork out with a satisfying pop and half-filled the two wine glasses that Zoe handed to him.

They sat on stools in the kitchen so she could keep an eye on the dinner and sipped their wine. Will thought it tasted nice.

'So, tell me Will, what is it like being a Customs Officer?'

He summarised his role and talked a bit about the excitement of finding drugs, and sometimes the disappointment when he was convinced something was being hidden and either he didn't find it or found something else. He explained that the reason he was in Switzerland now was because he had been hoping he was going to find drugs and it turned out to be watches.

Zoe was a good listener and smiled encouragingly, but he got the impression she was waiting to ask him something else. He was nearly right – she wanted to *tell him* something.

'I know about the other reason you are here,' she said, looking him straight in the eye.

Did he hear her correctly?

'I work for a government agency within the Federal Department of Justice and Police, I guess similar to your MI6,' she explained.

Well, this was a revelation, and it got better.

'I'm to be your contact in relation to your meeting with Elias,' she said.

Will let this sink in before responding.

'Well, I did wonder when I would be contacted, but I never suspected it would be the wife of my Police liaison,' he said earnestly. 'But I have to say, it is a pleasant surprise, and I never would have guessed. How much do you know about this?' He was conscious that, although relieved to have now met his Swiss contact, he needed to be cautious. As it turned out, he need not have worried as she gave him chapter and verse – and more.

'We've been working with a Branch of MI6 for a while now and it was us who alerted them to the arms smuggling. Our Intelligence officers had been working on a money laundering case involving Russians and had uncovered some unusual financial transactions into the account of a Swiss road transport company called EM Transport.'

Will interrupted, 'Elias Michaels?'

'Exactly.' she said. 'It's Elias's company. He'd been receiving large sums of money, at least six times more than you would expect, to transport loads to England. We initially thought that this was a mechanism for laundering money, but three days ago we decided to carry out some surveillance on the transport yard. We watched a Turkish lorry arrive and unload some long flat boxes from a concealment in the lorry floor. We also recognised an English driver, who is a known suspect. He was talking with Elias and pointing into the back of a lorry bearing English plates. We believe this is the lorry that will carry these goods to England. Unfortunately, we were at the wrong angle and not able to get close enough to read the registration number. I can't tell you how we know, but we know the consignment is due to arrive in England sometime next week. We just don't know the route or the exact date. This is where you come in. More importantly, we have reliable information that indicates that those boxes contain automatic rifles, ammunition, and possibly rocket launchers and bomb-making equipment.'

She was about to go on, when Jan entered the apartment with a cheerful greeting and apologised again for his absence.

'How are you two getting on?'

Will must have looked a little guilty as he wasn't sure if Jan was aware of what they had been discussing, because Jan quickly put him at ease.

'It is OK Will, I know that Zoe is your contact for another matter that has brought you to Switzerland. I don't know the details and don't want to know, but I do know what Zoe does for a living. Zoe was in "the network" before we got married and I've got used to not asking too many questions.'

Zoe nodded as she clarified. 'It was a little difficult at the start as much of what I do has to be kept secret, but Jan is a Policeman, that is how we first met. We both only share the outline of cases we are working on. It was no accident that Jan was assigned to look after you and was an ideal opportunity to arrange for me to meet you safely.'

Will thought back to the arrangements for his visit and it all fitted. A few weeks back he had been told that a detective named Hans Hopler, who had been the investigating officer for the jewellery case, would be looking after him. But two days ago he was told he would be met at the station by Jan instead. This did not seem out of the ordinary at the time, but now it was obvious.

Although it was a lot to take in, Will felt comfortable with all this, it all made sense and Jan and Zoe made him feel he could trust them. He was about to comment when Zoe spoke first.

'Jan, would you mind giving us a few more minutes whilst I finish briefing Will?'

'Of course, darling,' Jan responded cheerfully, 'I'll go and take a shower and freshen up,' he said as he headed for what Will assumed was their bedroom. 'Will, you are in safe hands with Zoe.' he said sincerely.

Zoe smiled at Will reassuringly and then got back to business.

'We urgently need to know what date the consignment is leaving, when it is due to arrive in England and the registration number. As the Freight forwarder, Elias will need to give you these details.'

He thought about this. 'Why can't you just watch when the lorry leaves the yard and follow it?' he said. 'Surely that would be easier than me meeting with Elias.'

'There are two reasons,' she paused in thought, 'no, actually three. Firstly, it is vital to avoid any suspicion and that Elias meets with the new Freight forwarder, Bill Mitchell, you. This would be normal and not to have the meeting might set alarm bells ringing for the crime group. Secondly, the surveillance of the yard is difficult. We were lucky last time to place an observation post inside a damaged trailer that was parked just outside the yard gates, but this has now been towed away. So, we simply cannot get into a position that would give us the view we need. And, thirdly, to put it bluntly, although we know the consignment is due in England sometime next week, we don't have the resources to watch the yard and follow the lorry all the way to England.

Will felt a little foolish now, as the problems were obvious, particularly the resource issues. Even in his own job, resources were always a problem.

'I can see your problems, that makes sense,' he said.

He thought Zoe had sensed that he was still a bit nervous about his task.

'Will, you don't need to worry. Your meeting with Elias should take no more than an hour and will reassure him that you can be trusted to do the paperwork that will minimise his risk in England. Then he will give you the details and you can pass them to me.' She thought for a moment. 'Actually, it will be easier if you just gave them to Jan to give to me.'

They could hear Jan was about to re-join them, so she gave Will some final instructions.

'My team have been busy in the last few days to provide you with some papers that will pass a cursory inspection should you need them, which I doubt.' She passed him an A4 envelope.

'In here are some publicity materials and other documents relating to Brighthouse Freight Forwarders, which includes some headed paper with a telephone number. Should anyone decide to call to check, the number will be answered by someone who will verify you as an employee. We have created a passport for you in the name of Bill Mitchell, it is the best we could manage in the time we had. It is not quite good enough to get you through immigration, but it will pass most inspections to verify your identity should anyone ask. And finally, there is an airline ticket that shows Bill Mitchell arriving in Zurich airport at 2pm tomorrow and returning the following day.'

Will was astonished by the preparation for what was to be a short meeting, the passport photograph even looked like the one in his real passport! But he also felt reassured.

'Thank you,' is all he could think of to say.

The rest of the evening went like any other meal with friends. They ate, talked about their jobs and their friends and families, and laughed at their differences. For the most part Will forgot why he was there.

After a very pleasant evening and some good conversation he left their apartment a little before midnight. Jan had offered to drive him, but he had got his bearings by now so knew the hotel was only about twenty minutes' walk away. It would also give him a chance to reflect on the evening.

Jan arranged to pick him up from the hotel at 08.30 and he said his goodbyes to Zoe.

'Good luck tomorrow,' Zoe said encouragingly, 'I am sure it will all go well. It was great meeting you, but I doubt we will meet again.'

She was wrong about that.

Six

The next day Jan collected Will from his hotel in his sporty Audi and drove him the short distance to the hotel where the theft of the watches had taken place. When he had started this investigation, he had assumed that the watches had been stolen from a jewellery shop, but it turned out they were stolen from a hotel display case.

This hotel was even more plush than where he was staying. Positioned on the edge of Lake Lucerne it had amazing views across the lake and of the mountains beyond. Will concluded that this kind of establishment would attract the rich and famous, as the cheapest rooms were 1200 Swiss francs, the equivalent of £500, per night. Dotted around the opulent reception area were a number of gold framed display cabinets containing jewellery, fur coats, artwork and other high value items. He was introduced to the hotel manager who showed him the display cabinet that had previously housed the Vacheron watches, but now contained a number of expensive watches from another Swiss maker. The manager explained that he had been on duty on the day of the theft and recalled a couple of men looking at the cabinet who he didn't think were guests. But then he got distracted. It was a few hours later that a cleaner reported that the cabinet door had been forced and the watches were gone.

'The cabinets are now alarmed,' he explained, 'but before this theft we hadn't taken these precautions.'

The Swiss police had taken statements from the hotel manager and the cleaner at the time, and Jan advised that they would provide them to him. They had also finger-printed, but this had not identified the thief.

Will advised Jan that he would need a witness statement from the investigating police officers who attended the scene. The statement needed to explain who they had spoken to and the actions they had taken to investigate. Jan said he would arrange this but was surprised by the need for it.

'In Switzerland if a policeman states to a court that he did something then it is accepted as true, we don't need to present witness statements. Can you not just tell your court what we did?'

Will agreed this was a good system, but unfortunately it did not apply to the UK justice system. Every officer involved in a case, Police or Customs, was required to provide a witness statement in the same way as the general public.

They drove from the hotel to Jan's police office on the edge of the city, stopping at a local bakery on the way to grab a sandwich. Jan introduced Will to his boss and his colleagues. They spent the afternoon together discussing the case and their respective justice systems. Witness statements were drafted by the detectives with Will's help and Jan confirmed he would have these and other papers ready for Will first thing in the morning.

Thankfully, all of this was straightforward, as constantly on his mind was his impending meeting at 5pm with Elias.

With business concluded in Lucerne Will could now visit Jan's colleagues in Zurich tomorrow. He made a call to his contact in Zurich, Stefan, to confirm arrangements. Prior to the visit Will had sent the Zurich police the photos of Michael and John in the hope that they might recognise some of the background scenes. If they could, this would be essential evidence of their presence in Switzerland, something they had denied.

'You and your colleagues have been most helpful,' Will said to Jan, 'I am very grateful for your assistance in the case and for your hospitality.'

'It's been a pleasure to meet you Will and glad we could assist. I know you have an appointment to keep, so let me drive you to where you need to go.'

'That is very good of you, but I'll get a taxi. Better to arrive that way I think,' he said. It was probably over cautious, but he decided it would be better than to be seen being dropped off. The yard was in an industrial area on the outskirts of town, about three miles away.

'No problem,' Jan nodded in understanding. 'Tomorrow I'll bring the witness statements to your hotel at 8am and take you to the railway station. Good luck.'

It was just starting to drizzle with rain as Will paid the taxi driver and walked through the large metal gates into the lorry yard. He could see a number of large sheds stretching down the yard for about eighty metres, each with a loading bay. Some trucks were parked in these bays and people were busy either loading or unloading, or checking things on clipboards. Other bays were empty and yet more lorries were parked further into the yard.

There was a buzz of activity. Diesel engines throbbed; drivers and workers shouted and pointed; forklift trucks pirouetted like sequence dancers, as they rounded on their next goal. They slipped their long silver arms under a stack of crates and swiftly hoisted them in the air, before swinging gracefully around to deliver their load to a lorry or to a loading bay. Will could see that the yard stretched for a further fifty metres beyond the loading bays, towards a three-metre-high wooden fence.

Above the sheds he could see the offices spanning the loading bays below. He spotted the external staircase off to the right and headed in that direction. No one took much notice of him as he crossed the yard, but he did spot someone at one of the office windows above. They seemed to be tracking his progress.

At the top of the stairs was a door into a small lobby, maybe eight feet square. The floor was covered in a scuffed brown lino, and the walls were a grubby beige. In the left-hand corner was a well-used metal chair that had scraped grooves in the lino, presumably as it had been shuffled backwards and forwards by many users. As the door behind him closed with a click, the sound from the yard was instantly muffled. Immediately in front of him was a counter marked 'Rezeption' with a door beyond. On the counter was a buzzer. He was about to push this when a slightly overweight man appeared through the door. The man was in his early fifties, about five foot ten in height and dressed in a checked shirt with a plain green tie He wore brown corduroy trousers. His bushy dark moustache matched his bushy dark hair; both were showing signs of grey.

'Welcome, I am Elias Michaels, and you must be Mister Bill Mitchell. Very good to meet you.' he said as he lifted up the counter on a hinge.

Like everyone Will had met so far, his English was good. Just as well, Will thought, as he could speak only a little German, the language of this particular area of Switzerland. He did speak a bit of French and some parts of Switzerland, such as Geneva had French as their basic language, but this was no help to him here.

They shook hands and Elias guided him through the door into a large open office. Sixteen desks were laid out regimentally. Will saw around eight workers dotted about, either on the phone or shuffling papers. It reminded him of a smaller version of the 'Long Room' in Dover Custom House, where all the import paperwork was managed. To the right it was all windows overlooking the rear of the yard that Will hadn't yet seen. Off to the left were several doors to other smaller offices; it was towards one of these that Elias led, chatting as they went about his flight and journey to Lucerne. Will was already telling lies as he described his flight and train journey from yesterday as if it were today.

Elias showed him into an office with **'Elias Michaels - Direktor'** stencilled on the door.

'I am so glad you have been able to visit us here as I wanted to make sure everything is ok for the shipment. I have a colleague who would also like to meet you. He works closely with the boss.'

Elias's office was large. As well as his desk and cupboards, the room contained a small conference table with six upholstered chairs. He ushered Will to sit down on one of them.

'Before we get started, can I offer you a drink, coffee or tea perhaps?'

'A coffee would be great, thanks.'

Will had been told by a colleague who had visited Switzerland on holiday, that the Swiss drink their tea and coffee black. Although he preferred coffee with milk, he could just about drink it without, but not tea. As it turned out the coffee came with a small jug of milk and some cubes of brown sugar, delivered by a pretty young lady in a short skirt. He could see Elias ogling her as she left the room and smirking at him knowingly. Will smiled back with the same knowing look. He now had to play the part of Bill Mitchell, but Elias's openly lecherous behaviour left him cold.

'Ah, here is Sergei my colleague. Sergei I would like you to meet Bill Mitchell,' he said, as a younger man, perhaps forty years old, entered the room. He walked in with a confident swagger and headed straight for Will. He was casually dressed in jeans and a dark blue plain shirt. The shirt was open at the neck, displaying a heavy gold chain.

'Pleased to meet you Bill Mitchell, I am Sergei Koskov,' he announced, holding out his hand. His facial features and accent had already suggested to Will that he was from Eastern Europe, but the name was almost certainly Russian.

Will stood and shook his hand. 'Good to meet you Mr. Koskov,' he said formally.

'Call me Sergei please, can I call you Bill?' He didn't wait for an answer, 'So good of you to come to Switzerland, Bill. Elias tells me you are the man who can get our lorry through the British Customs without problems, yes?'

Will took a sip of his coffee before responding. Not bad!

'That is correct,' he said confidently, 'I can *minimise the risk* of your lorry being stopped and searched,' he emphasised. 'I can do the paperwork that will make your consignment look uninteresting to them, and I am known and trusted by a number of Customs Officers. But, if they do decide to search then I have no control.'

Sergei looked unconvinced. 'But if the lorry still get stopped then what are we paying you for?'

He was straight to the point and clearly in charge – Will noticed Elias had not spoken yet and always deferred to Sergei so there was a definite pecking order here. It was time for him to play 'Bill' and get a bit assertive. He needed them to trust him, but to do that he needed to play hardball to show that he was the best they could get.

He stood up slowly for effect and walked towards the window that had a view of the front of the yard. After gazing out of the window for a few seconds, he took a deep breath to compose himself, like an actor about to go on stage, and turned.

He directed his speech to Sergei, slowly and deliberately.

'You are paying me because I'm the best there is,' he said emphatically, 'And just to be clear' his voice rising slightly, 'I understood from George that the deal was I only get paid, *after* the lorry gets past Customs, so I have a vested interest in making this work.'

Now he had Sergei's attention, he pressed on,

'I can do my bit, but you must do yours. I don't need or want to know what goods you are hiding but it is important that the goods are packaged in a way that looks like they match the paperwork. So we need to agree this. For example, if we decide that the load is "Cuckoo clocks" and the papers say that the crates contain "Cuckoo clocks", then the packaging needs to reflect this. And of course, if there is anything you don't want them to see, it must be well concealed.'

He saw Sergei glance at Elias and a nod passed between them.

'OK Bill,' smiled Sergei, 'I see now you know what you are doing, and we do trust you. It is very important to us that we get this lorry through Customs, so if there is thing you can do to help then we are listening.'

His chance to get the details he needed. 'Well for a start you can give me the exact date and time you expect the lorry to arrive in England. I can then make sure that I personally deal with the delivery of the paperwork to Customs, and I will be able to monitor the progress of the clearance. As I said, I know a few Customs Officers, so I can probably put gentle pressure on them to get the load cleared quickly. The sooner I know when the lorry is due the more I can plan. The quicker it goes through the system, the less chance it will be examined.'

All of this came out quickly, as he had pre-planned what he could say to convince Elias of the need to have the delivery details as soon as possible. He was now worried it sounded too rehearsed. However, they didn't seem to notice, instead they all sat around the table and discussed details. The first thing to agree was what the legitimate load would be. This was Elias's world as he had access to a number of commodities.

'I have a customer who makes chocolate and has just got a buyer lined up in England,' Elias said. 'I think this could work for us.'

Now that Elias was involved and leading this part of the arrangements Will didn't want to be negative, but chocolate might result in an examination, as the duty rates were higher than some other goods. There were also variants dependent on sugar and cocoa content, so it might result in Customs taking samples for testing. No, this was a bad idea, but he had to let him down gently.

'There might be a problem with chocolate,' he explained, 'Customs Officers have been known to open up the loads just to get some free samples. I think we might be better with something less attractive to them. What about second-hand furniture, could you arrange this?'

Elias thought for a moment, 'I had not thought of that, the greedy chocolate stealing bastards. But yes, I can arrange a load of furniture. And don't worry about the goods we do not want found – they will be well concealed.' Sergei nodded.

They discussed a bit more about how any crates could be marked. Elias confirmed that the lorry would arrive in Dover next Thursday afternoon, one week from now. With business concluded it was time to leave, but Sergei had other ideas.

'Now that we have a plan it is time to drink to our success,' he said. 'We go to bar, and I will buy champagne.'

This was definitely not what Will wanted at all, he just wanted out of there as quick as possible. But refusing would be difficult.

'That is very kind of you Sergei,' he said in the end, as he couldn't think of any excuse that was likely to change Sergei's mind.

The chosen bar was only five minutes' walk from the lorry yard. It had stopped raining, but the paths were shiny and wet in the street-light, and puddles had formed in places.

They arrived in what Will could only describe as a seedy part of town with neon lights and flashing picture signs, indicating offerings of drinks, food, and strippers. Sergei stopped at an open doorway with a foot high red triple 'X' neon above it.

There was a flashing red arrow pointing at a concrete stairway, lit with a low wattage red lamp. Clearly this was more than your average bar. Will could hear the steady thump of music rising from below. He followed Sergei and Elias down the stairs to a solid wooden door. Sergei opened the door and the sound level trebled.

They entered a large lounge, soft red lamps on the walls providing most of the light. Cigarette smoke hung in the air. There were lots of medium-sized round tables filling the room with plenty of soft comfortable chairs around them. Thick red patterned carpet gave a sense of opulence, but closer inspection revealed a number of dark patches. Drink spills probably. There were not many customers, it was still early. At the far end of the room was a small brightly lit stage. Will could see a scantily clad girl swaying to the loud music, to the delight and loud comments and cheers from those nearest her.

Sergei led them to a table that got them closer to the action. He shouted and waved to a buxom serving girl. She nodded and sashayed towards them. She was wearing what Will took to be a variation on traditional Swiss costume, a white ruffled blouse and red knee-length skirt. The blouse had the traditional two black stripes on the front that looks like men's braces. But there tradition ended. The blouse was completely see-through, the stripes just covering her nipples.

'A bottle of your finest champagne,' said Sergei, making no attempt to hide his lecherous stare. She returned swiftly with the champagne, complete with ice-bucket and glasses. Sergei tipped the girl with a $50 bill as he smacked her on the backside. She smiled sweetly as she tucked the note between her bosoms and sashayed off to the next table.

The scantily clad girl on stage had shed a few more clothes and was now dressed only in some thin sparkly knickers and sparkly tassels on her boobs which she swung into the face of the closest delighted member of the audience. The music ended abruptly and she gathered her discarded clothes and wandered off stage to more cheers from the minimal crowd.

'So, Bill, tell me about life in England.' shouted Sergei as the music started up again ready for a new act to hit the stage. 'I have not been there yet, but I go to London soon.'

As Bill Mitchell he needed to make out he was a man of the world and frequented places like this, even though this was Will's first ever exposure to a strip-club.

'You will love London Sergei. It is full of culture and art galleries,' Will said flatly, and paused as his comment had had the desired effect – he knew by now that culture was the last thing Sergei was interested in. Sergei was looking less happy, before Will continued, 'And the best strip-clubs and casinos in the whole world!' he said with relish.

'Bill you make joke, I like that,' he smiled and smacked him on the back. 'We are going to have a great evening,' he said as he topped up everyone's glasses. Will needed to be very careful now and avoid drinking too much somehow, or things would get dangerous. The music changed, a new girl arrived on stage. She was quickly causing a reaction amongst the audience as she suggestively dragged a scarf between her legs. Elias and Sergei were distracted long enough for him to empty his glass into the ice bucket. So far so good, but it might not be so easy next time. He needed a plan to get out of there.

They had been in the club only thirty minutes, but Sergei was already ordering another bottle of champagne. Will had managed to dispose of a second glass full into the ice-bucket when they were looking at the stage. But it was too risky now, even though they were getting a bit drunk. Both Elias and Sergei were now well-oiled, so he played along, laughing, and joking with them both.

The music was getting louder, and they were onto the third act, as another new girl hit the stage sporting some kind of national costume, a bit like the serving girl, but this time made of shiny leather that failed to conceal any of her finest assets.

'In Russia we have the best-looking girls,' Sergei said loudly, 'More beautiful and sexy than in this country. Look at her, she look like a dog.'

Will became aware that the four men at the next table were listening and showing clear signs of annoyance. They looked like they could handle themselves; three of them were well over six-foot and the fourth, although shorter, looked solid. Maybe they were Swiss and took offence at Sergei's comments. If he carried this on there could be trouble. Will decided that now might be a good time to visit the gents so left the table as Sergei continued to sound off loudly,

'Would you screw a dog like that Elias,' he heard Sergei say as he pointed to the act performing on stage, 'I would sooner screw my horse.'

As Will returned to the bar he could see Sergei on his feet shouting at the men at the table, they were starting to get up – this was going to turn ugly. As Will got closer he could see Elias grabbing Sergei's arm and saying something, but the music was too loud to hear. Elias looked like he was trying to get him to sit down, but Sergei was having none of it. Will then noticed that he wasn't the only one heading for the table. A man in a suit who looked like the manager, accompanied by a gorilla of a man wearing a much too tight dinner suit, got there before him.

Gorilla man approached Sergei from behind and pushed him easily into his seat, keeping his hand on his shoulder so that Sergei could not stand back up.

The manager spoke to the four men in German who begrudgingly all retook their seats.

'I think you gentlemen have out-stayed your welcome,' he said to Elias in broken English. Sergei was about to respond, but Elias got there first.

'We are just leaving, sorry for the disturbance,' he said meekly. Sergei again tried to stand but Gorilla man had him pinned to the seat. He started to speak, but this time Will was now at the table and bravely intervened.

'Our friend is sorry if he caused offence,' he said. 'We are celebrating my birthday and perhaps had too much champagne. We will leave now, is that not right Sergei.' He gave Sergei a stern but friendly look, a bit like a brother might, and this time Sergei just nodded lamely, although there was still anger in his eyes.

'Thank you gentlemen, we will show you to the door,' said the manager. 'This way.' He indicated with a wave of his arm and Gorilla man released his pressure on Sergei's shoulder.

They walked in single file to the exit, Elias leading, Sergei in the middle and Will bringing up the rear, but Gorilla man walked alongside Sergei, just in case.

Out in the fresh air and no longer chaperoned Sergei found his voice again. He shouted abuse in Russian as the door to the club closed behind them, but it was half-hearted, and he soon ran out of words.

'I am sorry Bill,' he finally said in English. 'These Swiss have no sense of humour. But we had last laugh I think – we did not pay for the champagne!' He laughed now, all trace of anger gone. 'Let us find another club, yes?'

This was Will's opportunity to make an exit, 'Thank you Sergei, I had a good time, but I have had enough excitement for one night,' he said. 'It was good to meet you and maybe we will meet again sometime.'

Sergei tried again to encourage Will to stay, but eventually accepted that he wasn't budging, so they wandered back towards the lorry yard, where Will got a taxi to his hotel.

Back in his hotel room he flopped down on the bed and breathed a huge sigh. That was a challenge, he thought, but he also felt exhilarated.

He had one last task that needed to be completed before bed – he wrote down all the relevant details for Zoe and put them into an envelope to give to Jan.

Seven

Will said his goodbyes to Jan, after handing him the envelope for Zoe, and jumped on the train to Zurich.

The journey back to Zurich was as picturesque as before, the sun shining on the lake and off the snow-capped mountains.

Will reflected on his mission. He felt very pleased with himself. It had not been straightforward, but he had improvised when needed and he had convinced Elias and Sergei that he was the real deal. The intelligence he had gained on the lorry movements should ensure that 'sharp-dressed man' would be able to arrange the intercept of the smuggled load.

Now all he had to do was finish his official task and get home.

It was no surprise to discover that Stefan had impeccable English when they had spoken on the telephone yesterday. He advised Will that he had examined the photographs and had short-listed four locations that he felt were most likely to be where they had been taken. They had agreed to meet under the station clock.

The train pulled into Zurich exactly on time at 09:46. Stefan was waiting under the clock as promised. He had described himself as thirty years old, six foot tall and wearing casual trousers, check shirt and a brown leather jerkin. There was no other person who looked remotely like this standing near the clock, so Will was comfortable that this was Stefan and walked over. They shook hands.

'Very pleased to meet you Will. I have high hopes that we'll find the location for you. Come, I've a car waiting.' Stefan sounded excited by the hunt.

'Thanks Stefan, I'm very grateful for your help with this.'

They spent the next few hours roaming the Zurich lidos in a large plush Mercedes. Will liked cars. First a sporty Audi and now a luxurious Mercedes. He enjoyed the experience of being chauffeured about, but would have loved to have also driven them.

The first lido they checked was definitely not the place in the photos. Too many trees. But they hit gold on the second. They were able to find the exact same spot in the photos, showing Michael and John sunning themselves. Will had brought a simple camera with him and Stefan took a snap of him in the same spot, to provide some clear evidence for the jury. When Will had spoken on the phone to Stefan yesterday he had explained to him the requirement for a witness statement. As an efficient Swiss police detective, Stefan had already drafted one and only had to add the finding of the location to complete it. If only Will's colleagues were always this efficient he mused.

'Stefan, you've been great,' he said sincerely. 'I'm so grateful to you and your colleagues.'

Stefan drove Will to the airport and they said their goodbyes; that was Will done in Switzerland. He was now able to get a mid-afternoon flight home. A great result on both fronts.

He called Alison from Zurich airport to tell her he would be back later that day. She sounded pleased and offered to cook them dinner. It had been a challenging few days, but he had succeeded in the mission, so hopefully sharp-dressed man would be happy. He found out sooner than expected.

***

It was just after 5 o'clock when he picked up his bag from the carousal and made his way through Customs at Gatwick. He didn't recognise any of the Officers on duty, but that was hardly a surprise as it would only be likely if someone had transferred here from Dover. Will wasn't aware of anyone who had. He strolled through the arrivals lounge and headed for the Hertz car rental office, but didn't get that far.

'I hear everything went well in Switzerland,' said sharp-dressed man as he came alongside, matching Will's step and taking him by surprise.

'News travels fast I see,' said Will, as he couldn't think of anything better to say.

Sharp-dressed man steered him away from the Hertz office towards the car park. 'I have a car waiting, we can talk whilst I give you a lift home.'

The driver of a black Ford Granada got out and greeted them and placed Will's holdall in the boot. Sharp-dressed man introduced him as John. Will doubted that was really his name and it was obvious that John wasn't going to engage in conversation.

He climbed into the back and settled into the plush leather rear seat next to sharp-dressed man. *Another different ride to experience.*

'Ok, Will, I think it is time I gave you a bit more information on what is going on. Firstly, I want to congratulate you. You handled yourself well by all accounts and it is only right that you get to understand the impact of your role. We now know details of the lorry and exactly when it is due to arrive at Dover. Well done! This will enable us to put the next part of the plan in place, but you don't need to know the details.'

Will did want to know the details, but it was clear he would not be told.

'Secondly, I feel that I should properly introduce myself, who I am and what my organisation does.'

Will glanced up at John as they entered the slip road for the M23, but John did not appear interested in their conversation.

'It is OK, John is one of us,' said sharp-dressed man as he sensed Will's concern. Will saw John in the rear-view mirror smile and nod, but he said nothing.

'My name is Clive Harrington, and I am head of an organisation that's sits within MI6 called Combined Organised Crime Group Sector, or COGS for short, but it is also known by the team as "The Network".'

'The Network' - where had Will heard that name before?

Clive continued, 'Our remit is to infiltrate organised criminal groups who are involved in multiple crimes, commodities and fraud, and provide intelligence to our colleagues to plan strategies for taking them out of business. The persons you met yesterday are members of one such group.'

Will let this sink in, then asked what he thought was an obvious question.

'So, these guys are involved in arms smuggling, but what else? From what you just said, and the Russian involvement, I'm guessing they're involved in lots of crime.'

'You guessed right, they're involved in a lot of crime; prostitution, extortion, bribery, fraud, drugs, you name it they're probably doing it. This is why we were formed, as there is not one single law enforcement body that deals with it all, so we need to coordinate and marshal our resources effectively to counter these high-level groups.'

Then Will remembered where he had heard 'The Network' mentioned, it was Jan when he was talking about what Zoe did. Maybe he shouldn't know this and to reveal it might get Zoe and Jan into trouble. But he could ask a general question that might confirm, couldn't he?

'Does that include using resources that are based overseas?' he enquired.

Clive paused, as if deciding how much he should confide. In the end he said, 'Let's just say that we utilise resources from a range of organisations, and this includes within other countries. But this leads me to the main reason I wanted to have this little chat.'

They were now on the M25, traffic was heavy as it was rush hour, but still moving quite well. He would be home in just over an hour. He was tired now, only half listening to Clive as he was thinking of Alison and how he might explain how he had got home without a hire car. He was about to raise this issue when Clive dropped a bombshell.

'We are very impressed with the way you handled yourself during this mission and would like you to join The Network.' He must have seen Will's surprise but continued anyway. 'Many of our operatives are recruited from organisations outside of MI6, but we operate in a different way.'

Will was now fully awake and listening intently.

Clive continued. 'The Network is made up largely from persons who, on the face of it, continue to work for their existing organisation, but secretly work for us. We find this gives us an edge. Firstly, it is good for security. Apart from a very select few, no one knows, either inside or outside of MI6, that you are an operative working for COGS. Secrecy is paramount in this game,' he said with emphasis. 'Secondly, the skills and knowledge our operatives already own are fairly unique, but by continuing to work within their own organisation they will stay up to date and these skills remain current. We have found to our cost that when we recruit new operatives full time, their past knowledge and skills diminish quickly after one year. What was an asset can then become a risk to our type of work, if you know what I mean?'

Will could relate to this point as this was the reason why trainers in Customs were not full-time. They came from the uniformed ranks at the ports and airports. By using them for only a few weeks a year to deliver the courses, they remained current in their uniform role.

'And thirdly,' Clive explained, 'we have the advantage of flexibility. We generally use operatives from The Network on only a few occasions per year, sometimes only for a few days and sometimes a few weeks.'

Will let all this sink in. Although what he had just done in Switzerland had had its scary moments, he did feel exhilarated to have got through it, proud that he had been able to think on my feet when it got challenging.

This was a very tempting offer, but he couldn't see how it would work.

'So, if I agree to do this, how will I be able to work for you without causing suspicion with my colleagues?'

'All in good time my boy, all in good time. If you decide to join us you will soon discover that we've ways and means of achieving things that others wouldn't credit. But to partially answer that question, we have a plan that will place you in a position where you would have opportunities to be absent from your normal duties without causing suspicion.'

A curious answer and Will wanted to know more, but clearly Clive wasn't ready to explain just yet. The other query he had was about the whole issue of secrecy. Would he have to keep this whole thing a secret from Alison, could he do that? Clive must have read my mind.

'I need to remind you that you have signed the Official Secrets Act. Whether you agree to join us or not you would of course not be able to share this conversation with anyone outside of The Network. *And I mean anyone,*' Clive stressed, 'Not friends, not colleagues, not family, not your girlfriend. If you do agree to join us then everything about your role and the role of this organisation has to remain secret. Could you do that?'

Clive was looking at Will closely now, waiting for an answer.

If Will said no to joining, he could tell no one, but would miss this opportunity. If he said yes, he could tell no one, and would be required to tell no one probably forever. And that included Alison. He thought back to a number of discussions that he and Alison had had in the last few months. He had never lied to her, but recognised that he had already been keeping the details of his work from her. Some of the intelligence he dealt with was confidential and simply inappropriate to share outside of immediate colleagues. It had been a bit of a joke at first. 'If I tell you I'm going to have to kill you,' he'd said. It became clear to both of them that some of his work, and some of hers, was not for discussion. They both easily accepted this. But joining The Network was taking this a step further. It was true that parts of his past he had not shared with Alison, but this would almost certainly lead to actually *lying* to her. He valued their relationship, but convinced himself that she would understand if she ever found out (which she couldn't).

All of these thoughts chased back and forth in his head in a matter of seconds, but it felt like hours before he finally replied.

'Yes, I can do this and yes I would like to take this opportunity,' he stated emphatically whilst looking Clive straight in the eye.

'Excellent,' Clive said. 'Now I can give you some further information that should answer some of your questions; but first a toast.' He pulled a silver hip flask from his pocket, took a slug of its contents then passed across to Will.

Will could already smell it was whisky and was surprisingly grateful for the gesture. He didn't drink much but did enjoy the occasional Scotch; right now he decided he really did need a drink and took a healthy sip, enjoying the burning sensation as it slipped down his throat.

Clive returned the flask to his pocket and Will spotted John in the rear-view mirror giving him an encouraging smile, a kind of 'welcome aboard' expression.

Clive settled back in his seat. He gave Will a twenty-minute run-through of the important things he needed to know. Will listened attentively. He thought he had got it all (no notes allowed), but Clive told him not to worry. One of the key points he mentioned was Will's COGS training, where a lot of the important stuff would be re-visited.

The main revelation was the groundwork that had already been planned and executed in the background to secure Will a position which would give him, and them, the flexibility needed for any missions. They had arranged for him to be transferred to the HM Customs and Excise training centre in Southend on temporary promotion. This would enable him to travel around the country without much oversight. He would be conducting training, monitoring other trainers and courses, and arranging venues. Part of the newly designed Preventive training for uniformed officers was residential so most events were conducted in hotels with conference facilities.

Clive explained to Will that he would be approached by the Senior Officer in charge in Southend, Dave Campbell. He would get a job offer which he should accept. The job was one that Will might have applied for anyway if it had been advertised. But often jobs like this were not advertised and were allocated on who you knew. As it happened Will had already met Dave last year when he attended a 'train the trainers' event to train on the new Preventive course, so it would not be an unusual request.

Will noticed that they had passed the M2 services a while back. They had just left the motorway to join the A2 to Canterbury. This was familiar territory for him as he had been born and grew up in Canterbury, moving to Dover only when he took up his job in Customs. So he was quite surprised when John turned off towards Rough Common, a small village on the outskirts. John pulled the Granada into the side of the road and stopped.

'This is where we part for now,' said Clive. 'I will be in contact soon, but in the meantime you must go about your business as if nothing has happened. See that Ford Escort in front?'

Right in front of them was a new blue 'H' registration Ford Escort.

'This is your hire car, the one you should have collected from Gatwick. The papers inside show that you did collect it; one of my team has driven it here for you. You can now complete your journey and arrive home as expected.' Clive was right – Will was yet to understand the planning and resources they had at their disposal.

Eight

Stopping the lorry and seizing the arms and ammunition at the docks would now be easy, but would not meet the objective of exposing and arresting the crime heads. Another solution was needed. Clive set his best team on solving this challenge.

The problem for the COGS team to solve was how to intercept and secure the arms and ammunition without the crime-gang becoming suspicious as to how they had found them. They had to make it look like just bad luck. They were not about to let a lorry load of weapons get into the hands of the IRA, but at this stage they didn't have enough evidence to arrest the big players. Taking out this consignment would not stop the gang from regrouping and continuing their illegal activities. There was also the risk to the COGS operatives if the gang became suspicious.

As usual in these situations the problem solve started with a 'brainstorm'. The COGS operational intelligence team was led by Tony Blunt. It was an unfortunate name considering that Anthony Blunt was a well-known Soviet spy during and after

World War Two, but Tony was used to the ribbing he got from colleagues, it was all in jest.

Tony worked with his team on brain-storming a range of common sense as well as wacky ideas, as this was a way of creative thinking. Sometimes a crazy idea would spawn a workable solution.

The biggest problem, amongst many, was how to secure the arms and ammunition without anyone knowing they had been secured.

They considered a hijack by an unknown competitor. They quickly dismissed this as it would likely create an unwarranted hunt for the unknown group by both the Russian Crime gang and the IRA. This might get dangerous and uncover the ruse. They considered the lorry having an accident and its cargo being destroyed, but understandably this was also quickly dismissed as far too dangerous.

But staging an accident that *gave the appearance* that the cargo had been destroyed was a possibility. This idea was developed and honed. The team worked out all the angles and after presenting to Clive they got the green-light and started planning for Operation Hangover. No plan is perfect, it would rely on a lot of different factors, but they were confident they could adapt the plan at short notice, as necessary. In the end the moves made by the crime-gang made their overall plan much easier.

***

It was 3pm, a week after Will had returned from Switzerland and he had just finished his shift. He was in the General Office checking his pigeon-hole for messages as he always did before heading home. Mostly it was updates to operating instructions, or details of next week's shift pattern, but this time he was surprised to see a sealed envelope marked 'Confidential'. *Today was the day that the lorry was meant to arrive at the docks. Could this be something to do with Clive?* Clive hadn't mentioned when and how he would make contact, but had indicated that there would be some training for him to attend sometime soon, so maybe this was it? Will looked around him and noted that the office was busy as usual at shift changeover time. Conscious of the secrecy that Clive had drummed into him, he decided to pocket the envelope and open it when he could be sure that no one could pry.

Five minutes later he was sitting in his car in the staff car park, excited to see the contents of the envelope as he eased open the flap. It contained a single A4 sheet. Typed at the top was a short paragraph. Will read the words and his heart raced. They were instructions and were followed by a hand-written word – "Clive". Other than this the sheet was blank. Will read the instructions again.

It is the start of your training. Go to Langdon cliffs car park overlooking Eastern docks. Park next to a 'G' registration Blue Ford Sierra at 15.30 hours. Do not leave your car until approached by a man called Tony.

Will checked his watch; a quarter past three. Langdon cliffs was only a short drive away, but he needed to get moving if he was to be on time. He knew the spot quite well, a great place for observing the docks, with beautiful cliff-top walks. At this time of day it was likely to be quiet, probably just a few dog-walkers, he thought. At weekends it got busy with tourists and families out for a picnic and in the evening the car park was popular with courting couples. Will smiled to himself as he knew this from personal experience. *The smile vanished immediately when he remembered it was with Rachel. He blinked the memory away – it hurt too much.*

He spotted the Sierra easily. Apart from an old Volvo it was the only car parked up. It was close to half-past three, so as instructed he pulled up next to it, sat in his car and waited. He could see that the car was occupied, and he didn't have to wait long for the driver to emerge and tap on Will's window. Will got out to meet him.

The man was in his late thirties Will guessed. He was dressed in dark jeans and a dark polo shirt. He was average height and average build and average looking. The sort of person you would pass in the street and not notice. Exactly the sort of person who would be good at merging into the background, hiding in plain sight.

'Hi, I'm Tony,' he said with a friendly smile. 'You must be Will, glad to have you on-board.'

They shook hands.

'Nice to meet you Tony, and looking forward to whatever it is we'll be doing,' Will said.

'Ah, so Clive hasn't told you then. No surprise there,' Tony said with a smile. 'Lock your car up and come and join me in mine, we've a lot to discuss.'

As they sat in the front of the Sierra, Tony checked his watch. 'Ok, first things first. We need to move to another location, so I will brief you as we go.' He started the car and they headed for the car park exit. 'Remember that lorry you identified in Lucerne,' Will nodded. 'Well it's currently sitting down there in the docks.' Tony waved his hand at the docks below as they headed along the cliff road. 'It'll soon be cleared and we plan to follow it.'

Will had already worked out that this was a likely scenario. Stopping and searching the lorry at the docks might confirm it was loaded with arms and ammunition which would be seized, but he knew that Clive was after bigger fish.

'I guessed that this might be part of the plan,' he said, 'Clive wasn't prepared to tell me last week, but I understand why. What's my role in this?' he asked.

'Your role is simple, observe and learn.' Tony drove down the hill, heading back towards the docks. 'I've a team with me, and we'll have the lorry under surveillance to wherever it goes. You'll be with me the whole time, watching a master at work, you could say. I've been doing this kind of thing for years now, so what better way for you to learn than see a live operation in action.'

Will could tell that Tony wasn't being cocky, he was just setting out his credentials. He was self-assured and Will was excited to learn from this man.

'I might have some dumb questions as we go along,' he said seriously, 'This is all new to me, but I'm keen to learn.'

'I couldn't ask for more,' Tony said, 'No such thing as a dumb question as far as I'm concerned.'

Tony parked on the promenade with a good view of the dock exit. 'The rest of my team are close-by and ready to move on my radio command,' he said. 'All the surveillance team have 'call signs'. We are 'Romeo's' and all targets are called 'Tango's'. I'm Romeo 1 and Fred, Henry, Dave and Chris are the other Tangos. You'll soon recognise who's who,' he said.

Will nudged Tony as he spotted the target lorry exiting the dock gate and slowly climbing up Jubilee Way. Tony pressed a button next to the gear lever and spoke.

'All call-signs, Tango 1 mobile, Romeo 1 has eye-ball,' He announced as if talking to himself, then let go of the button.

There must be a hidden microphone in the car, Will surmised.

The lorry faced a climb up the hill of nearly a mile before reaching a roundabout. As it rounded the long bend over the docks and disappeared from sight, Tony explained to Will that he would take another thirty seconds before they left their parking spot. The lorry had no other turning options, so it was a safe strategy. 'Also,' he said with a smile, 'one of the team is parked in the lay-by half-way up the hill!'

As if on cue a voice came through on the car radio. 'Romeo 2 has eye-ball.'

When Tony judged it was time, they set off up Jubilee Way. In less than a minute they both spotted the 'tango' three hundred yards from the roundabout at the top. As expected it took the second exit and continued along the A2.

'Our Intelligence suggests that the lorry will stay on the A2 and then up the M2 towards Dartford Tunnel, so I'll swap places with other vehicles on the team as we follow it,' he told Will. 'This will avoid being noticed as it would be unusual for a car to stick to lorry speed when there is a chance to pass.'

Will was soaking up this information. Surveillance was clearly a skill and he hoped he would get the chance to actively participate one day. Not today though, this was purely an observation exercise for him. Still exciting though, he thought.

Over the next thirty minutes Will listened to Tony giving updates and positioning his four-vehicle team. Several times Tony hung back and others in the surveillance team took 'eye-ball' for a few miles, changing again when it was felt necessary.

Tony explained that his main concern was how to keep his team from being detected if the lorry came off the motorway and proceeded on single track roads. 'What I'm hoping is that the driver will stop to take a break before then,' he said.' If he does then I have a plan that would assist greatly assist us.

The driver obliged. Halfway up the M2 at the Top Rank services the lorry pulled in.

'Timing is excellent,' Tony said. 'It's just getting dark.'

The lorry came to a stop in the lorry park and the driver jumped from his cab and headed into the facility.

Tango 1 on foot. Romeo 3 has eyeball,' said Fred over his covert radio, as he leapt out of his car to follow the driver.

'Roger, Romeo 3 - Romeo 2, you are go to deploy the brick,' instructed Tony.

'Roger, Romeo 1,' said Henry.

'What's the brick,' Will asked, intrigued the by language they were using.

'It's a tracker, so called because it is the size and shape of a small brick.' Tony explained how Henry would deploy the brick and how it was important for all those doing surveillance to have a back-story. 'If Henry gets questioned about what he is doing he needs to give a plausible story. If it was me I'd probably say something like, "I'm desperate for a piss".'

Will could see Henry as he climbed out of the back of a blue Transit van carrying a holdall, and sauntered, indirectly, towards the lorry. Tony told him that all Romeos wore a covert earpiece, their radios concealed in a holster under their jackets. There were few other lorries in the park and no sign of other drivers, but Henry clearly knew his job and seemed to melt into the shadows. He made his way to the rear of the lorry without drawing attention.

'Tango 1 in Gents,' Fred said over the radio.

Will couldn't see what Henry was doing now, it was too dark, so Tony explained. 'Henry will climb under the lorry, locate a section of chassis and offer up the brick. It is magnetic. He will then cover the tracker with grease to conceal it and that's it, job done.

'Tango 1 on move heading back to lorry park,' Fred announced over the radio.

When Henry returned to his van Tony pressed a switch near the radio. A green screen lit up just above it. A few seconds later a small white blob started flashing on the screen showing the output from the brick. Tony explained that the four smaller blobs on the screen were the surveillance vehicles.

'Now we can afford to stay further back out of sight, as the tracker will show how far away the lorry is and when it stopped.'

Tony controlled the surveillance team positions by radio and kept them back, all the while describing to Will the reasons why he performed certain actions. For the most part he was able to keep the lorry in sight on the main roads without drawing any attention to his car. He would occasionally let one of the team take eyeball just to avoid any risks. But for most of the journey he stayed up front. Using his years of experience, he would hang back for a few miles whilst following the tracker, then close up when a junction was near, just to make sure.

'The tracker is good, but trackers had been known to lose their signal sometimes,' he said. 'It would make our task much more difficult if we didn't have eyeball at the right time.'

The lorry passed through the Dartford Tunnel and after a few miles on the M25 it joined the A12 towards Ipswich. With the tracker in place, the team stayed well back, but one vehicle always kept a visual. The lorry ploughed on through the evening at a fairly steady pace, briefly joining the A14, before turning onto the A140 to Norwich. At about 8pm it took a turn off to the west onto the B1134 towards Attleborough. This suggested he was getting close to a destination. Tony had seen the lorry indicate from his position about five-hundred metres back and had alerted the team. He didn't need to tell them what to do, they knew the drill. Dave and Chris were a few miles back and Dave quickly checked the map. He told Chris to take the next left. It was a last-minute instruction. Chris had to brake hard and make the turn at a much higher speed than he had wanted, but his advanced driver training got him safely around the corner. He sped along an adjacent B-road with the intention of getting ahead of the lorry.

'Romeo 4 has taken alternative,' Dave announced over the radio, so that the rest of team could plan their own positions.

'Romeo 3 standing ready to take point,' Fred advised. He was now fairly close behind Tony.

'I could let Fred take eyeball now, but I'm comfortable we are not showing out so we will continue with eyeball for now,' Tony said. 'But that is good to know the team are well placed.'

'Received,' was all he needed to say.

For the next 5 minutes the radio was mainly silent as the lorry, now driving much slower, navigated the country road. Twice the lorry passed a junction. Tony simply said, *'No change'*.

'Romeo 4 at junction of B1134 and Common Road,' Dave announced over the radio.

'Received,' said Tony. *'When Tango passes Romeo 4 to take eyeball with Romeo 3 as back-up.'*

Tony got confirmations. When he saw Chris exit the junction to take eyeball he hung back and slowed to allow Fred to overtake.

Five minutes later Dave was back on the radio., *'Tango is left, left, left onto unmade road,'* he announced. *'Romeo 4 flying by.'*

'All Units – Stop, stop, stop!,' announced Tony.

He explained to Will that the map suggested a track that ended in a dead-end after about half a mile, so no need to follow. Or more importantly, to follow would put them at risk of being noticed. The 'Stop' instruction, he said, was for all units to find a spot where they could observe the junction or be in a position to recommence the surveillance should the target move again.

The white flashing dot was now moving much slower; after four minutes it stopped moving. 'This looks like the destination, but we shouldn't assume anything. However, I've felt confident enough to alert Clive. They drove half a mile back down the B1134 to a telephone box Tony had noticed earlier. 'Come with me, you can listen in to the call.'

Will guessed that there must be some kind of hotline to Clive, as otherwise Clive would never leave his office.

'We think the lorry has got to its destination,' Tony announced to Clive when the line clicked through. 'The map suggests it is some sort of small farm or depot,' he gave Clive the coordinates. 'I recommend we get the CARS boys mobilised,' Tony advised.

'Yes, agreed.' said Clive. 'I'll put the call in and get them moving ASAP. In the meantime, I'll pass the coordinates to the Mapping team, and see if we can get some satellite imagery of the site. This should help the CARS team with their planning. If this is the site then we need to make the most of the darkness.'

'OK, we'll keep monitoring until CARS get here,' Tony said. 'I guess it's time for Will to go home,' he said looking at Will.

'Yes, I agree. I hope he's gained a lot from the experience. I will send a car.'

Clive ended the call.

'OK Will, you heard the man,' Tony said, 'this is the end of your education for today. And I bet you want to know what happens next? Well, there is good news and bad news. The good news is that I'll tell you all about CARS whilst we wait for your lift. The bad news is I can't tell you what is going to happen after. You've had some valuable experience today Will and it should be useful going forward. But there is a term you will hear a few times in the future – "need to know". And right now you don't need to know!'

Whilst they waited for the car to return Will to Dover, Tony outlined what the CARS team did.

CARS stood for Countryside and Rural Surveillance, he told Will. They were a team of surveillance experts who were skilled in getting very close to a target in rural situations. This involved them moving on foot very slowly and deliberately through terrain such as woods, trees, vegetation, bushes, and undergrowth, disguising themselves by wearing camouflage. Often the moves would take place under cover of darkness. They would then hide in natural ground positions close to the targets, not moving during daylight hours. For this operation they would use two CARS operatives to get a greater view of the targets with the intention of getting close enough to take photographs.

The car arrived and Will thanked Tony for all his tuition, it had been an eye-opener. Before midnight he was climbing back into his car on Langdon Cliffs, ready for the ten minutes journey to his house on the edge of town. He was itching to tell Alison about his experience, but Clive's words still echoed in his head. 'Tell no-one, not even your girlfriend.'

Fortunately she was fast asleep when he got home. They both worked odd hours, so his absence was not unusual, and she had been on a late shift so would not have missed him. *Just as well she was asleep he thought, as I would have been tempted to tell her everything.*

Nine

By midnight the CARS operatives, Bill and Nick, call signs Charlie One and Charlie Two, had arrived by VW Campervan. They parked up in a layby on the B1134 some two miles west of the lorry location. Tony met with them to brief them on the latest position, which hadn't changed. According to the tracker the lorry had not moved and according to the map there was no road exit other than where it had entered the track, which had been under constant surveillance. Bill and Nick had already met with the Mapping team on their way to the site. They had been furnished with the latest satellite image, which confirmed that the lorry was still in situ. More importantly the satellite image had shown what looked like a small freight yard, with two freight containers and some outbuildings, maybe maintenance huts. There was also a house, which probably contained offices. This had been enough for Clive to authorise CARS deployment.

At 00:30 hours they left their Campervan wearing camouflage clothes and carrying small camouflage rucksacks on their backs. They wore night-vision goggles and made their way through a hedge, across a ploughed field towards their target.

They then split up. Both spent the next 4 hours slowly taking different routes across fields, hedges, and ditches to get close to the depot. They had satellite navigation equipment which they checked periodically. Every hour they made brief contact over their covert radios to check progress. At 04.40 they were both in position. Bill was thirty metres to the southeast of one of the containers, in undergrowth behind some oil drums. Nick was about the same distance to the north on a small hillock beneath a slightly raised hedgerow, well concealed by brambles.

Nick heard the crackle of static in his earpiece and then a whispered message from Bill.

'Keep eyes and ears up......commencing plan Alpha.'

The great thing about trackers is that they are able to keep covert track of targets, but at some stage the tracker needs to be retrieved. The first task for the CARS was to recover the brick from under the lorry to ensure it did not get discovered later.

Bill moved very, very slowly, his night vision goggles providing a clear view of the lorry he was crawling towards, although the view was eerily green. The goggles were the latest 3rd generation and apart from the eerie green tint they were an enhancement on the previous model. He had a good view of his surroundings up to about one hundred metres. The lorry was about forty metres away to his left. He slowly moved his head from side to side to take in the landscape in front of him. Further to the left about sixty metres away was a large farmhouse, which looked like it had been converted into four accommodation units, maybe offices. Further to the left still he could make out a track, probably the track that the lorry had taken when it arrived. Moving his head back the other way brought a view of two shipping containers and a container lifting cradle. Beyond he could make out a few large buildings.

Suddenly his goggles picked up some movement to the right of one of the containers. He realised it was a small animal, probably a fox, but too far away to be sure. He noticed he had been holding his breath. He breathed out slowly. He wasn't worried about the nightlife, but he did worry about dogs. It was unlikely a dog would be roaming about in the open. But they could be a real big problem if they detected his presence and started barking and woke the household. He continued on his slow journey towards the lorry. Nick tracked him from his raised position in the hedge. He was also wearing goggles. He was looking and listening for any signs of movement.

By 05:30 Bill was back to his position behind the oil drums. Although not yet dawn there was a hint that dawn was coming, the dark was less dark. He had managed to secure the brick and had also checked out the containers, recording some of the markings and numbers on them, just in case this became relevant later.

It was time for both him and Nick to withdraw to a safer distance, to positions a bit further back, perhaps seventy-five metres from the lorry. This would ensure that they could be safely concealed throughout daylight, but were close enough to observe any activities and where they could take photographs of the targets if they came into view. On his earlier approach Bill had already noted a safe observation point (OP) he would use, a natural indentation in a small clump of bushes. He knew Nick would have located his own OP. At 06:15 Nick checked in with Bill. They were both now fully holed-up in their selected concealments. Nick had agreed to take the first two hour-watch to allow Bill to rest, but neither would sleep that day until the mission was complete. From now on, as voices, even whispers, could carry, it would be radio silence. They would revert to a pre-arranged simple click code if needed, to alert each other of any activity.

At 18:00 hours it had been dark for almost two hours, so Bill and Nick decided it was safe enough to extract. They worked their way slowly and carefully back to the Campervan.

Throughout the day they had seen and photographed six persons who had been in the house. They had observed the transfer of the crates from the lorry into one of the shipping containers. The lorry had left three hours ago, and no activity had been seen since as everyone else had returned to the house or offices.

Now that the goods had been transferred to a container, COGS got to work to revise their plan. Their original plan had involved the lorry, but now they were dealing with a container, the idea they had to stage an accident would probably work much better. But it did involve a bit of 'smoke and mirrors'. They put money on the fact that the container would be taken to Felixstowe, as the nearest container port. But, as usual, they were flexible and prepared for any change if necessary.

Ten

Mikhail somehow had suppressed his anger when Sergei had given him the news, but he wanted the detail, and ordered Sergei to investigate. Sergei had told Mikhail that the shipment had failed to reach Ireland. This was unbelievable.

Mikhail now had the embarrassment of calling the Irish customer and explaining that the goods would not be delivered as planned.

The customer was not happy, not happy at all. The customer understood, of course, that the non-delivery was not Mikhail's fault. But as the customer he wanted the problem redressed as soon as possible. And, of course, as the customer, he was looking for some compensation. Mikhail had controlled his anger, his grip on the receiver tightening. The nerve of these people. I'm the loser here, he thought angrily, they haven't even paid yet.

But he could see it from their point of view. Despite his anger he still had the ability to think straight. He rationalised that he would probably have reacted the same way, probably worse. He agreed that the next consignment would be arranged as quickly as possible. He promised some additional pieces of equipment at no extra cost. The deal was done, the customer sounded happy, but there was the expected veiled threat in the customers voice.

'And we would not want this delivery not to happen, now would we?'

Mikhail replaced the receiver down gently into the cradle. Then he stood up, picked up the whole telephone, and with all the power of his right arm he threw the appliance against the wall. The telephone plastic splintered into a thousand pieces and spilled it's electronic guts over the deep pile carpet. The crashing sound had Sergei run into the room. He saw the telephone in pieces, he saw the almost purple complexion on his Mikhail's face. He wished he was somewhere else right now.

'The nerve of those Irish bastards,' Mikhail almost spat, 'Do they know who they are dealing with? When this shipment is delivered and we get paid I'm going to blow these bastards up with one of their own bombs,' he stormed.

The thought of revenge always had a calming effect on Mikhail, he started to feel better already, an evil grin now forming from the corners of his mouth. Sergei had seen this 'Jekyll and Hyde' transformation several times before. Although still cautious, he was glad that Mikhail seemed to be calming.

'Do you remember Sergei, when you joined my gang, how I dealt with the man responsible for my father's accident?'

How could Sergei forget. He was only thirteen years old when he joined Mikhail's gang. Even at that young age he himself was not been averse to torture and violence. But that particular brutal act still gave him nightmares. The man had been beaten half to death, his legs had been badly damaged by some heavy blows with a baseball bat, but this wasn't enough for Mikhail.

The man was unable to stand without two of the gang members holding him up. Sergei recalled looking on with horror as Mikhail picked up an axe and approached him. With a swift and accurate blow he had chopped down on the man's left foot. The front of the man's shoe came clean away - along with his toes. Sergei recalled the blood-curdling scream, before Mikhail repeated the action on the man's right foot and the man passed out.

But that wasn't enough for Mikhail. He had ordered his men to place the man inside a large cement mixer. The blades inside the cement mixer, designed to turn the sand and cement mixture, proved to be excellent at slicing a body into smaller parts. As the cement mixer grinded and turned the screams of the man echoed around the drum before they abruptly stopped, as his head was severed on the second turn.

'That is how I will deal with those bastards,' his evil grin growing more pronounced.

Mikhail had been brought up within a crime family.

Uncle Nico and his father were cousins, his father a few years older. Although they both grew up in a poor rural community, Nico and his father had followed different paths. Both had done well at school, but Nico was the more academic, graduating from High School with a Silver Medal. He had become a candidate member of the Communist party while he was in high school having proved his loyalty by his passionate involvement in the Young Communist League. This led to full party membership a few years later when he graduated from Moscow university with a Business and Economics degree. He set up a construction business with the help of his party contacts. He also owned and ran a Cement Works on the outskirts of Moscow.

Mikhail's father, Alexander, gained a reputation at school for being a tough guy. He was smart enough to stay out of trouble, so his teachers never caught him doing wrong. But his classmates knew to keep out of his way, or they would suffer for it. He bullied the younger ones, stole their roubles, but threats of violence stopped them grassing.

At 18 years old he was called up to serve in the army. It was early in 1944, the war with Germany was still at its height. He quickly established himself as tough and ruthless so was given a position in the 'Barrier troops', a group of soldiers who served just behind the front line to 'encourage' other soldiers to engage the enemy. If they tried to retreat he was part of the group who shot them, a motivation to others to keep up the attack on the enemy.

In 1948 he left service and returned to the community farm that was his home and laboured on the land, but two years later got into trouble for stealing a horse. He was sentenced to five years hard labour. However, after three years he was released with a pardon. He was amongst eight million other prisoners who were released as a result of Stalin's death and the change of Communist leadership.

By then Nico had established his legitimate construction business, although was already earning extra money from burglary and dealing in black market goods. Mikhail's father decided to join Nico and help develop the crime business.

Whilst he had been in prison Nico had taken Mikhail under his wing.

As a teenager Mikhail quickly established himself as a leader amongst the gangs that roamed the streets. His gang was seen as the toughest. And Mikhail was the rottweiler in charge.

By the mid-sixties Mikhail's reputation and that of his family was notorious. Black market activity was protected by Nico's corrupt party officials. The crime family had moved on from simple burglary and dealing in stolen goods, to 'protection' and 'extortion'.

When Mikhail's father was killed Mikhail became Nico's right-hand man and quickly developed a taste for the finer things in life.

Mikhail eased himself slowly back down again into his chair behind his desk and poured a healthy measure of brandy.

'Sergei, you need to find out more,' Mikhail took a sip of his drink and said finally. 'I still can't believe the non-delivery was an accident, there must be more to it.'

Sergei was pleased that Mikhail had calmed down at last. He promised to leave no stone unturned to find out what had gone wrong.

***

It was now three weeks since Mikhail had been given the bad news and Sergei explained to Mikhail, for the second time, what he had managed to find out. He knew that Mikhail didn't trust him, he didn't trust anyone. As far as Sergei knew he had not given Mikhail any cause, so far everything he had promised he had delivered. But despite their long friendship he was aware he needed to be careful.

'As you requested Mikhail, the lorry driver has been spoken to. He's one hundred percent certain he was not followed to the depot. When he unloaded the crates into the container everything was ok. When he drove back to Dover there was no sign that he was being followed or monitored. The container was picked up at the depot by our second driver as planned. He's done a number of delivery jobs for us and is paid well to keep his mouth shut and the guys at the depot have no concerns. He's never told what he is hauling, and he never asks. I didn't speak to him directly, but according to our boys at the depot, they quizzed him about this delivery. He reported nothing out of the ordinary. He dropped the container into the designated shed at Felixstowe dock and drove his flatbed truck back to his own depot in Harwich. He's been driving containers around for nearly 10 years, everything was normal as far as he was concerned.'

Mikhail held up his hand to pause Sergei's report and stood up from his desk. He turned to look out of the window across Lake Balaton, whilst he absorbed this part of the story, looking for holes. There was always a possibility that the boys at the depot had something to do with it, but unlikely – they were Hungarians. He had known their leader, Zoltan, for nearly a year and Mikhail was sure he would not be stupid enough to cross him. Anyway, that wouldn't explain the accident.

Mikhail's gang had spent many hours debating the safest way to get the arms to Ireland. They had decided that using a container was the safest. Security forces at borders between England and Ireland were on high alert due to several provisional IRA bombings in the Province and on the mainland last year. So they were searching a lot of lorries that were using the ferries across the Irish sea. Therefore the idea of using a container had several advantages. Firstly, nearly 2,000 containers a week arrived at Dublin Port and very few were searched unless Customs had suspicions. Secondly, if the worst happened and the arms were discovered it would be near impossible to trace back to them as they had set up a bogus exporting company to cover their tracks. They also felt that leaving the container for a few weeks before shipment (which was a fairly normal scenario) was a way of checking that there was no undue interest from UK authorities before it shipped.

Sergei waited patiently and after two minutes Mikhail turned back to look at Sergei and said 'Ok, continue.'

***

Switching the containers was easier than COGS expected, helped by the fact that the container containing the weapons was not delivered to Felixstowe Port for another four days. This gave them extra time to prepare.

When the container arrived at Felixstowe, it was taken to the usual holding place. Containers got moved around a lot in the Port depending on when and where they were to be shipped. That night this particular container was moved to a shed where it sat next to a very similar looking container (courtesy of the CARS information and photographs). Overnight some minor touch-ups were completed. Next day an empty container that looked exactly like the one that contained crates of guns and ammunition, was collected from this shed, and placed on the stack ready for shipping.

It was nearly three weeks before this dummy container was moved again to be placed on the container ship, the Baltic Star, for its planned two-day trip to Dublin. The ships route was out into the North Sea, then through the English Channel before joining the Irish sea and into Dublin port.

The toughest parts of the COGS plan relied partly on the Captain of the container ship, and partly on the weather. With nearly three weeks to plan they identified who the Captain would be and did some background checking – was he a man who would readily assist them or would he need to be coerced? They struck lucky. Their Captain had previously spent ten years serving in the Royal Navy, working his way through the ranks to Lieutenant Commander before deciding to switch to the Merchant Navy. He had seen some action during the Falklands War in 1982 whilst he was serving on HMS Sheffield, which was hit by an Exocet missile. He had survived unscathed, but twenty of his colleagues were killed and several more badly injured. He loved being at sea, but the warfare and loss of so many friends and colleagues had had an impact on him. The opportunity of leaving the Royal Navy, but still having a seafaring job with the Merchant Navy, was very tempting. He worked hard and became Master of a general cargo vessel. After four years he gravitated to Captain of a container ship. When he heard what was required he was more than willing to help as he saw it as a way to still serve his country. He also suggested using one of his trusted crew to assist him. This avoided the need for a COGS operative to carry out the final function of releasing the locks and ensuring that the container was in the right position on the ship. It couldn't have worked out better.

***

Sergei finished his story. There wasn't much more to tell that wasn't already public knowledge.

'The container was loaded onto the ship as planned, the logs confirm this,' he said. 'Everything else is as it stated in the newspapers, and I've found nothing new. The Captain is a well-respected and experienced mariner, there is nothing to suggest that this was not just an unlucky accident. It turns out that across the world this happens much more than anyone had thought, we just don't get to hear about it. I've done some digging and the estimates suggest that around 500 containers per year are lost overboard in this way.'

Sergei went on for a few more minutes describing to Mikhail what the newspapers had reported.

During the night of 14th October, it was quite stormy in the English Channel and the Container ship, Baltic Star, reported that a container had been lost overboard in heavy seas. An examination had shown that a 'twist lock' had failed to lock in place when it was loaded. The container underneath had a damaged corner that had gone unnoticed at loading. As the container was on the top of the stack it was therefore not properly secured, and the stress on the other locks of the ship rolling in heavy seas was enough to cause it to topple sideways into the sea. It sunk almost immediately.

According to the shipping records the container contained furniture. The exporter would be reimbursed in full by the ship's insurance company. The investigation and initial findings of the Maritime and Coastguard Agency did not find anyone to blame. It concluded it was 'an unfortunate accident', but no doubt when the final report was complete some new rules and regulations would emerge.

What Sergei couldn't have known (and couldn't therefore tell Mikhail) was that there were many unnoticeable holes drilled into the container. This had ensured that it quickly filled with water - COGS could not risk the container not sinking.

Mikhail wanted someone to blame, he wanted retribution as always, but who? As much as he didn't want to believe this, he had no evidence that it was anything other than an accident.

Eleven

January 1991

Alison looked sad 'I'm going to miss you, she pouted. They hugged and kissed.

'I'll miss you too,' he responded. 'Perhaps we can go out for a meal when I get back on Friday?'

'I'm on lates on Friday,' she replied apologetically, 'but I'll see what I can book for Saturday if you like.'

Will climbed into his pride and joy, a 1975 Triumph Spitfire in racing green, a present he had bought for himself last year. The engine burbled to life, the sound always put a smile on his face. Alison waved enthusiastically and he set off.

It was a bright but chilly Sunday afternoon, and Will was on his way to Southend to start his new job on Monday morning in the Training Centre.

A month after returning from Switzerland he had been telephoned by the Senior Officer for Preventive training, Dave Campbell, and asked if he would like to work with them. Dave needed someone to cover for at least 6 months as one of his team was due to go on maternity leave. Will had met Dave a few months back when he attended the 'Train the Trainers' for the new Preventive course. Dave told him he thought Will would be ideal for the role. The post was only temporary and would mean staying in a Bed and Breakfast during the week and going home at weekends.

It had been nearly 3 months since Will had had the opportunity to observe that surveillance operation, but Clive had not made any further contact. Will might have wondered if Clive had had second thoughts about his recruitment, if it wasn't for the fact that he was now moving to the job that Clive had apparently lined up for him. They had not discussed how Clive would get hold of him and he had assumed it might be a letter like last time, or a phone call to the office, but so far nothing. He also had no idea what had become of the lorry. Clive and The Network would had done whatever it was that they needed to do, but he couldn't fathom what that might have been. Tony had told him that a specialist surveillance unit was on their way to relieve Tony and his team, but would not say more. 'We have a plan that will ensure that the arms and ammunition do not get to their destination,' was all he was prepared to tell Will. He had said that if Elias tried to contact Will through Brighthouse Freight Forwarders, then his team would 'deal with it', whatever that meant. So Will just tried to put it out of my mind.

His B&B was situated on a road just behind the Training Centre and less than two minutes' walk to the office front. Mrs. Hollis, a pleasant short plump lady in her seventies, welcomed him in and explained the rules, which were few.

'You will have your own key and breakfast will be at 07.30 sharp. As long as you don't play music too loud,' she said, 'we will get along famously.'

After a restful sleep, Will awoke at 6am. This was quite usual for him, but as he wasn't expected at the office until 9am, he decided to go for a stroll into Southend before breakfast. He dressed and showered, grabbed a hat, scarf and gloves and crept out quietly. It was cold and dark, but dry. He knew his way into town from his previous visit to Southend fifteen years ago for his Assistant Officer training course. Nothing much had changed. The shops were the usual mix of high street brands and small local enterprises. Will remembered with amusement a couple of local jewellers that were situated next to each other under the railway bridge that traversed the street. They must have been in constant competition. He was delighted to see they were both still there, the fight for customers no doubt still raging, he thought. Apart from a few early commuters heading for the railway station and a couple of sleeping tramps in shop doorways, it was quiet. The only noise came from a powered roadsweeper that was cleaning up the litter.

Twenty minutes later he was standing at the end of the town overlooking the estuary. It was still dark, and he could see a few ships lights out in the channel and some flashing buoys, marking wrecks or sandbanks he assumed. His thoughts jumped back to happier times and a similar scene in Dover, as he strolled hand in hand with Rachel along the White Cliffs. He could never love anyone the way he loved her.

The police had explained that she had not suffered and must have died instantly. 'Pronounced dead at the scene,' the coroner had subsequently reported, '...multiple injuries caused by her body colliding with an automobile travelling at speed.'

His parents made all the right noises when he telephoned to tell them, but weren't much support. He wasn't close to them. They had moved to Chester ten years ago with his dad's job and he barely saw them. They visited only a handful of times and only met Rachel once when she insisted that they went to visit them after announcing their engagement. His mum was pleasant to Rachel, but showed no real warmth or affection. This was no surprise to Will as she had not shown him much as he grew up. His boss was really supportive though. 'Take all the time you need,' he had said. 'If you need anything just ask.' His colleagues were similarly supportive, but he didn't really have any close friends. He enjoyed his work life, the banter, the parties, but had never really come to see them as friends. His one true friend, Ed, was working in Germany for a telecoms company. Will didn't really know what he did, but he seemed well paid for it. They had met at Secondary school and remained friends ever since. Will would tell Ed when he saw him, but he wasn't due back in the UK for two months.

After he had got over the shock, a few days after her death, Will learnt from the police that a man had been charged with 'death by dangerous driving'. A witness had stated that the car that hit Rachel was a red Porsche travelling at speed. He said that Rachel could not have seen the car as it sped around the corner as she stepped into the road. Rachel had been visiting her best friend and chief bridesmaid Emily. They had spent the evening at her house at the other end of Kearsney, the village where they both lived, near Dover. They had been making wedding plans.

The police advised him that on the night in question they had managed to track the Porsche to an address in the nearby village of Whitfield (there were no other red Porsches listed on DVLA in this part of Kent). But it was 1am before they got to talk to the driver. He admitted he had driven through Kearsney earlier that evening, but had not seen a woman. He was clearly intoxicated but he denied that he had been drinking and driving. He had drunk half a bottle of whisky since getting home about 11pm, he said. The police did not believe him, but could not prove otherwise. However, based on what the witness had said and some impact damage noticed on the front nearside wing, they took him to the station and questioned him further. Later, forensics would prove that it had traces of blood and fibres that were a match to Rachel. He then admitted that he thought he might have hit a cat or small animal, but thought little about it at the time. The police decided there was enough to charge and after a brief appearance in Magistrates court, Gary Busby (known as Gazza) was sent for trial at Crown court.

The Crown court case had occurred some months after Rachel's death, but Will made a decision not to attend. He did not want to hear the details of Rachel's death again, or any attempt by Defence or their client Gary Busby to plead any sort of mitigation. He knew how it worked, he had been a witness in several Customs trials. There was always half-truths or smoke-screens spread by Defence to try to influence the jury and get their client freed. But the police were confident that he would be found guilty and get a custodial sentence, so Will relied on that and stayed away.

When the police told him later that Gary had been found 'not guilty', Will was shocked and angry. The Police were very sympathetic and privately said that they were convinced that he was drunk, and driving dangerously, and were equally surprised by the verdict.

The police explained that the witness, Harry Carpenter, a retired farm laborer, stated in court that the Porsche had been driving too fast through the village. The woman could not have seen the car race around the corner as she stepped off pavement at the wrong time. She was spun around by the impact and fell to the ground.

But when the witness was cross-examined by the clever high-paid Defense barrister he was made to look unreliable. It transpired that he had just left pub when he saw the accident. Defense called the landlord of the pub to give evidence who confirmed that Harry had been in the pub all evening and drunk at least six pints. Furthermore, they then called Rachel's friend Emily. She reluctantly agreed that she and Rachel had shared a bottle of wine together. Will could imagine the way that the barrister would have twisted this new information – something like,

'You have heard the evidence of the landlord, members of the jury. The witness was the worst for drink and would not be capable of determining if the Porsche was speeding. Sadly the poor woman staggered into the road because she was intoxicated. A most unfortunate, but nonetheless, accident of her own making.'

The Jury felt there was not enough evidence 'beyond reasonable doubt', that Gary was driving dangerously or speeding, so they found him not guilty.

Justice had not been done. **But justice will be done Will vowed.**

Every day since Rachel had died he thought of her. Sometimes he even spoke to her when he was alone. He told her that he still loved her and that it wasn't her fault. He told her not to be cross with him for what he had done to seek justice. He had done what needed to be done. Life had got easier since he had met Alison, she seemed to understand. But some things went unsaid and other things would not be shared, he decided.

It was getting cold standing still, so he made his way up through town and along Victoria Avenue back to the B&B. As he entered he could smell the familiar aromas of a cooked breakfast. Mrs. Hollis shouted from the kitchen that breakfast would be ready in five minutes. Will dumped his outdoor clothes in his room and made his way back down the stairs to the dining room. The breakfast was delicious, with cereal followed by bacon, egg, mushrooms, sausage, and fried bread, and all the toast he could eat. If he ate this every day he was going to be like 'Michelin man' within three months, he thought.

Twelve

The Training Centre offices were in one of several office blocks that shouldered the main road into Southend. Will felt a flutter of anticipation, but was not at all nervous as he entered the building. Reception booked him in, and two minutes later Dave stepped out of the lift to greet him. He took Will up to the 5th floor and into his office. The ashtray was overflowing with Benson and Hedges butts and the aroma of cigarette smoke hung in the air.

After some brief small talk, they settled down with a coffee and Dave lit up again before getting straight down to business.

'Really glad you decided to join us, we've a lot of Preventive courses to organise and run, so your background will be immensely helpful. I'll introduce you to the team in a minute, but first let me give you an outline of what I expect from you.' Dave went through some general information and then focused in on the key roles he had lined up for him.

'Firstly, we need to get you to start looking at some venues for the May and June courses. That might seem a long way off, but you'll soon learn that we need to be about 6 months ahead in booking accommodation, so we're already behind. Good venues are hard to find as we approach Summer, so we've got to get cracking. We've some possible hotels in mind in Brighton and Eastbourne, so I want you to do the groundwork on them this week for suitability. Don't worry, I've got Paul on the team lined up to help you get to grips, but after this week I expect you to get on with it and make decisions for yourself. Next week we've got a hotel in Cheltenham we want checked out, so you'll be on your own for that one. Any problems with that?'

'None at all.' Will said. 'Can't wait to get stuck in.'

Will had heard that Dave had previously been in the Royal Navy as a Lieutenant, and was known to treat his team like he was still on-board ship. Will had been expecting this style, but he actually quite liked it. At least he knew exactly what was needed from him.

'That's the spirit, now let's go and meet the rest of the crew.'

The crew was made up of two other Higher Officers (HO's) like Will, a couple of Executive Officers (EO's) and three Assistant Officers (AO's), who generally dealt with the course administration, copying papers, delivering material to venues, booking students onto courses etc. Paul was one of these, a 20-year-old in his first job, but it quickly became apparent that Paul was very fast and efficient, knew his stuff, and would soon be promoted, he had no doubt.

The two HO's were out of the office, but Will was introduced to the rest of the team and made to feel very welcome. He recognised one of the EO's as she had been a role-player on his train-the-trainers course. Cathy was her name. She was in her late thirties, with short dark brown hair cut in a pageboy style. She clearly remembered him and took it upon herself to start sorting out his building pass and other admin that he needed to enable him to function. John was the other EO, a much quieter and less confident individual Will thought, but still pleasant enough. He was twenty-eight he discovered, and appeared to be the Office manager. Will later learnt that he managed all the AO's. The other two AO's were in their late fifties. Steve, who was seriously overweight and sweating constantly, and Beryl, who was stick thin, with long dark hair almost to her waist.

Introductions over Will was shown to his desk in the HO's office across the corridor, which he would share with the other two HO's. The office was huge, so he was more than happy.

The day rolled by, and he was introduced to a ton of other people in the building as he was shown around by Cathy. Will doubted he would remember half their names, but the welcome from everyone was genuine and he knew he was going to enjoy it here. He had built up a good rapport with Cathy, as she escorted him around, whilst they chatted about his job in Dover and her previous role. She had been in uniform at Harwich as an Assistant Officer so knew the job well.

As he was in a B&B with no evening meal provided he had to venture out in search of a suitable takeaway. The guys in the office had suggested a good Indian about five minutes down the road, which they had nicknamed the 'Green Chicken'. Querying the name Will was advised that it was due to the owner previously being fined by public health for preparing food that was past it's best. He thought he might give this a miss. Instead he decided on pizza and bought a spicy pepperoni to take back to the digs. By 8pm he had eaten and watched a bit of telly but was already bored so decided that a trip to the pub for a pint was in order. He had seen the Spread Eagle whilst searching for the pizza shop and it looked like his kind of establishment, just outside of the main town. He didn't fancy heading into the town tonight, he would save that pleasure for another time.

As expected on a Monday evening it was quiet. A handful of customers, mostly older than him, congregated around tables, with a couple of young lads propping up the bar. Will was completely ignored as he strolled to the bar. He ordered a pint of London Pride from the tired looking, but cheerful fifty something landlord, and he took it over to the fruit machine in the corner. He wasn't a great fan of these machines as felt he was certain to lose, but he had a pocket full of change from his pizza and beer transactions so he thought it might amuse him for a while. He settled onto the stool in front of the machine. He had just entered five 10p coins and was studying how the machine worked, when he was interrupted by a voice to his right.

'Will, hello, fancy meeting you here.'

Will nearly fell off the stool as he looked up quickly, startled by that familiar Etonian tone.

'Clive, where did you spring from?' he blurted.

'You'd be surprised,' Clive smiled. 'Finish your game and your pint and let us go for a stroll,' he said.

Will gulped his beer down, pressed the machine buttons and lost fifty pence, as expected. Then he followed Clive out the door. The stroll lasted all of a minute as they arrived at what looked like the same Black Ford Granada that picked him up from Gatwick. It looked identical, but Will knew it wasn't. Being a Customs Officer he was trained to be observant. He specialised in car traffic and had a thing about number plates; he tended to memorise those of interest – this one was different.

But the driver was the same guy and he smiled and nodded as Will and Clive climbed into the back seat.

'Best to talk away from prying ears,' Clive said, with a chuckle at his own deliberate use of ears. 'How have you been?'

Well it was good of him to ask, Will thought. 'I've been fine thanks, but I wondered when you'd make contact. As usual you've popped up unexpectedly,' he exclaimed, but he said it with a smile as he was actually pleased to see him.

'That's good, I'm glad you are ok, because we've a situation brewing and need you to be available sooner rather than later. It has to do with Elias, but more on that in a minute. How's your new job going, have you settled in?'

Will was taken aback with the switch from a conversation about Elias to his new job, but he was starting to understand Clive's style and knew that this was a deliberate act on his part. Clive would get to the point in his own way when the time was right.

'As I'm sure you know this is my first day, but everyone is really supportive, I think it was a good move. Dave knows what he wants from me, and it seems he expects me to just get on with it, at least after I've been shown the ropes this week.'

'Excellent, excellent, just what I'd hoped. I'll cut to the chase - we need you, or rather "Bill" to meet with Elias next week in Lucerne. Elias has requested the meeting, so it looks like another consignment might be on the move. You clearly impressed him and the Criminal gang, so your stock is good.'

This was all moving a bit fast, and Will had a dozen questions, but Clive hadn't finished yet.

'When you meet with Elias, we've a task for you. You will need to receive some specialist training to achieve it, so we've arranged for you to do this in Cheltenham next Tuesday, as this is where you will be assessing a new hotel venue for your Customs Prevention training.'

How did he know this? Had he bugged Dave's office?

'You must have lots of questions, so fire away and I will do my best to answer them.'

Will launched into his queries. One thing he wasn't clear on was the communication with Elias – how did they know Elias wanted him to visit? It turned out that Elias had called the Brighthouse number, and as Tony had explained to him, someone from COGS had fielded the call. He then discovered that Elias had phoned three times since Will had met him, the first call was a week after they had met, to congratulate him on getting their lorry through Customs. Will wanted to know what had happened to the lorry after they had followed it to Suffolk, but Clive was still not prepared to tell him.

'Our goal was to convince the Crime gang that a pathway had been developed for regular illegal traffic, but don't worry dear boy, the guns never made it to their destination – I can't give you details but let us just say that an unfortunate accident meant that the buyer did not receive the goods. Oh, and a cheque was sent to Brighthouse Freight Forwarders for £1000 in the name of Bill Mitchell, so we know they were happy with the job you did.'

Clive then advised that Elias had called again a couple of weeks ago asking for a call back, and again last Friday. Each time Elias had been advised that Bill was unavailable, but on the last call he had insisted that Bill called back and had asked that Bill go to Lucerne next week. The first and most important task was for Will to call him back and arrange this for next Wednesday.

The specialist training was his next concern – what task did he need to complete that required this and what was it? He was right to be concerned.

'We need you to search Elias's office and find details of any customers who are based in Ireland and photograph the documents you find.' Clive explained. 'That will mean gaining access out of hours. Before you ask, yes, we did consider using one of our operatives, but you're the only one who has been inside the building. Although you could have described the layout there is no substitute for first-hand knowledge.' He looked at Will as if daring him to object then continued. 'The yard sometimes stays open during early evening for late lorry arrivals but is always closed and locked up by 10pm, so we suggest going in after midnight to be sure. The main gate is padlocked, and the main office building is alarmed, but we have the code. No doubt Elias locks his office and his desk drawers, which is where your training comes in – you're going to learn how to pick locks,' he said with a flourish, like Will had just been awarded a cracking prize in a TV game show.

'What if I get caught,' Will blurted out. His first outing to Lucerne on behalf of Clive and his gang was fair enough, but now he was going to be 'Bill the Burglar'. If he got caught he felt sure that the Swiss would be as equally upset, or even more robust than the British justice system when it came to punishment.

'Part of your training is how not to get caught,' Clive responded, 'but in the unlikely event, we've enough sway with the Swiss authorities to solve the problem.' He emphasised *solve the problem* in a way that suggested some underhand dealing or bribery.

'What if it is Elias or one of his men who catches me in the building? I suspect they might not bother with the Police!' Will could hear the panic in his own voice now and knew he was over-reacting, but this whole scenario had caught him off-guard.

'Will, my dear boy,' Clive said in a fatherly tone, 'the reason you've been chosen to join my organisation is because you have already proved yourself to be resourceful and shown you can think on your feet. The training we give you will only enhance those qualities. I will admit,' he said in a quieter almost apologetic tone, 'that some of that training comes later, but in the meantime we have to react to the time pressures that this Criminal gang are placing on us.' Then Clive's normal happy confident tone resumed. 'However, I can give you my assurances,' he stated cheerfully, 'that we will be watching your back the whole time.'

Will did not feel reassured at all, but Clive advised that he would be more fully briefed next Tuesday, and it was clear Clive was about to end the conversation and kick him out of the car. He gave Will a telephone number for Elias and another number to call at 08:30 on Tuesday morning.

Will watched the Granada drive off and stood for a moment in the yellow light of the nearby lamppost whilst he reflected on the conversation that had just happened. *What had he got himself into?* But it didn't stop him feeling a little bit excited.

The rest of the week went fairly smoothly. He called Elias on the number Clive had given him and apologised for missing his earlier calls. He confirmed he would be happy to go to Lucerne next Wednesday. He asked Elias the reason for the meeting, but Elias was cagey and just said, 'We have some more work for you, following your last success.'

Making plans for the following week took a bit of thought and preparation. His covert role required Will to be in Cheltenham on Tuesday, Lucerne on Wednesday, then returning to the UK on Thursday, all without his work colleagues knowing. And of course, fit in the visit to the hotel that he was meant to be assessing. Because Cheltenham was a fair distance from Southend it was expected that he book into a hotel for two nights next week (not the hotel he was reviewing), which gave him some scope and flexibility to manage everything. Dave had made it clear that he expected Will to manage his own time and there was no need to bother him with what he was doing. As long as he got the job done Dave wasn't going to be looking over his shoulder. Will quickly learnt that days out of the office were perfectly normal for the HO's and as long as everyone else knew that they were out on business and broadly where, then that was OK. He had never had this level of freedom before, but it was most welcome in the circumstances.

He worked out that if he travelled to Cheltenham on Monday afternoon he could probably visit the hotel and make his assessment that day. This would then free him up for his work for Clive. He had booked a pool car, a Vauxhall Cavalier estate for collection on Monday, so getting around wouldn't be a problem.

Thirteen

He left the office at 4.30pm on Friday knowing it would be a slow journey back to Dover in the rush hour. He had been mulling over his impending trip next week and was finally happy he had prepared as best he could. But he remained uncomfortable with keeping the whole scenario from Alison. Since he got recruited by Clive back in September, his relationship with Alison had continued to flourish. Lying to her now would be difficult.

As he drove out of Southend along the busy dual carriageway arterial road towards the Dartford tunnel, he came to a decision. He would ignore Clive's rules and planned to tell her everything. Part of this decision was linked to what Zoe had said. She had told Jan because she felt it was the right thing to do. He felt the same. All he needed to do was pick his time over the weekend. He was sure she would be OK with it. Afterall, as a policewoman she was no stranger to challenging and threatening situations. Every day she faced new and unexpected risks. The only issue might be the fact that Will hadn't told her earlier.

He was shaken from his thoughts as suddenly his car lost power. One second he was cruising at seventy, the next he had no acceleration. The road was busy and cars were moving up fast behind him – he needed to get off the carriageway straightaway. He spotted a turn off thirty yards ahead, indicated and swiftly took the turn into a narrow lane. The car limped on at thirty miles an hour, then started kangarooing. It managed another two hundred more yards before giving one final lurch and coming to rest. That was a bit hairy, he thought.

He tried to start it. The engine turned over but wouldn't fire up. He gave up after four attempts as he knew it would only drain the battery. Probably a fuel blockage.

Damn. He had owned the car for a couple of years and had had a few minor issues, as expected from an old classic car, but nothing like this. He flipped the lever to open the bonnet before rummaging around the glovebox to grab his screwdriver, the only tool he had in the car. He tried to see what might have caused the breakdown but despite a nearby streetlight and his headlights on, it was too dark to see anything obvious.

There were some houses about a hundred yards further up the street so hopefully he could find a telephone to call the AA. He switched off the lights, locked the car and headed for the houses.

The car had mis-behaved just after the Basildon turning so this must be the outer edge of town. Not a place he wanted to be for sure – rough and very rundown. He noticed that the streetlight close to his car was the only one working between the main road and the houses up ahead. The broken glass he passed probably explained why the others were inoperative.

It was just before 5pm. He could hear the heavy traffic from the main road he had just been travelling on, but now only a few hundred yards away, he felt isolated and unsafe. There were no walkers about and no cars moving. It was eerie.

As he reached the first few houses, he saw two large blocks of rough concrete positioned in the road. They were the size of big bales of hay. In his haste to get off the main road he hadn't noticed that he had entered a no through road. That at least explained the lack of cars. The blocks had grass growing from underneath and blown litter was strewn all around them. They had clearly been there some time. Probably some years ago the council had decided that this route onto the main road was too risky. He could understand. He could foresee the problems he was going to have getting back onto the carriageway into the fast-moving traffic. But first, of course, he needed to get his car mended.

The first house looked in a state of disrepair. A light blazed in the uncurtained front window, a good sign perhaps? But it looked uninviting. A broken washing machine and haphazard black sacks of rubbish adorned the front lawn, next to a rusting car up on blocks.

Will moved on down the street, but the next few houses were similarly unkempt. Then a few yards further on he spied a telephone box. He didn't loiter and increased his pace. No one was using the phone. This turned out to be no surprise, when he opened the door to see a smashed handset and wires hanging from the earpiece. What now? He looked around and noticed what looked like a small shop fifty yards further up the road. As he got closer it proved to be a newsagent.

Five minutes later after a helpful shop assistant let him use the phone, he was on his way back to his car. The AA estimated 45 minutes.

As he re-passed the concrete blocks his car came into view. But the car was not alone. Two men were showing an unhealthy interest in her – they appeared to be trying to get the drivers' door open.

'Oi,' he shouted as he started to sprint towards them.

Initially they froze and turned to run in the opposite direction. But then when Will was still fifty yards away, they slowed and turned back. Will had a better view of them. One was white and one black, both in their late teens. The white guy was the bigger of the two, easily six foot, but carried a bit of weight. He wore a black leather bikers jacket over a grubby white t-shirt. The black guy was shorter and wiry. He was wearing a denim jacket covered in sew on patches and wore a black baseball cap.

Will wasted no time considering the risk this presented and kept up his run. They had clearly decided that he wasn't a threat and that he would likely back off. They didn't know what he was capable of, he thought.

He got to within twenty feet and stopped, got his breath back. The teens just stood there next to his car – a Mexican stand-off. 'I suggest you guys go on home and leave my car alone,' Will said with authority. 'We wouldn't want anyone to get hurt now would we.'

The black guy with the baseball cap laughed, 'We were going to break into your car, but now you are here you can give us the keys,' he said cockily.

Will looked at them closely. 'Baseball cap' was not very big, only about five feet eight, but he looked quick. Will would need to take him first. 'Leather jacket' looked big, but it was mostly a beer belly. If he had a weapon it would be trouble, but otherwise his reactions would be slow and a kick in the right place would put him down easily.

Will had trained in martial arts as a teenager and achieved a black belt in karate. But his karate teacher was also keen to equip his students with some street survival techniques. 'Karate is a discipline,' he said, 'but to survive on the street you need to be ruthless.' Will remembered the advice. 'Go in first, go in hard and don't hang around to admire your handiwork.'

Will started a slow walk forwards. They looked surprised. They had expected Will to back-off, but now this man was coming towards them. They looked less confident.

He stopped, now less than five feet from them. They were standing together. Dumb. If they had separated it would have made it harder for him. Baseball cap was to the right and Leather jacket to the left. He anticipated that Baseball cap would react first.

'This is your last chance,' he said, 'Beat it home or you will get carried out of here by ambulance,' Will said levelly. He stared at them, unflinching. He breathed slowly, relaxed his shoulders but stood with feet apart and slightly on the balls of his feet. He mentally rehearsed his moves. *A stride forward on his left foot, then a roundhouse with his right leg to the head of Baseball cap, followed by a right punch to his kidneys. Then a side kick to Leather jacket to his thigh – a dead-leg, followed by a double punch to his head.*

Baseball cap looked at Leather jacket, presumably to get some unsaid agreement, but Will didn't wait for a response. They had briefly distracted themselves, so he moved in fast.

By the time Baseball cap had looked up the kick was already on the way to his head – too late to avoid. The kick sent him reeling, but the punch to his kidneys put him down.

Leather jacket was still trying to process what had happened to his friend, but he recovered quickly. But not before his leg went dead from Will's side kick. He tried to parry Will's punches, but was off balance. He took the double punch, but remained standing. It took two more punches, one hard to the face and another to the stomach that doubled him over. He went down whimpering in pain. Baseball cap was starting to get up so Will kicked him full face, not too hard. He was out for the count.

Ordinarily Will would have followed his teachers advice and left, but he had to wait until the AA arrived. He checked them out. Leather jacket was still down, moaning and holding his stomach. Baseball cap was unconscious, blood was oozing from a split lip, but he was breathing ok. These two were not going anywhere soon. He hadn't wanted to hurt them, but he had warned them. Six years ago he would have walked away, but personal risk and conflict didn't bother him now. Perhaps they would think twice in future about trying to steal someone else's possessions.

Five minutes later an amber flashing light announced the arrival of the AA man. He was flabbergasted by the sight of the two teens.

'I'm glad you are here quickly, 'Will said. 'Can you call an ambulance before sorting my car. I found these guys by my car. I think they must have been mugged. It seems like a dangerous place to be hanging out, if you ask me. Who knows, I could have been next.'

He could tell by the look on his face that AA man didn't believe him. AA man looked again at the teens, looked at Will then looked at Will's car. 'It's a dodgy area around here,' he said. 'I was here a few weeks back on another breakdown and a couple of lads tried to nick some of my tools out the back of my van.' He looked at the teens again. 'They were probably up to no good and should've known better.' He radioed in a request for an ambulance.

'Ok let's see about your car,' he said.

Will explained how the car had behaved and AA man came to the same conclusion – fuel starvation. It took him minutes to strip out and clean the fuel filter. When he had finished the car started and ran perfectly.

'You don't mind if I leave you to wait for the ambulance do you,' Will said, 'I am already running late due to the breakdown.'

'No problem, I will take care of this,' he said, looking down at the still prone lads.' They probably deserved it. You take care now.'

Will jumped into his car and headed for the main road. As expected it was hard to get a gap in the fast-moving traffic, but a gap appeared as an ambulance slowed to make a turn into his road.

Fourteen

The weekend did not go well. Will had thought a nice meal out with Alison on Saturday night would give him the perfect opportunity to discuss his role in the Network. As it turned out circumstances conspired against this, and the conversation never happened. It was one of those times when, whatever could go wrong did go wrong, as the 'queen of bad luck' paid them a visit.

Being away all week meant he needed to get his clothes washed, dried and ironed before returning to Southend on Sunday afternoon. After his disrupted journey he got home at 7pm. Alison was at work, but said she would be staying over tonight, so should back about 11.30pm. Chance to get his clothes washed. He unpacked his case and threw the laundry into the machine. Then he had a thought. His trousers and shirt had some spots of blood on them, so he decided to strip down to his underwear and throw them in as well.

Alison spent time at his house when he was around, but hadn't been there all week, so the fridge held nothing appetising.

A short stroll to the fish and chip shop was in order. He pulled on a fresh pair of jeans and jumper, slipped on his jacket and was back home in ten minutes with cod and chips. He was hungry, but as he stepped into the kitchen all thoughts of food went out of his head. A large puddle of water had formed on the kitchen floor, getting bigger by the second. Water was spurting out of the washing machine door. He grabbed the towel and tea towel to mop some of the water, but they quickly became soaked as more water flowed out. He ran upstairs to the bathroom and grabbed all the towels off the rail and nearly fell down the stairs as he raced back to the kitchen.

By now most of the floor was covered with water, but he could see that the water had almost stopped flowing from the machine. He threw the towels down and grabbed the bowl from the sink as he soaked up the water and wrung the towels out into the bowl. Several full bowls poured down the sink and he finally had most of the water mopped up. He breathed a sigh of relief and yanked open the washing machine door. He noticed that the trousers he had thrown in last were partially hanging out; could this be why it leaked? He pulled the still soaking clothes out into a wash basket and had a closer look at the door. Seemed ok, but then he saw it. A large rip in the rubber door seal. This was clearly the cause of the flood, but how did that happen – he hadn't noticed the rip in the seal when he loaded the machine? Then he had a thought. He rummaged through the washing until he found his trousers. In the pocket was a screwdriver.

When the car had broken down and he had grabbed the screwdriver out of the glovebox he had stuffed it into his pocket. The trousers must have caught in the door and the screwdriver had clearly done its worst and ripped the rubber seal. That will teach him. At least the fish and chips were still warm.

Alison got home on time and Will regaled her of his eventful day (leaving out the encounter with the teens). She laughed at his misfortunes, and they snuggled up together. Will had really missed her. She was on earlies tomorrow, so there was not much more chat.

Next morning, with Alison at work, Will needed to arrange a washing machine repair. But first he would have to go to the laundrette with his wet, but unwashed clothes. The laundrette was straightforward, if a little boring. Getting someone out to fix the washing machine, however, was harder. Yellow pages showed three possible repairers in the area, but none of them were answering. Then he spotted an advert for a shop that sold spare parts. He gave them a call. They were very helpful and explained that the seal was an easy fix and had his seal in stock.

By lunchtime he had fixed it himself and checked it didn't leak. Result. By the time Alison walked through the door he had finished ironing and had his clothes neatly stacked ready for packing tomorrow.

'I see you've been a busy boy,' she said as she grabbed him for a hug and a kiss. 'How do you fancy a little shop in M and S. I thought I might buy some new underwear for our evening out,' she said, a glint in her eye and her tone of voice betraying what was on her mind.

How could he refuse?

She was not at all embarrassed as they trawled the aisles, with Will quietly making suggestions on what she would look good in, and eventually she chose some sexy red lace underwear and suspender belt, items that were guaranteed to make the evening a very pleasant one indeed. Things were definitely looking up.

The evening started well as they prepared to go out. Will put on his usual smart trousers and casual shirt instead of jeans and t-shirt, and Alison spent over an hour getting ready. When she came down she looked gorgeous. There was an anticipation in the air as he imagined the sexy lingerie he knew she was now wearing. Then the phone rang. It was Alisons sister, Tina, and she sounded in a flap.

'Hi Will,' she said, sounding a little distressed. 'Is Alison there, I need to talk to her urgently.'

Will passed the phone over. From the responses Alison was making it was clear that something was very wrong, and that Alison's help was needed. It sounded like Alan, Tina's husband, had had some sort of an accident. Alison ended the call by saying. 'I'll be there in ten minutes.'

She put the phone down and explained the issue. 'I'm really sorry Will, but Tina's husband has been in a car accident and is in hospital. He's not badly hurt apparently but Tina needs to get there and needs someone to babysit little Jack.' Jack was Tina's three-year old son and Will loved the little fellow. He wasn't normally great with kids, but had taken to this bright and cheerful lad and they seem to have bonded.

'Of course,' Will said, 'You need to go. Do you want me to come too?' he asked.

'Yes, if you' sure. Perhaps we can get ourselves a take-away. Can you call the restaurant and cancel.

So, Will's best laid plans to tell Alison everything had been scuppered. As well as a promised night of passion, he thought. Never mind, maybe tomorrow morning as Alison is on lates.

But the queen of bad luck had not finished.

It turned out that Alan's injuries were superficial, but he was kept in overnight for observation, so Tina had come home.

Alison offered to stay, but Tina said she would be fine, so Will and Alison left, getting home at 1am. They were both tired, so the promised night of passion had fallen off the agenda.

It had been raining all night, including some heavy bursts. Will had a disturbed sleep, mainly because of the thundering rain on his conservatory roof. Let's hope it copes with this deluge, he thought.

The conservatory was already part of the house when he bought it a couple of years ago, but it was more like a lean-to than a proper conservatory. He had always thought he should get a professional one built, but up to now it had been sound and waterproof, so he hadn't got around to it. He had often checked during heavy rain to see if it had leaked and was always gratified to see that it had stood up well to the elements. But not today.

Where the conservatory met the house wall, water was pouring down the inside. When he got up at 8am there was already a healthy puddle spreading across the floor and there were streaks of water down the wall spanning about three feet. Will's guess was that the flashing, the join between roof and wall, had given up its fight with the rain. Not an easy fix whilst it was raining. All he could think of to do was try some sort of temporary fix inside the conservatory roof until the weather improved.

He left Alison mopping up water whilst he headed for the shed looking for inspiration on what would help stop the leak. He came across some tape he had used last year to fix some leaking guttering, which might work as he recalled this stuff could be used even when wet. But he also recalled it had the constituency of fibreglass resin and was very messy to use. This wouldn't be noticed on the outside, but would leave an unacceptable looking gash on an inside repair, so he dismissed the idea.

Alison was shouting at him to hurry up as the rain seemed to get heavier, but there was simply nothing else in his shed that was likely to solve the problem. Reluctantly, there was only one solution. He grabbed the tape and his stepladder, donned his waterproof and set about repairing the problem from the outside. The rain lashed down.

An hour later, after he had gotten completely soaked to his skin, he was now soaking again, only this time in a hot bath. Alison brought him a steaming hot cup of tea as he lay there in the suds recovering his body temperature. All in all Will felt pretty satisfied. He would admit he was not the greatest at DIY, but despite initially making a bit of a mess with the resinous tape, he had finally stopped the leak, and the finished job did not look too bad; unless you craned your neck out of the bathroom window to look.

He padded out of the bathroom naked and entered the bedroom. The sight before him suddenly made all the drama of the last two days melt away. Alison was languishing on the bed dressed in the lingerie she had bought yesterday.

'Couldn't have you leaving me for another week without something to remember, now could I,' she said, a sexy leer on her face.

Will didn't need a second invitation and leapt on her. The fire was ignited in both of them and in seconds they were joined and lost in a passionate exploration of each other's bodies.

One hour later and completely sated they laid together gently stroking each other in the post-coital after glow.

Will felt the urge to open the subject of his role in The Network, but knew it would spoil the moment. There is always next weekend, he told himself. He really was falling for Alison. Was this love? Could he even love again after Rachel?

Fifteen

It was 8:35am on Tuesday and Will had just finished a call with the contact Clive had given him, a man who called himself Matt. He would be outside Will's Cheltenham hotel in his car in ten minutes, so Will had to get his skates on and finish packing his bags. He was due to return to stay at the hotel that night, but had been advised to bring all his belongings just in case there was a change of plan.

Late yesterday he had managed to see the hotel he was there to assess, the Queens Hotel. He met with the Assistant Manager who showed him around the facilities. The hotel was looking tired and in need of refurbishment, which was no doubt why it was available in May and June and was offering good conference rates.

The four-week Customs Officer course, known as a 'Preventive' course, had lots of requirements – twenty students and four trainers would be residential during weekdays. There was a need for one big 'classroom' and at least six smaller rooms to conduct 'role-plays' which were filmed on video cameras.

The action would be piped live to a TV in another room to enable those outside of the room to watch. In addition, during weeks three and four there were a lot of visiting role-players who would stay overnight, so additional bedrooms would be needed.

A lot of hotels struggled with this provision as in some cases the course virtually took over the place, but Edward, the Assistant Manager was falling over himself to be accommodating. He clearly saw this as a lucrative opportunity and wasn't going to lose the contract by being awkward.

Will's main concern was the lack of additional rooms, and he shared this concern with Edward.

'The main conference room would work as a classroom, but we need more other smaller rooms to meet our needs,' he explained.

Edward pondered this for a moment and then flashed Will a smile as if a lightbulb had gone off in his head, and said, 'Follow me, I have just the thing that will solve this.'

He led Will down a corridor outside of the conference room away from the direction you would normally go to reach reception and the lifts, and headed down a further, less well-lit corridor. There appeared to be eight hotel bedroom doors off to the left. They were clearly not in use as the corridor was very grubby and unkept and was mainly filled with ladders, old paint pots and dust sheets.

'We have a plan refurbish this part of the hotel,' he explained, 'and convert these rooms into luxury suites, but the plan is on hold until next winter. The rooms are large, and we can clear them out and tidy this area and you could have sole use of this part of the hotel.' he said.

Will had to admit he was attracted by this idea, as a lot of the training delivered was a bit sensitive. To be away from the general public was useful. Edward opened up one of the rooms, and apart from the clutter and peeling paintwork, the potential was clear. Will checked out two more rooms which were much the same, and Edward assured him the others were of equal size. It looked like this might just meet the need.

Over a cup of coffee, they discussed rates and after a bit of haggling Will got a price that was better that some of the other hotels they were currently using, so was pleased with the result. They agreed dates for the first course starting in May, with an expectation (but no promise) of repeat business if it went well. They shook hands on the deal and paperwork would follow to cement it, but for Will it was a good couple of hours work, and more importantly it now freed him up for his other job!

***

Will was not surprised when Matt pitched up outside his hotel in a black Ford Granada. He guessed the organisation had bought a job lot, but this one was a little older and had a few minor dents and scratches. They shook hands and swapped greetings and after stowing his bags in the boot Will jumped into the passenger seat and they set off to who knew where. Matt was a few years younger than Will and dressed casually in jeans, a black crew neck jumper and black leather jacket. He had advised Will on the phone to dress casually, so Will was also in jeans and jumper, but wore a blue anorak. He didn't own a leather jacket but thought he might buy one now as he could see how versatile they could be. They were common so he wouldn't stand out, and could look smart or casual. And unlike jackets or anoraks, leather would not get easily creased so would look good for longer.

'We're going to our training facility, which is about five miles out of town, so should be there quite soon,' Matt advised. 'I'm sure you don't need to be reminded that the location of this facility mustn't be divulged to anyone,' he said seriously.

'Of course,' Will responded.

'Great,' he said, the serious tone now gone, 'Have you been to Cheltenham before?'

They chatted about trivia; the weather, football, the traffic, anything other than the business that Will was there for. A few miles out of town they turned onto a winding gravel track and drove through some woods for about half a mile before approaching a series of farm buildings. Matt pulled up outside a white-walled farm cottage surrounded by a picket fence and shrubs and announced they had arrived. Not quite what Will expected, but he guessed this was some kind of reception building.

'You can leave your bags in the car if you like, they'll be quite safe, and I'll take you back to your hotel later,' Matt offered.

Will thanked him, got out of the car and Matt did a well-practiced fast U-turn, throwing up a shower of gravel, as he headed back down the track. Will strolled up to the front door of the cottage and couldn't see a bellpush or a knocker, so he rapped on the solid oak door. The door was opened almost immediately by a lady in her 50's wearing a tweed skirt and matching jacket. A white blouse, and spectacles hanging on a cord around her neck completed the ensemble. She was generously built, her cheeks glowed with that look of an outdoors lifestyle and her voice was solid and commanding.

'Welcome Mr. Mortimer,' she almost boomed, 'Please follow me.' She turned and strode down the surprisingly wide hallway and Will followed. He could see the hallway led towards a large country kitchen and off to the left and right were open doors to small, typical front-rooms, found in any country cottage. In the centre of the flag-stoned kitchen was a large wooden table surrounded by six wooden chairs. On the table he noticed some papers, pens and files neatly placed at one end, next to a cup and saucer.

'My name's Joan,' she said with a broad welcoming smile, 'May I call you Will?'

'Yes, of course,' he said, 'Pleased to meet you Joan.'

She motioned him to sit at the end of the table with the papers and files and without asking filled the cup with fresh coffee.

'Milk and sugar?' she enquired.

'Thank you.'

She brought over a small jug of milk and a bowl of sugar cubes and sat on the chair next to him.

'Shortly I'll take you to the main facility to meet the instructors, but first, there are some papers for you to sign.' She opened up the file that sat in front of him and passed him the top sheet. 'This is simply a form for you to sign that says you'll never disclose the whereabouts of this facility.' she explained. 'As you might imagine it would cause us a lot of problems if the opposition or general public became aware of what we do here.'

He dutifully read and signed this non-disclosure form and she moved on to the next bundle of papers.

'This is your security vetting.'

This was news to Will, as he didn't know he had been vetted. He had a vague idea that vetting existed as some of his colleagues who worked in the Investigation Division had mentioned it once, but he wasn't quite sure what it meant. Joan enlightened him.

'There are different levels of vetting,' she continued, 'that enable you to have sight of confidential and secret material and all of our agents are vetted to a high level to ensure they can be provided with sensitive intelligence. And because of some of the techniques they'll use that must not be made public.'

Agent? Is that what he was?

'As you can see, we've already carried out comprehensive checks on you and determined that you should receive a high level of vetting. Actually, this should have been done months ago and Clive has been a bit naughty in not arranging sooner, but not to worry, we can get you to sign now to say you will abide by the rules of the vetting. Think of it as 'Official Secrets Act' plus, which you signed when you first started work in Customs and Excise.'

He thought back to that first day in the job nearly sixteen years ago and how excited he was to be asked to sign the Official Secrets Act. He had fantasised then that this was somehow a first step to becoming James Bond. Childish of course... *but maybe not quite so ridiculous now.*

Will read through the next ten pages and was astonished at the detail - his life history was summarised into these ten sheets. They described his family background, Alison's background, his finances, even down to the large credit card bill he had carried a couple of years back. He had had to fund some repairs on his house and had no other way of finding the money. Thankfully, with some effort he had managed to pay this off, but it was a hard slog. It also mentioned, *'the tragic death of his fiancée six years earlier in a hit-and-run.'*

It was clear there must have been a lot more background material that supported this summary and Will felt a bit unnerved by just how much they knew about him. There was even a brief note of his Grandad, on my mother's side, spending a week in an Australian jail for stealing a sheep. Will's Grandparents had moved to Australia before his first birthday and returned when he was ten years old. His Grandad died a year later, his Nan soon after, so he didn't really know them. He certainly didn't know about this family secret. But, of course, he would now have to keep this to himself.

Will dutifully signed the vetting form and Joan placed it back in the file.

Joan stood up 'Ok, Will, now let's get you trained!'

She led him out of the back door, and they headed across to a large barn, twenty metres away. It had a brown-coloured metal roller shutter door, fully closed. However, to the right was a standard-sized brown painted door. They entered.

Inside it looked like a large workshop with tools and machines of various types around the walls, including what looked like a lathe. There was a mixture of desks, tables, whiteboards and chairs in the middle. At the far end were about ten cupboards or lockers and a few filing cabinets. It reminded him a bit of a larger version of his old school metalwork lab. Two men, dressed in brown lab coats, turned and greeted them. They were both about Will's age and both, like Will, around six foot tall.

'Will, this is Alan and Gordon, and they'll be your instructors for today.'

Alan and Gordon both said, 'Hello Will.' in unison and then both laughed at their unintended duet.

Alan continued, 'Very pleased to meet you Will and looking forward to taking you through your paces. We've a lot to get through, so OK if we get started?'

'Of course,' he said eagerly, 'good to meet you both'.

"Great, and thanks Joan,' Alan said, turning to Joan, 'we'll bring Will back later when he has had enough.'

'Don't work him too hard, boys,' Joan said playfully, 'he has important work to do tomorrow.' With that this turned and left.

Gordon led Will over to a table and chairs in the centre of the room and they all sat down.

'Before we get started we need to check with you what you believe your mission is. Clive has given us the outline of the task and we have some good intelligence on the property you'll be entering, but it is always good to know what you are expecting. We'll be honest with you, this is a very unusual training request – normally we would take a full week to give you the basics and somehow we've got to get you ready in one day. But we love a challenge, so I hope you are a quick learner.'

So do I, Will thought, but didn't say it. He repeated to them what he had been told.

'Clive has explained that he wants photographs of any papers in the office of the owner, Elias Michaels, that pertain to Irish customers. He advised that the lorry yard would be closed and locked by 10pm, so I would be best to go in around midnight. Beyond that I was expecting you guys to fill in the gaps. He did say that the building was alarmed, and once inside I'd need to open cupboards in his office, but that's about all I know.'

"Ok that's good," said Gordon 'That is pretty much what he told us. So in the limited time we have available, we propose to teach you a number of things.' He raised a finger. '*One,* how to open a padlock without a key,' then more fingers, '*Two,* how to open locked doors, *three*, how to disable the alarm, and *four*, how to open drawers and filing cabinets. How does that sound?'

'That sounds like just what I need, I think,' he said, his tone perhaps betraying his uncertain feelings. 'But as we go through this, I might think of other needs.'

'We're here to help,' said Alan sincerely. 'We do appreciate that you've been somewhat thrown in the deep end, but between us we we'll make you ready.'

Although this was still daunting, Will felt much reassured by these guys. They were genuine, helpful and clearly knew their trade.

Over the next hour they talked him through how padlocks worked. Then how to open the drawer and cabinet locks that he was likely to encounter. They had decided to train him in the common ones as there was no time for him to learn them all. They all hoped that he would encounter one of these and not something different – if he did he was sunk. On the plus side they had already identified the padlock to the gate. In the next hour they got him to practice picking this type of padlock until he found he could open it within ten seconds. Another two hours of practice on a range of cupboard and drawer locks and he felt like he was getting fairly good at this.

They stopped for a short lunch, that they had provided, some sandwiches, crisps, and coffee. But the break was short, and they were quickly back to it.

The first session in the afternoon was led by Will. They wanted to understand the layout of the inside of the office building, so Will drew a diagram on their whiteboard as best he could. He was not the greatest artist, but it wasn't a bad representation. By the time he had finished it gave the instructors a feel for what he was about to do.

'We know the office building is alarmed,' said Alan. The good news is we've managed to get the code. The bad news is that when you open the door to the building you only have sixty seconds to enter the code and we don't know where the code panel is situated. It should be just inside the door, but you may have to hunt for it. The alarm code is four numbers which you'll have to memorise.'

He gave Will the number and he recited it in his head several times until he was sure he had got it. Some years earlier Will had read some books of how to improve memory. It had come in useful when recalling registration numbers of suspect vehicles when working in the channels. Most of the techniques involved imagining visual prompts, the more outrageous the better. This number for the alarm was 1288. In his mind he visualised throwing a dozen eggs at two fat ladies.

'Now you'll probably have two doors to defeat,' said Alan, 'the office building door, and the door to Elias's office. They'll have different locks, so let's go through the types of lock and get you to practice defeating them.'

They spent the next three hours on door locks and the instructors patiently explained everything he needed to know and how he could hone his technique. By the end Will had just about mastered how to open them, but was tiring now and could feel a headache coming on.

'Will, you've done brilliantly, Gordon said sincerely. 'It's a lot to learn in such a short time, but I really think you've got it. And now I think it is time to give you a couple of presents - to be returned after your mission of course.'

Gordon handed him a pack of Benson and Hedges cigarettes and a stainless-steel Zippo lighter with a venetian design engraved on its front and back.

'Thank you,' Will said, 'but I don't smoke.'

'That's good.' said Gordon. 'It is a filthy habit, but I wouldn't try to smoke these.'

He opened the flap of the cigarette box and went to pull out a cigarette. But as he pulled on a cigarette, a cover that looked like the tops of 20 cigarettes came off in his hand. Underneath the cover it revealed some small instruments – lockpicks.

'It wouldn't be sensible for you to go equipped with lock picking tools in your pocket, so we devised this miniature set instead. It's the same tools you have been using all day, just a little smaller.'

Will was impressed, but this wasn't all.

'You'll also need a camera. Do you know anything about photography?' Gordan asked.

'A little, I have a manual SLR at home, but to be honest I'm a novice,' he admitted.

'No problem,' said Gordon. 'For what you need to do you'll not need too much skill. Have you heard of digital cameras?'

Will had not and shook his head.

'They're fairly new,' said Gordon, 'But I think they'll be all the rage in a few years' time. They don't use film, they record a digital image on a chip inside the camera. You don't need to know the technicalities, you just have to know how to use it.'

He opened the top of the Zippo lighter and pulled the flint section up by half an inch. This revealed a tiny lens and a small button next to it. Gordon held the lens about a foot above an A4 sheet of paper on the desk and pressed the button gently. A small light shone onto the paper, and he adjusted the height of the lighter until the whole sheet of paper was bathed in light and pressed the button harder. There was a reassuring click and the light went out.

'I have just taken a picture of the piece of paper. Now you have a try.' He handed the Zippo to Will.

Will followed the same steps as Gordon, flipped the lid and pulled out the top by half an inch, then held the lens over the paper. It was a bit tricky to hold as it was so small; he pressed the button. Unfortunately, the light came on and the shutter clicked before he had realised.

'Just a gentle push first,' Gordon advised.

Will tried again and this time he got a better grip and a gentle push turned on the light. He was able to adjust the height to get the whole page in before he pushed the button harder; the shutter clicked, and light went out.

'Excellent,' commended Gordon. 'Don't worry about how many photos you need to take, the chip on here should do two hundred at least. Oh, and one more thing,' Gordon picked up the Zippo flipped the lid and scraped his thumb across the light-striking wheel and a one-inch flame flickered into life. 'Just in case you need to use as a real lighter,' he said with glee. 'It only has enough gas for about ten strikes, so don't waste it.'

'One final piece of advice,' said Alan earnestly, 'You need to be aware of your surroundings at all times, particularly when going to and from a location. So, when you approach a premises always try to use counter-surveillance. To learn this properly you'll need a full training course. You'll get to do that soon, but some key things to remember; never go directly towards your goal and never the same route twice. Double-back several times as if you've forgotten something or made a mistake. It's hard to follow someone who suddenly reverses direction. And use all your senses. Do these things and you stand more chance of not being compromised.'

Will thanked Alan and Gordon for their excellent instruction and patience, pocketed his new toys and Alan led him back to the cottage. It was dark by now, but the kitchen light was blazing to guide the way.

Joan asked how his day had gone and before he left she gave him a black leather briefcase for his trip to Lucerne tomorrow. Concealed in the lining was an opening which she said would be ideal for hiding the false passport and airline ticket that she then gave him, both in the name of Bill Mitchell. She also gave him the genuine ticket in his name and reminded him not to mix them up. The briefcase had some of the Brighthouse headed paper in it that he had been given by Zoe on his last mission.

Matt was waiting in the Granada and drove him back to the hotel. Will was shattered. It had been a long and tiring day and he could not wait to take a shower and possibly a nap. The shower was refreshing and relaxing, but, as usual, he could not sleep.

Sixteen

Yet again half of the plane seemed to be filled with the Jewish jewellery community as he settled back into his seat ready for take-off to Zurich for the second time. Unexpectedly Clive had called him at the hotel that morning to ask how yesterday had gone and to wish him luck. Clive re-emphasised how important it was for Will to get the information and the photos. *No pressure.* He said he looked forward to the de-brief. Will hadn't been told about any de-brief, but with Clive's record so far he guessed it would happen at some unexpected time.

The flight was uneventful, and he touched down in Zurich on time. As this was meant to be a, there and back in one day trip, he was only carrying the briefcase. He sailed through Swiss Customs and passport control and headed for the railway station. Before buying a train ticket he entered the toilets. Once safely in a cubicle he swapped his passport and air tickets for the Bill Mitchell documents hidden in the lining of the briefcase.

Seated on the half-empty train he was once again impressed by the efficiency. The train pulled out of Zurich station on the exact second of the big station clock. It was now 10.32am so he should arrive at the EM Transport depot in Lucerne at around midday.

As it turned out he was spot on with his estimate and was standing at 'Rezeption' at exactly noon. Elias appeared as before, and they shook hands and exchanged the usual pleasantries. Elias seemed a bit happier than when they had last met; his confirmation that Sergei would not be joining them this time was probably the reason. Will was also somewhat relieved. They chatted a bit about that night in the club and Elias apologised.

'No need to apologise,' Will reassured him, 'I think Sergei was just out for a good time and had too much to drink.'

'Sergei is always having too much to drink and can get very angry,' Elias said darkly, 'but somehow you managed to keep him calm, not many have managed that before.'

As Elias had opened up the conversation Will took the opportunity to try to find out a bit more. 'Does Sergei live in Switzerland?' he enquired casually, 'He's clearly Russian.'

'Yes he is Russian, from a rich Russian crime family,' Elias said, with a hint of venom, 'That's why he gets angry quick, I think, because he is used to getting his own way. I should not tell you, but he put one of my drivers in hospital once because the driver questioned his orders. Sergei is not a big man, but he has big friends and a bad reputation. He is from a "family" with connections in Russia, so everyone knows not to cross him. The driver was new and did not know.'

Will absorbed this information and took a risk to probe a bit more. 'Why do you deal with him Elias if he has a bad reputation?'

Elias looked straight at him as if deciding if he was going to answer him or not, and in the end he moved his head a little closer and said confidentially, 'No one messes with the Russians, and I didn't know what I was getting into. I wish I had not, but I can't change that now.'

All at once Elias changed the subject, as if he realised he had said too much, and they got down to business.

'OK, we need to discuss the next shipment,' he said, all business now. 'You did a good job last time, and we need you to do this again.'

He did not mention that the last shipment had not arrived at the destination and, of course, Will didn't ask as he was not meant to know. They talked about when and where the next lorry would be arriving in the UK and how he might ensure it got through Customs.

Whilst they talked Will surreptitiously studied Elias's office.

There was a filing cabinet against the left-hand wall and although he couldn't be sure, the lock looked like one he was now familiar with. Elias was sitting behind his desk and from the chair Will was sitting at he couldn't see the desk drawers. There was also a tall metal cupboard in the corner behind his desk that looked quite substantial and with a lock he did not recognise, so he hoped this did not contain anything useful.

He reminded Elias of his limitations in getting the lorry cleared through Customs.

'I don't want the blame if it goes wrong,' he said. 'Don't forget Elias, I can minimise the risk, but I can't cover all situations,' he explained again. 'Last time I was able to ensure the clearance was quick and without interference because a Customs Officer I know well was on duty. I told him I was keen to get the lorry cleared quickly as I didn't want to hang around as it was my daughter's birthday, and he was happy to do me a favour. But I can't do that again, although of course I'll do my best.'

'I understand,' said Elias. In a serious tone he said, 'My employers will be very unhappy if you don't get the lorry through Customs, so for your sake and mine please arrange for this to happen. I've been instructed to give you £2000 this time as an incentive.'

Bill Mitchell would not want to lose out on this sum of money so he readily agreed that he would make it happen.

Will somehow found it easy to be Bill, a confident no-nonsense character. In reality he felt he wasn't like that, although he knew his work colleagues would disagree. And making up a daughter? Was this something he might have had with Rachel if she had lived? How he missed her. He was sure a Psychologist would make something of his need to create a non-existent family.

'The next shipment will be planned to arrive in Dover next Wednesday. Can you be ready?' Elias asked.

Will's thoughts were jolted back to the room and task in hand. He nearly missed what Elias said.

'Next Wednesday you say,' he said for confirmation. Elias nodded. 'Yes, I can be ready. Is it furniture again?'

Elias confirmed that the load would be furniture as this seemed to work and he provided him with papers showing the load and shipping details and Will popped them in his briefcase.

'We've arranged the load similar to last time so that even if the lorry is opened the goods we want to conceal will not easily be found. Let me show you something in the yard, it might reassure you that we've taken your advice and hidden the goods well.'

'Ok, but if we're all done I will take my briefcase with me and get off straight afterwards. I could do with getting to the airport early to buy a gift for my wife. It is our anniversary in a few days,' he lied, not wanting to prolong the meeting any longer.

Will followed him out of the office as they headed downstairs to the lorry yard. As they walked through the main office and through the door to the stairs Will scanned the walls for the alarm panel, but it was nowhere to be seen. This might be a problem later, but nothing he could do right now. They got down into the yard and headed over to one of the sheds just past a Turkish registered lorry. On the floor of the shed was a large empty crate.

'This is where we hide the goods,' he said.

Will didn't quite understand what he meant – this was an empty crate. But…was this an illusion or did the inside space look smaller than the outside? Now Will understood, but as Bill Mitchell he probably wouldn't have noticed this, so best to play dumb.

'I don't understand, you're hiding the goods you don't want found in an empty crate?'

'Not quite,' said Elias with a smile, 'Watch this.' He pressed on what looked like nails close to the bottom corner of one side of the outside of the crate; they popped out by about an inch. He then pressed the base of the crate on one side and the whole base came loose. He removed this false base to reveal a space underneath, a space about ten inches deep. The crate stood about three foot high so over a quarter of the inside had been hidden by this false base. Very clever.

'That is brilliant,' Will commended. 'So just as I advised, you have concealed the goods so even if Customs do a search they'll be hard pushed to find them. Well done!'

Elias looked proud, but then he got distracted as he looked over Will's shoulder, 'Here comes Peter, the lorry driver that will making the trip to Dover,' he indicated, 'I'll introduce you to him.'

The UK registered lorry had entered the yard and Will saw the driver getting down from the cab. The driver was about fifty metres away and he waved across to them and shouted. 'Just need to book in and nip to the toilet and I'll be back in a minute.'

Although they were a distance away the driver looked familiar to Will. The man strolled over the yard towards the toilet. Will froze – *he knew him*. Will had met and spoken to the driver when he was working on Export Freight about eight years ago. Although the driver had obviously aged a bit, it was definitely him.

Eight years earlier the Customs Investigation Division (ID) had arrived at Will's office as they had been following a lorry they suspected of being involved in large scale tobacco smuggling. They knew the driver would need to get his export documents endorsed by Will and were keen that Will do what he normally did when presented with papers. They also asked Will to try to engage the driver in conversation. They had said that this might provide some useful information. Maybe the driver would lie about his movements? Whatever was said would be useful if the driver finally got arrested and interviewed.

Will had chatted to the driver when he arrived at the counter, with the ID officers sitting out of sight around the corner of the office listening in. The driver told Will he was travelling to Belgium but coming straight back later that day. He didn't have a load to pick-up so he would return empty. This proved to be useful intel for the ID, as later in their investigation they uncovered a major tobacco smuggling operation using empty lorries with false floors. *I wonder where Elias got his idea for the false bottoms of those crates?*. For his part, the driver got five years in prison.

Will had to think fast as he couldn't risk that the driver would recognise him.

'Elias, if you don't mind I'm going to leave now. I don't think it is a good idea if the lorry driver knows who I am, or that I've been here – if he gets caught then he might identify me, and I really don't need that.'

Elias thought for a moment and then nodded. 'We are all taking risks and if he gets caught then I'm also worried, but I understand and won't mention you. Go now before he comes back, and I am sure we'll do good business again. I'll contact you soon.'

Will headed quickly for the gate. which fortunately was away from where Peter had gone, but he did spot him out of the corner of his eye heading towards Elias. Will avoided turning to look as he didn't want the driver to see his face.

'Who was that?' the driver said to Elias, indicating in Will's direction as he exited the yard, 'he looked familiar.'

'Oh, just an agent for one of my customers,' said Elias quickly. 'Now, are you ready to earn your money and help with the unloading.'

***

First task completed and it was only 2pm, so Will had a lot of time to kill before his next task later that night. His flight back to Gatwick was not until 9am tomorrow, so his first job was to find a cheap hotel within walking distance of the yard. He wandered up and down a few streets and found himself not far from the red-light district where they had been thrown out of the club. A bit further on he found a small hotel that advertised rooms for one hundred Swiss francs (about forty pounds). Not cheap, but nothing in Switzerland was cheap, and he made a mental note to ask Clive about expenses. He booked in and was shown to a basic, but clean room and thought about his next move. He decided that it was time to go shopping and that Clive would have to pay for what he needed.

His first purchase was a torch and he decided on a mini-Maglite that he found in a shop that sold Swiss army knives. It was sturdy, reliable and small – just the job. Next he found a department store and kitted himself out with some dark jeans, black t-shirt, and a black polo-neck jumper. He also bought a small holdall to put them in. He toyed with the idea of buying a black leather jacket, but although he felt confident he could get the money out of Clive, he didn't have enough cash with him for such a purchase. He would have to wait until he found a cheaper one in the UK. His final purchase was back in the first shop where he decided to buy a Swiss army knife. It might come in useful tonight, he thought, but if it didn't he had always wanted one and it would definitely be useful in the future.

On the way back to the hotel he picked up a few snacks in a local food shop; some sort of sausage pastry, an apple cake, and a few chocolate bars. He didn't feel like eating much, and wasn't keen on going to a restaurant later, so this would have to do.

It was now nearly 6pm so he took a shower, set an alarm for 9pm and tried to snooze. But although tired, sleep just wouldn't come. He thought through the planned night excursion and all the things that might go wrong. Maybe looking at all the negatives was a bad thing, but for him it was a useful mental exercise in planning different scenarios in his head.

By 8 o'clock he had given up all hope of sleep, so he ate half of his sausage pastry and decided to go for a walk around the nearby streets.

It was all quiet outside the hotel as all workers had long since gone home. It was also far too early for night revellers, particularly in this part of town. But remembering the very brief advice from Alan, he practiced some counter-surveillance. He went around the block and then suddenly reversed his direction and headed back towards the hotel. He recalled doing something similar when he was a teenager, playing games in the woods as an army cadet. They would be set up in teams to try to reach the opposing teams flag at the other end of the woods. One tactic they often used then was to confuse the enemy and pretend to go one way. Then, if they thought they were being watched, to suddenly change direction.

When he was almost at his hotel he took an unexpected turn into another side street and almost immediately changed his mind and headed back towards the hotel. He was only practicing, but at one point he was convinced he saw someone dive into a shop doorway, as if they were trying to avoid being seen. Will dismissed this thought and put it down to his imagination. Enough of these games he thought, and he went back to his hotel room.

Seventeen

Just after 11pm he left the hotel again dressed in his new dark clothes, plus his blue anorak. It was too cold without, and it would look strange if he didn't wear a coat. Just like earlier he practiced some counter-surveillance by taking an indirect route and making several double-backs and sudden changes in direction. Oddly, he again thought he saw someone who might have been following him. He thought he saw them make a sudden change of pace. They were some way off and he only got a glance before they turned off down another street, but he was fairly sure it was a woman. Was he being paranoid? He continued to make some swift changes in direction and pace for the next ten minutes to see if she reappeared, but didn't see anything unusual.

It was half hour to midnight when he arrived at the yard. There were a few floodlights in the yard and a streetlight near the padlocked gate. The office was in darkness and there was no sign of life. He scanned around him and there was no activity on this side of the gate either, so it was now or never.

The streetlight was an advantage but also a curse. He would be able to see what he was doing without the need of his Maglite, but equally if anyone happened by, they would see him trying to pick the lock. He took one last look around before taking out his cigarette pack of lockpicks, and headed for the gate. When leaving the yard yesterday he had recognised the type of lock as one he was now familiar with, so he was fairly confident he could get it open quickly. He went to work and in just thirty seconds he heard the satisfying click as the lock opened.

Just as he was about to pull the lock off a voice behind him said, 'Do you need some help?'

Will nearly leapt in the air. He turned quickly, but he had already recognised the voice,

'What the hell are you doing here?'

Zoe smiled and said, 'Nice to see you too Will, but can we get inside before anyone sees us.'

He was speechless, but quickly pulled himself together and opened the gate to let them in and closed it behind them, putting the lock back in place, but not locking it, just to make it looked untouched. They hurried across the yard and up the stairs. The outer door to the lobby was unlocked and they were now comfortably out of sight in the reception area. Now to get some answers.

'You frightened me half to death, now tell me, what are you doing here?' he said a little too sharply. He realised he was shaking a bit from the adrenalin rush.

Zoe smiled again. 'I heard you were on a mission and thought you might need some help.' she said happily. 'You did well with the gate lock, but I too have had the course and thought it might help when we get inside.'

Despite his near heart-attack Will was actually pleased to see Zoe and was not too proud to accept her help.

'That's nice of you, but I wish I'd known. Was that you following me earlier?'

'Yes it was, and I have to say you took me by surprise when you started doing counter-surveillance. I pride myself on being good at this stuff, but you nearly caught me. You've clearly learnt more skills that I gave you credit for.'

This was good to hear, but didn't change the point.

'But why? You could have spoken to me instead of following me.'

She looked sheepish. 'I'm sorry,' she said. 'But I thought you might turn down my offer of help, and I'm not exactly meant to be helping with this.'

He didn't know what she meant, but now wasn't the time to argue. 'Ok, let's just get this done and we can talk later.'

The first job was to open the door to the offices. Will was very conscious of the need to disable the alarm once they had defeated the lock. Although he had the code he had no idea where the alarm panel was located inside. He explained the problem to Zoe. It was agreed that they would each take a different direction when they entered, and search for the panel. Will would go to the left and she would go to the right. They knew the panel would not be far from the door as legitimate persons would need to disable it within the sixty seconds. He examined the lock, it was of a type he recognised, so he pulled the appropriate tools from his specially designed cigarette packet and got to work.

'Nice toolkit.' Zoe smirked. 'Beats my manicure set.'

He wasn't looking at her as he was now focused on the task in hand, but he guessed she was smiling.

Two minutes later the lock clicked. He made ready to open the door. He motioned to Zoe and then threw the door open and they both bundled in. Will headed left as planned and quickly scanned the walls as he went, looking for the alarm panel as a loud beeping started. The sixty seconds had started. Sixty seconds to disable it before probably some much louder noise would start. Then they would be in all sorts of problems. For all they knew the alarm could be linked to the police or another security firm.

There was enough light coming through the windows from the floodlights to see clearly, so no need for a torch. Will's initial scan did not detect the panel. Out of the corner of his eye he could see Zoe still searching. They went further into the office and continued looking desperately around, but no luck. By now they were both about twenty feet into the main office. He judged that thirty seconds must have passed and still no sign of anything that resembled an alarm panel. Will was close to panic, but kept his head. He told Zoe he was going to backtrack and look closer to the entrance, as he felt they must have missed something. He moved slowly back towards the door and ran his hands over the wall space a few feet at a time. Moving around a painting on the wall of a snowy mountain scene and onto the next section of wall. *Wait. The picture.* He went back and tried to lift the bottom edge of the picture, but it didn't move. *Strange.* He pulled the right-hand edge, and it swung out into the room on hinges. Behind the picture was the alarm panel showing a number keypad and a countdown clock that read 15. He had fifteen seconds to enter the code. He entered 1288. Nothing happened. The beeping continued. The countdown continued. Was the number wrong? Then, from behind Will, Zoe reached over and pressed a green button on the panel with a 'B' on it and the beeping stopped. The countdown clock showed 5. That was close.

'How did you know to press the B button,' he asked Zoe.

'I guessed that the B stood for *Bestätigen*, which in German means *Confirm*,' she said.

Zoe followed him to Elias's office and as expected the door was locked. It didn't take Will long to open it. Now that they were in the office Will decided to close the blinds as they were now overlooking the yard. If anyone happened by and looked up they would almost certainly be seen.

In the semi-dark Will could still make out his surroundings and his first target was the filing cabinet, which surprisingly was unlocked. He guessed that as Elias locked his door he was comfortable leaving this cabinet unlocked, but that might also mean there was nothing of interest in there. He was wrong. Using the Maglite to look at the contents the very first folder he looked in had details of customers in Ireland. He quickly laid these out on Elias's desk and set to work with his Zippo camera. Zoe wasn't paying much attention to what he was doing because she seemed otherwise engaged under the desk.

'What are you doing Zoe?' he enquired, only vaguely aware that she was pulling something from her bag, as he set the camera up to take the first photo.

'Nothing for you to be concerned about Will. Just keep doing what you are doing.'

He was curious, but he needed to focus on the photographs, so he let it go for now. When he had finished the first folder he carried on searching the files, but nothing else of interest caught his eye. Zoe was still fiddling with something under the desk, so he moved on to Elias's desk drawers. He managed to pick the locks easily. But there was nothing in them that seemed relevant, so he relocked them and turned to look at the tall metal cupboard behind the desk. He had noticed this at his meeting with Elias only twelve hours ago so he knew that the lock on it might be a challenge. On closer inspection he was now convinced it would be beyond his meagre lock picking skills. Too bad, as this looked like a place that would hold some interesting and important papers.

Zoe had finished fiddling around under the desk and Will's curiosity now needed satisfying so he looked under the desk to see if he could assess what she had been up too. Well concealed, but still visible if you looked hard was a small black object.

'Are you going to tell me what that is, or do I have to take it off and look myself,' he said sternly.

Zoe looked worried, but also sheepish, like she had been caught with her hand in the sweetie jar. Then resignedly she said, 'It is a listening device. It doesn't have much range, but I should be able to hear what is being said from my car if I can park just outside the gates.'

'Did Clive ask you to do this, because if he did I need to have words. I don't like being kept in the dark and this mission has enough risk without adding to it by bugging Elias's office.'

'Please don't say anything to Clive,' she pleaded, 'He knows nothing of this. When we get out of here I promise I'll tell you everything.' She looked over his shoulder. 'Now are you going to open that cupboard and finish taking pictures with your toy camera so we can get out of here?'

'I would if I could, but I can't. That lock is not one I recognise, the lock is too difficult for me to crack, so we'll have to leave it.'

She walked over to the cupboard and studied the lock and said, 'Pass me your torch and your toolkit.'

He gave her his cigarette packet and torch. With the torch gripped between her teeth she selected a couple of picks and set to work. It took her just two minutes. She removed the torch from her lips, smiled in triumph and pulled the cupboard door open.

The first thing Will saw took him by surprise. Sitting on the top shelf was a revolver and next to it a box of fifty rounds of ammunition. He tried to ignore this and looked at the other contents. On the shelf below were some folders similar to those found in the filing cabinet. He took these out carefully and made sure he kept them in order as he thumbed through the contents. They contained some more details of Irish customers, but different to the ones he had already seen. There were names, addresses, telephone numbers and some hand-written notes on some of these in German. He quickly, but carefully took the papers out one by one and photographed them – there must have been at least thirty pages. Then he put them back making sure they looked undisturbed. Zoe in the meantime had been looking at the rest of the cupboard contents, but apart from details of consignments from Turkey which he quickly photographed, there was nothing further on interest.

Tasks now complete they checked and re-checked that they had left the office as they had found it. As they turned to relock the door Will froze. He had nearly forgotten that he had not re-opened the blinds. Such an easy mistake, but they had both missed it. As he re-locked the door something else was nagging at the back of his mind that he hadn't thought about, but he couldn't see anything else. So they walked back up the office towards the main office door. Then it hit him. How would he reset the main office alarm? No one had thought to tell him this and he had no idea.

Will shared his concerns with Zoe, but she just gave him that happy smile and said, 'Leave that to me.' She pulled the picture out on its hinges and studied the alarm panel for a moment.

'What was the code please?'

Will told her the code which she entered. She pressed another button and the beeping started. They headed out the door and this time Zoe did the re-locking. She put him to shame by doing so in just ten seconds.

They walked quickly down the stairs and headed for the gate. They were halfway there when they both saw some car headlights appearing from around the corner and approaching the yard gates. Zoe reacted quickest. She pulled Will behind a large rubbish container, just as the headlights panned the position they had been standing only a second before. Then the car stopped, its headlights still burning. This wasn't good. The driver got out of the car and walked towards the gate. He was wearing some sort of uniform and carrying a large torch, but he wasn't police. A security guard maybe.

The man stood for a minute looking into the yard, but didn't turn on his torch, he could probably see well enough without, as they had. Then he turned around, got back in his car and drove away. Thank goodness he didn't try the lock.

They agreed it was probably a security guard doing his rounds and nothing to worry about. So lucky. A few seconds earlier or later and he would have certainly seen them and raised the alarm.

Outside the gates now, and with the padlock securely back in place they headed back towards the hotel.

'Now I think you've got some explaining to do Zoe,' Will said as they walked. 'Shall we go somewhere warm, and you can keep your promise and tell what on earth is going on.'

Eighteen

Thirty minutes later they were raiding the minibar in Will's hotel room, and he was enjoying the warm sensation of a scotch whisky as it gently burnt his throat. Zoe helped herself to a Brandy.

'Ok Will, as promised I'll tell you everything, but I need you to promise me that you will not tell Clive. I don't trust him, and I urge you to also be careful of him. He's a clever man and has a gentle manner, but don't be fooled. He may look out for you, but he may not.'

Will pondered this for a moment, then agreed that he would not tell Clive that they had met. But he warned her that he might be forced to tell *someone* what he had learned if anything she told him had an impact on others, or on his safety.

She agreed and assured him that what she was doing would not affect others, it was personal. She sat down on the chair by the window, Will perched on the end of the bed as there was nowhere else to sit, and Zoe told her story:

'I was born in Hungary,' she said, 'but moved with my parents to Switzerland when I was six years old. My Uncle Janos was a farmer in Hungary and lived near Balliton lake. In April last year he narrowly escaped a car accident. The car that nearly hit him as it rounded a bend, hit a tree instead and the two Russian occupants had been killed. The police investigated the accident and decided it was not Janos's fault and that was the end of the matter. Janos went missing a week later. Searches of the area around his farm revealed no trace of him, and no connection was made to the accident. The police kept the file open as they could find no reason for his disappearance, but they'd no leads and were no longer actively looking for him.'

She explained that she had started her own investigation – she had access to many sources as a member of the Federal Department of Justice and Police, but also as a member of The Network. Although she also saw no link to Janos's disappearance and the car accident she had to start somewhere. She investigated the background to the two Russians who had died. What she discovered made her blood run cold.

The driver was from Moscow and had a military background but also a criminal history – he had been a Private in the Russian Army and after beating a colleague to near death after an argument, he went to prison for five years. On his release he got a job in security at a Moscow nightclub. Then got hired as a driver-come-bodyguard, to a known Russian criminal gang leader by the name of Nico Brodsky. Nico Brodsky turned out to be the other person killed in the car crash. But what shocked Zoe was that Nico Brodsky's name had been linked to the money laundering investigation she was working on.

The Department for Foreign Affairs (FDFA) in Switzerland was responsible for Security Policy and a heightened risk had been identified from Russia over money from Eastern Europe that was flowing through Swiss businesses. The Swiss President (who through a quirk of the political structure in Switzerland was also the head of the FDFA), tasked the Department for Justice and Police to investigate the suspected money laundering from Russia, and Zoe was on the team. It quickly became clear that corrupt high-level officials in the Russian Government were involved, and the Russian mafia were behind most of the serious organised crime, and of course, laundering the proceeds.

'As I told you when we first met Will, our money-laundering investigation uncovered some suspicious transactions involving Elias Michaels and that led us to the arms smuggling. It's now clear that Elias is working for the Russian mafia.'

'Ok, I can understand about the Russian involvement,' he responded, 'I met Sergei Koskov when I went to see Elias last October and Elias has told me he is in deep with some heavy Russians. He told me he's not happy about this. But what has that got to do with your Uncle, and why bug Elias's office without telling Clive?'

Zoe looked like she was about to cry, but she didn't. She took a deep breath and continued.

'I am very close to my Uncle, actually he was my father's Uncle, but as my father didn't have any brothers I always see him as my Uncle. As a very young girl I would stay at his farm regularly, with him and my Auntie Kitti - they were such happy times. Auntie Kitti died from cancer three years ago, she was seventy-one, the same age as Uncle Janos. Every year I'd go back to Hungary and stay for a few weeks on their farm. As I got older, I went back less, but it did not stop us all being close. The last time I saw Uncle Janos was in February last year, a couple of months before he disappeared. He hadn't coped well initially when his Kitti died, but time had passed, and he'd come to terms with his loss and was happy again. The police had suggested that he might have still been grief-stricken and had decided to end it all somewhere, but that was not true, not from the way he was in February.' She paused for a moment to compose herself. 'I don't believe he would have taken his own life. But I'm sorry to say that I do believe he is dead. And I believe he was killed by Nico Brodsky's family.'

Will could see she was upset, but felt he had to state what was on his mind.

'I am really sorry that your Uncle has disappeared and from what you have said it doesn't look like he will now be found alive, but don't you think it is a big step to believe that he was killed by the Russian mafia?'

'I know it sounds crazy, but I've further information that would suggest he was killed by Nico Brodsky's family as some sort of retribution, even though Brodsky's death was not my Uncle's fault.' She took a sip of her Brandy before continuing, 'We're talking about some very bad and ruthless people. Let me tell you what I have learnt.' Zoe then described what her investigation had uncovered.

Nico Brodsky had been identified as a crime boss involved in lots of criminal activity which included drugs, arms, prostitution, extortion and murder. The money laundering investigation that she was working on had shown that Nico had corrupted some high-level government officials. When he died the investigation team expected that they would lose their way, as often in these circumstances another crime gang would breeze in and take control. They thought they would lose a lot of leads and have to start again.

'But that didn't happen, she said, 'because Brodsky had a nephew who saw the opportunity to take over and moved quickly into Brodsky's shoes. We found out his name was Mikhail. By all accounts he was reported to be even more ruthless than Brodsky, but he's also very cautious.'

She paused, stood up and paced the room, before continuing.

'We've been investigating Mikhail for months and we still don't know his last name. His reputation in the underworld is renowned, he's a very bad and dangerous man. But he's always avoided being caught as he is so careful, and he has friends in high places. However, there is now some strong evidence that he personally murdered two drug dealers who were trying to rip him off,' she explained. 'Although there is a lot of corruption in the police, there is still a core of decent and non-corrupt police officers and through them the team found out about the murdered drug dealers. A witness to the murders, a brother of one of them, had approached the police and offered to give them information if they would give him a new identity as he was frightened that he would be killed next. He told the police about the whole drugs organisation, names, dates, places, everything. The business was part of Nico Brodsky's, now Mikhail's, empire, and the information he gave to the police was gold dust. In exchange they agreed to provide him with a new identity.'

Zoe took another sip of her brandy and continued.

'During the interview with the police, the man had described how some men had come to his brothers country house and dragged his brother and another associate outside and executed them with bullets to the back of the head. By luck he had been upstairs when they arrived and managed to hide in a loft space, and he recounted what he'd seen. From his position he had a perfect view of everything, and he recognised the leader, the one who directed and then carried out the execution, a man called Mikhail. This man, Mikhail, had made a point of meeting with all of the local drug leaders in the region and telling them that he was now in charge after the death of his Uncle Nico. He would heavily punish those who didn't follow his rules or decided to do business behind his back. There was no doubt among the drug dealers that Mikhail meant what he'd said. His brother didn't listen and paid the ultimate price.'

Will had listened intently to what Zoe had said and thought he'd worked out why she had come to Elias's yard and bugged his office, so he tested his theory.

'Ok Zoe, let me tell you what I believe.' It was his turn to stand up and pace around the room as it helped him think.

'You've now found out who the top man is behind the organised crime gang and believe he's also responsible for your Uncles disappearance?'

She nodded.

'And from what you have said, you also believe that despite evidence of him committing murder that he won't be arrested and charged by the police as the witness will never agree to testify – how am I doing?'

'That is my belief,' she said.

'So you are now intent on doing your own investigation to gather evidence to make sure that Mikhail is finally brought to justice, and you think that bugging Elias's office might lead you to Mikhail. Ultimately you get the evidence you need to convict him.'

'Very good Will, that is my plan,' she agreed.

Will had other questions but he felt he needed to be supportive.

'I am a great believer in justice,' he said, 'So it would seem right to me that you get the chance to put Mikhail in prison. But what I don't understand is why you didn't approach Clive?'

'I did.' she explained. 'I told Clive everything I have told you, but he wasn't interested. He's concentrating on the Irish end of the crime as this is currently the UK Government focus. I can understand that of course, with all the recent IRA activity, but why not also commit to catching the leader of a major Russian crime gang at the same time. He made it clear that this wasn't his aim and wouldn't listen to my proposals, so that is why I've taken matters into my own hands. If I can get the evidence to convict Mikhail then he won't be able to ignore it.'

She appeared close to tears again, but it looked more like tears of frustration this time.

'I know I'm playing a dangerous game, but I have to. I'm convinced that Mikhail is responsible for the murder of my Uncle, and I won't rest until he is behind bars.'

Will paced up and down in the small room and thought about the implications. After all, he knew firsthand the burning need to seek out and punish those who had hurt (killed) someone who you had loved. If it was possible to arrest and put Mikhail in prison then he felt duty bound to assist.

But now she had told him her story he was feeling uncomfortable. Will had found Clive to be frustrating and never quite knew what his game was, but up to now he had no cause to mistrust Clive or his motives. If he kept quiet about this would he become complicit in undermining Clive's authority. And where would that leave him if he was found out? But not pursuing Mikhail, regardless of Zoe's personal motives, did seem wrong to him. He made up his mind. He would keep quiet about this whole affair. But he did need her to answer one more question.

'Why do you not trust Clive. Is it because he wouldn't agree to your proposal?'

She looked directly at him and paused, as if considering if she should tell him and then he detected a decision in her eyes.

'When I first met Clive it was to be welcomed into The Network. I suspect, like you, he had done his research and I quickly discovered that he knew a lot about me, which was somewhat unnerving. But I was pleased to have been chosen and was quickly inducted into the way the group operated and how I would effectively be leading a double life.' Will sat down on the edge of the bed, and it was her turn to get up and pace up and down as she spoke.

'Clive insisted, for reasons of security, that I told no one of the arrangement, not even Jan. I agreed to this, but after a few months I decided that I couldn't keep this from Jan anymore as I felt that keeping secrets from him would eventually ruin our relationship; so I told him. Jan as you might expect was initially concerned that I was putting myself at risk. We talked it through and in the end I got his agreement to carry on. We now have ground rules that we follow, as you know. I tell him the broad outline of what I do, but never the detail. This works for us.'

Will could relate to this. It was partly Zoe's decision to tell Jan that had led him making the decision to tell Alison about The Network. *Which should have happened last weekend.*

He could see Zoe was conflicted, but he knew it wasn't this that was the issue, it must be something else.

She sipped a bit more of her brandy. She looked Will in the eye, a sincere expression on her face.

'What I'm telling you now I have never told anyone,' she said with feeling. 'After six months as part of The Network, I attended a surveillance course in England. There were six other Network operatives and Clive was there. The course was held in a residential college for a week and all the trainers and students, and Clive, stayed at the college during the week. There was an incident, and it was not pleasant.'

She looked down as she spoke, clearly re-living the moment.

'On one evening during the week Clive asked to see me in my room with some excuse about concerns over one of the other Network members on the course. He then tried to force me into sex with him. He was very persuasive and would not take "no" for an answer. Eventually I physically forced him out of my room. I think he was surprised that I could do this, but all members of the Federal Police receive self-protection training. I had learnt some fancy moves. I didn't tell anyone about the incident and the next day Clive behaved like nothing had happened, so I decided to just put it down to experience. I blamed myself, as I thought that I had somehow made him think I wanted his attention. And for being daft enough to let him into my room in the first place.'

Will was shocked by the revelation. She continued.

'For weeks after I reran the events in my head. I couldn't think of a single thing that would have encouraged Clive to think I was interested in him. I was angry, but vowed to put it behind me. I had almost put it out of my mind when something happened that brought it all back. Some months later I met with another female operative whilst we were on a mission together. She was a bit younger than me and much prettier, but we hit it off immediately and instantly became good friends. She was from Madrid and worked in accounts for the 'Guardia Civil', the Spanish police. She was a civilian worker, not a policewoman. On the evening after the mission, when it was all finished we had a meal together. That was when she confided in me. Like me she had received unwanted attention from Clive. But she also revealed that she was unable to repel his advances and was forced into sex. That is why, Will, I do not trust him.'

She sank back into her chair and waited for his response, but she appeared calm and controlled now, like a weight had been lifted.

'I don't know what to say Zoe, I'm so sorry you've been treated this way,' he said, 'that is appallingly.' He was shocked. He saw Clive in a whole new light now, and did not doubt for a moment that Zoe was telling the truth. 'I know that this must've been hard for you to share,' he said sincerely, 'I promise I won't tell anyone else, and I'll certainly watch my back where Clive is concerned.'

Zoe stood up and walked across to Will. She stared at him, relief in her face. She kneeled down in front of him whilst he sat on the edge of the bed and grasped his hand. Her hand was soft but firm.

'You are a good man Will,' she said. 'I hope we get to work together again. Please take care of yourself. And thank you for listening.'

She left soon after, but not before Will vowed to keep his promise and not tell anyone of her help tonight. They agreed to keep in touch.

The evening had been full of revelations. He would clearly need to be very careful where Clive was concerned. And he fully understood Zoe's need for justice. Despite everything he was a strong believer in law and justice, except he often found that when you applied the law correctly it did not always result in justice.

Sometimes you have to apply your own law to achieve justice. Like he did six years ago.

Nineteen

Dover, 1984
It wasn't difficult for Will to find out where Gazza lived. He knew from what the police had told him that Gazza was located in Whitfield village; one of the PCs even commented that his house was 'a bit rich for a young guy like him to afford'.

Whitfield was located just off the main road to London and was fairly small. Most of the properties were bungalows build in the fifties, but a fairly new housing estate was located on the edge of the village. In another part newer luxury houses had been built in the last five years, as the village continued to expand. On the main street through the village there was a pub and nearby a couple of shops, one was a newsagent the other small grocery store. There was also a fish and chip shop. Further down the main road was a post office.

After a slow drive around the streets Will finally spotted the Porshe on the driveway of a large, newly built detached house, situated at the end of a quiet cul-de-sac. The house overlooked open-countryside and woods. There were only three other detached houses in the close; all were very luxurious.

How could he afford a house like this at his age, Will thought? And a shiny new red Porsche?

Over the next two weeks Will did some digging. He had some information sources as a result of his occupation, and a few contacts he had cultivated in the police and Special Branch who owed him favors. Slowly he built up a profile of Gary Busby.

Gazza had left school with no qualifications but was now apparently a successful businessman who had an import business involving 'bric-a-brac' purchased at Antique Fairs and Brocantes in France. He received regular shipments into Dover, according to paperwork Will had accessed, courtesy of his colleagues in the import freight team. He had a small unit on a business park in Coombe Valley, on the outskirts of Dover, where he stored the goods before selling them on to local antique and curiosity shops. On the face of it all very legitimate. But Will was by nature very suspicious, a great trait for a man in his profession. And he was motivated. If Gazza was a criminal, as he suspected, then Will had a lot to gain by proving it.

He decided to spend some time covertly watching Gazza in the hope of seeing something that might be useful to pass on to the police. It was early November, so by 5pm it was dark. Parking in the road near Gazza's house was not possible as he would stand out like a sore thumb, but to the left of his house Will had noticed a farm track. A look at an ordinance survey map and a further recce identified that the track could be accessed by car from a campsite situated a quarter of a mile to the rear of the property. The site was closed for the winter, but the gate was not locked. Will drove through the site and followed the track until he was nearly at the cul-de-sac. He found a spot on the track under some trees, where he had a good view of Gazza's house. It was 6.30. He waited. The car soon got cold, but Will barely noticed, his concentration on the house never wavering.

At 7.30 Will noticed movement at the front door. Gazza appeared, wrapped up in a dark padded coat, and left his home on foot. Will left his car and followed. Gazza walked up the main street, past the shops and entered 'The Archer' pub. Will followed. The pub was fairly full and noisy. Music was playing loudly, and voices were raised to be heard.

Gazza was clearly a regular. Will heard him exchange some banter with the barman and then he joined a group of mates at a table. Will got himself a beer and sat quietly out of the way in a corner, but close enough to overhear the conversation at the next table. Gazza seemed to be holding court.

What Will heard made his blood boil. '…she looked a right tart and was probably on the game, legs always open if you ask me, so couldn't keep them on the pavement. Silly cow walked right in front of me…' Lots of laughter from his mates.

Will vowed he would avenge her death in some way. This man had no remorse for what he had done and needed to suffer, as Will was suffering since Rachel had died. But how could he make him suffer? He was certain Gazza was involved in something criminal, but he had no evidence. If he could find some then perhaps the police would open up an investigation. But he knew the constraints, so unless it was something solid enough to get Gazza convicted he doubted they would be able to do very much.

His fiancée was dead, so he didn't feel he had anything to lose anymore. If justice was to be served he decided it was down to him to serve it.

On the following night Will repeated his surveillance and was again sat in his car close to Gazza's place at 6.30. Just after seven o'clock, Gazza left his house and jumped into his Porsche. Will let him get out of sight then followed, not turning on his headlights until he saw Gazza turn right, out of the cul-de-sac and onto the main village street. Will had a good view of the Porsche as it headed towards the roundabout on the main A2, but then suddenly his view was blocked by a slow moving lorry maneuvering into the petrol station. By the time he reached the roundabout there was no sign of the Porsche. Will had used this roundabout often, so he knew that Gazza would have had four options. He could have taken the main A2 to Dover and the docks or gone the opposite direction and headed towards

Canterbury? The third option was a small local road into Dover; the fourth led down the hill towards Kearsney, where Rachel used to live (and where she died). Will made a snap decision and headed for Kearsney. Gazza's business premises was in this direction, so it seemed the most likely.

The road twisted and turned down a long hill and Will put his foot down. There wasn't much traffic, and he gained some ground. Then in the distance he just caught sight of the taillights of a car turning left at a junction five hundred yards ahead. Will was fairly certain that this was Gazza and increased his speed. If there were police around he was in big trouble as the needle on his speedo hit seventy before he braked hard to negotiate the turn. But it paid off. A few hundred yards ahead he could see the red Porsche. It had turned towards Dover town. It passed the road to Gazza's business and headed onwards toward the Western docks. Will hung back as he saw Gazza pull into a poorly lit car park near Snargate Street, close to the dock gates. Other than the red Porsche, and a burnt out car up in the corner, the car park was empty. What was he up to?

Will, pulled into the side of the road and switched off his lights. He knew this area. It was very run-down and frequented by prostitutes who got some trade from the small number of freight ships that docked here. The pubs here also had a bad reputation, drunken fights were commonplace, and most normal citizens would not choose to be out wandering alone in this part of town.

Will stepped quietly out of his car and moved in the shadows to get a closer look. Gazza sat in his car. He appeared to be waiting for someone. Will found a spot behind a broken wooden fence, about fifty feet from him. There were no lights here and he was confident he couldn't be seen. Through the broken slats he had a good view. Five minutes and nothing happened, but then Will spotted a teenager, probably only fourteen years old, walking into the car park and up to the Porsche. He was wearing a faded green colored parka with the hood up to hide his face. The window of the Porsche dropped down, and the teenager passed a large envelope into Gazza's waiting hand. Gazza passed back a carrier bag. From his vantage point Will could tell the bag was bulked out. He had no doubt what it was. This was a drugs deal. But not just a dealer selling to a user, as Will first thought. No, this was bigger. Gazza wasn't selling drugs to a user; he must be using the teenager to do the dealing for him someplace else.

If Will was right then he needed to follow this teenager to verify his suspicions. Will waited in the shadows as the teenager left the car park and passed him on the opposite side of the street. He followed. Sure enough the kid darted through a couple of backstreets and entered Pencester Gardens close to the center of town, a known drugs-user hang-out. He saw the kid approach a lone figure over by a park bench and the transaction was made. 'Gotcha!'

***

The following night he decided to visit to Pencester Gardens, but nearly got himself into problems. It was drizzling with rain, so few people were about. Maybe those he was looking for were sheltering. Then a group of four drunk teenagers spotted him. He was a man alone in a dodgy place. Prime target. They shouted a few obscenities from a distance. But as he drew closer, he noticed them blocking his path.

They were no more than sixteen. Two of them were short and slight and were very drunk. No problem. But two of them were about Will's height and they oozed trouble. The closest wore a black t-shirt, despite the November chill and had a large tattoo on each of his muscled arms. The other one looked flabby and slow but seemed to be holding a solid stick about two feet long. Not good.

'Hey, shitface,' tattoo man shouted, 'you look like you want to donate us some dosh to buy a drink,' he said with a smile, his mates laughing like hyenas and egging him on. 'Just give us your wallet and we can let you pass.'

Will tensed. He wasn't about to hand over his wallet. He was not afraid to get rough if needed. He knew he could handle tattoo man, but the man with the stick could be a problem. Although they were drunk, he would struggle to take them all on. He decided on a different tactic.

He stopped and stared directly at tattoo man, but was aware of where the others were positioned, just in case. Instead of pulling out his wallet, he pulled out his Customs ID and held it up.

'Now then lads,' he said loudly and with authority and confidence, 'You don't want to be upsetting me now do you.' The reaction was what he expected, hesitation. They wouldn't be able to see his ID, but the doubt was sown. Was he Police?

'I don't have time for this right now but pull a stunt like that again and I will nick the lot of you. My boys are dotted around the park and will be here in seconds if I radio them. We are after bigger fish tonight, so do yourselves a favor and get out of here.'

More hesitation.

'Now!' Will commanded loudly. It was enough. Tattoo man glanced at Stick man and after a few muttered grumbles, but they all turned and slunk off.

Will let out a sigh of relief. Phew, that was close. He couldn't see anyone else lurking, and the rain was getting heavier, so he decided to call it a night.

On the next night it was dry and clear. He had better luck. No sign of 'tattoo' man or his buddies for a start. He spotted a drug-user on a park bench, possibly the same one he had seen dealing with the teenager two nights ago. Will had seen dope users many times, but this lad had all the features of a heroin addict. He looked about thirty but was probably much younger. His jeans were stained and ripped, and his black t-shirt hung off him, like he had purchased one two sizes too large. The track marks down his arms confirmed Will's assessment. His face was blotchy and unshaven with sunken eyes and bad skin. He appeared a bit spaced-out, which was a good thing as he must have recently 'shot-up'.

Will, approached the man, keeping his pace and manner unthreatening. 'Hey man, mind if I sit here,' he said.

The man looked up through glazed eyes. 'No problem man,' he said in a sleepy response, 'it's a free country so they say.' He smiled a happy smile.

Will sat down. 'Yeah, so they say, although not everything is free. I need to score some coke. Any idea where I can get a bag?'

The man eyed him a bit suspiciously, but then his face switched back to happy-man. 'Sure, but it will cost you,' he chuckled. 'Like a finder's fee maybe?' he suggested.

'If you can hook me up with a seller I am sure I can make it worth your while,' Will said sincerely. 'I heard Gazza can supply what I need.'

Happy-man turned and looked at Will, but now had a serious head on. 'Gazza can do you some coke, I know, but he needs to be careful as coke is not his bag normally, and he will be treading on toes. I used to work for Gazza, but he wasn't happy when I started using the merchandise, if you know what I mean.' He chuckled again. 'The local coke man is Gilroy and his troop of black kids. I heard that Gazza is trying to muscle in on Gilroy's coke and speed business, but Gilroy is really bad news, he is connected, if you know what I mean. It would be a big mistake for Gazza to start a turf-war.'

This was useful information. He could take this to the police, and they might be tempted to start an investigation? But he was starting to develop another option in his head - if he could stir things up with the rival gang, Gilroy might just do Gazza some harm, a good beating might just feel like justice. At the very least it would seriously harm Gazza's drug business, wouldn't it?

On the next night Will found the addict again and for a few pounds finder's fee he got directed to one of the kids who worked for Gilroy's gang. Posing as an addict he sought to buy some cocaine. Will was offered a 'bag' for thirty pounds.

'That's over-priced,' he said to the kid, 'I am told that Gazza only charges twenty. You go back to your boss and tell him I will deal with Gazza from now on.'

Will then walked away from the deal and left the park.

He didn't know if he had done enough, but he hoped his plan would annoy Gilroy enough for him to give Gazza some grief? If he hadn't heard anything in a weeks' time he would come back and try again.

Will learnt Gazza's fate two days later in the Dover Gazette.

Police were called to Pencester Gardens in the early hours of this morning following the discovery of a dead body by a dog-walker. A man aged 24 was found stabbed to death. He was identified as Gary Busby, a local businessman. No arrests have yet been made, but Police are looking for two black men in their late teens who were seen arguing with the deceased. They are not ruling out the possibility that the murder was drug-related. If anyone has any information that might assist please contact...'

Did he feel any remorse? Not one bit. Sometimes actions have unintended consequences. He didn't expect Gazza to be killed, but he was not sorry.

Twenty

Will fully expected Clive to pop-up when he arrived at Heathrow airport, and he wasn't disappointed. Only this time they just sat in Clive's car in the multi-storey car park, as Will had a Vauxhall Cavalier pool car to drive him back to Southend. John, as usual was sat in the driver's seat and greeted him as he climbed into the back of the Ford Granada next to Clive.

'So Will, tell me about your trip. Did it go well?'

Will settled himself into the comfort of the leather seats and started his report.

'Yes, it went well I think.' He handed him the 'Zippo' camera. 'I found a number of documents that related to Irish customers, just as you asked for, and found out some other useful information from talking to Elias.'

'Tell me more,' said Clive as he pocketed the Zippo. 'You can hold onto the cigarette packet by the way, you might need it again soon,' he said tantalisingly.

Will explained to Clive about the Russian involvement, how Elias had said he felt scared working for them and how he now wished he had never got involved in their business.

'That's useful,' Clive remarked thoughtfully, we might be able to put some pressure on Elias in the future. What else did you learn?'

He described the concealment that they were using to hide the goods and also mentioned the British driver he had recognised from a few years ago, who had been convicted of tobacco smuggling. Clive perked up at this and said that he would follow up with Customs and Excise Investigation Division to get the background intelligence.

'Well yet again Will you have done a great job, anything else?'

He immediately thought about Zoe and the bugging device, but he had promised Zoe he would not say anything. He was now looking at Clive in a very different light. Here was a man who abused women and maybe abused others. He took care to mask these thoughts by changing the subject.

'No, that's it, apart from the fact that I'm currently out of pocket. I assume you'll be paying my expenses very soon?'

Clive laughed, My dear boy, of course.' He took three twenty-pound notes from his wallet and handed them to Will. 'This is to tide you over for now.' Then he handed him a piece of paper and a pen. 'Scribble down what you've spent, and we'll get you the funds by tomorrow morning,' he said.

Will thought about his expenditure, the hotel, the clothes, the meals, the torch, and wrote it all down and handed it back. It came to £120. Clive took the sheet, made a note on it and passed it to John.

'We're not worried about receipts, but just be sensible what you spend. There may be occasions in the future when you have to spend a lot more, but then we will arrange for you get funds up front if we can. We have to keep the bean-counters happy of course, but my budget it quite large.' Will did not doubt it.

'Thanks again Will for a job well done. This operation is far from over, so you can expect some more missions quite soon. In the meantime we need to arrange some further training for you. There is a three-day course I would particularly like you to attend next week. Your boss, Dave, has already been told that you need to attend a pre-arranged drugs refresher course next Tuesday, Wednesday and Thursday near Heathrow. He is fully supportive as it will help with the delivery of some of the new Preventive courses that you'll undoubtedly need to do sometime soon.'

As usual Clive had done his homework. In theory his role now was to help plan courses and monitor the trainers who were delivering to make sure the quality was maintained. But currently there were some gaps in the schedule as they couldn't get trainers released from their stations due to the pace at which they were trying to run the courses. So the backstop was for Will, and some of his colleagues in the office, to fill the gaps and train on the courses instead. He didn't mind this at all. He enjoyed being the trainer and it made sense to refresh his knowledge and skills if he was to be remain effective.

Clive continued. 'You won't be doing this course, of course.' He laughed at his own joke. 'We've arranged for you to receive some other training that might be more useful; just down the road is one of our establishments, in Harmondsworth.' He handed Will a hand-drawn map and an address. 'Be here at 8am on Tuesday please.'

That was it, meeting over. Will got out of the car and it disappeared down the ramp and he headed over to the long-term parking to collect the pool car and head back to Southend. Clive had seemed pleased with the result of the mission and more importantly Will had kept quiet about meeting Zoe and her involvement. Clive did not seem at all suspicious. He hoped he was doing the right thing, but it felt right and that was what mattered to him.

When he got back to the office it was mid-afternoon on Thursday. He updated Dave on the hotel he had secured for the May course in Cheltenham and Dave told him about the drug refresher course he would be attending next week in Heathrow.

That evening he planned to have an early night but decided a quick pint would be in order and headed off to his usual pub. It had been a busy day, and the tiredness was creeping up on him so an hour later he was back at the B&B and ready to turn-in. As he entered the front door he noticed an envelope on the doormat addressed to 'Will Mortimer'. Mrs. Hollis was in the front room with the telly up loud, so clearly she hadn't heard the letter drop through the letterbox. Inside the envelope was £60, the residue of the money that he was owed. Will had to silently congratulate Clive, he and his team were very efficient. Time for bed. As he drifted off to sleep he wondered what training course Clive had in mind for him.

Twenty-one

Elias had been looking forward to his weekend for a bit of rest and relaxation, but his weekend did not go well.

After a very busy week managing his legitimate business, as well as his illegitimate business, he was keen to spend some time hiking around the hills and lakes where he lived on the edge of Lucerne. He had been married, but five years ago he had lost his wife to cancer. Since then had become a bit of a loner, enjoying the isolation that walking in the hills gave him.

He had earlier personally supervised the packing of the arms and ammunition into the crate concealments with the help of Peter. The packing had been overseen by Sergei who had insisted on being present. Mikhail was clearly not going to take chances with this load and planned to monitor it's delivery every step of the way. Sergei had flown in especially to check on the consignment, and would be flying back that evening. As usual Sergei felt that Mikhail was overdoing it, but he was not about to argue. Elias was not about to argue either and not for the first time he wished he had not got involved with the Russians.

He had always been prone to stretch the rules and make some extra money on the side. His late wife had often warned him that he would get caught out one day, but they were minor misdemeanours. He did not think he would ever get caught, or would only get a warning or a small fine if he did. But he had got himself dragged into serious crime and a toxic relationship with the Russians.

It had started simply enough with him being paid money for a small and straightforward role, but he was suckered into more tasks, and now it put fear in his heart whenever he engaged with them. He knew he could not now escape. They were ruthless and he was in no doubt that he would pay with his life if he ever crossed them.

Initially he had been approached and offered five thousand Swiss francs to divert one of his lorries to pick up some goods that would not be on the manifest. He didn't know what the goods were and didn't want to know, it was easy money. This happened a few more times, but then he was asked to take part in the loading of the packages. He had guessed they must be drugs, but again he did not want to know and simply assisted as he was asked. At this point there was no going back – it was made clear to him that he was now 'in-deep' and to refuse to do as the Russians asked would not be an option. So he complied. There was nothing else he could do.

Before he left, Sergei warned Elias that there had been a change of plan and Mikhail would be calling him shortly to explain. As they had finished their loading task, Elias let Peter go and went back to his office to await the call from Mikhail. Peter would no doubt be spending the weekend in Switzerland as he usually did, Elias thought. Using the money the crime group paid him, on prostitutes and getting drunk. His own weekend was planned to be far more relaxing, walking around the hills. He was contemplating which route he might take when the telephone rang and brought him back from his reverie. It was Mikhail.

The lorry would leave the yard on Monday morning, Mikhail explained, and would travel to Dover for Wednesday. But then instead of unloading in Norfolk, Mikhail had decreed that it would go directly to the Irish customer at a location in Northern Ireland, somewhere near Newry close to the Irish border. The last consignment, although meticulously planned, had gone badly wrong. The customer was getting impatient. It was true that a direct delivery posed a higher risk, Mikhail had explained. But he could not follow the lengthy approach this time, or he would lose the customer and probably his reputation.

Elias felt uncomfortable with this decision but, like Sergei, he knew better than to argue.

Mikhail had also decided that he would have some of his men following the lorry in a car all the way to Calais, and see it onto the ferry to make sure it stayed safe. He had lost tens of thousands of dollars on the last shipment, and he was taking no risks this time.

However, he felt that four Russians travelling in a car through British Customs might look suspicious without some very good reasons. So he had hired Zoltan's Hungarian team from the Norfolk depot to follow it from Dover to Liverpool, and see it onto the Belfast ferry.

***

Zoe was parked just outside the gates to the yard on the other side of the road. She felt quite sure she was unseen in the shadows as she was some way from the glow of the yard's floodlights. She had parked here for a few hours yesterday afternoon in the hope that she would overhear a useful conversation from the bug under Elias's desk.

She knew it was a longshot, but she had to try. She also knew that today was probably the last chance for anything meaningful to come from her eavesdropping, as the battery in the bug would only last about 48 hours, probably not much longer.

The bug had worked well. She had heard everything said in the office through her earpiece yesterday and today, but nothing so far had been of any value.

It was getting late. She was about to give up when she heard Elias's phone ring in her earpiece. She struck gold.

She could only hear Elias's side of the conversation, and at first she thought it was Sergei on the call. But then it was confirmed she was listening to a conversation with Mikhail, as Elias called him by name. They were planning for the next arms shipment. She now knew from their conversation that plans had changed. This was going to be a problem.

Despite her unapproved bugging of Elias's office, she would have to find a way of letting COGS know of this development. She would worry about that later. What she really wanted to hear was some clue as to where she could find Mikhail. All the intelligence they had so far indicated he was in Russia, possibly Saint Peterburg, but no one had been able to verify this. She had the feeling he was no longer in Russia, but where would he go?

The call ended, and she was left frustrated. No clues. In hindsight she should have placed a bug into the telephone handset, then she would hear both sides of the conversation, but it was too late now. All she wanted was to locate Mikhail so that she could get a confession from him that he had killed her Uncle.

She reflected on what she had learned about Mikhail so far – Mikhail had taken over from Nico Brodsky, his Uncle. Where would he go to run the business?

Nico Brodsky had been killed in that accident in Hungary, so was it possible that Nico had been living there? She had never thought to investigate this as she had assumed, as the Hungarian police had, that Nico and the driver were visiting from Russia and were not residents. The assumption was based on the fact that the car had Russian number plates. But it made some sense that they were actually living in Hungary at the time of the accident, and that Mikhail had now moved there to take over the local business interests.

She needed to return to her office and call the contacts she had built up in the Hungarian Police to see what they knew. However, she still had the more urgent task of how she was going to tell COGS about the information she now had that the arms shipment would be delivered directly to Ireland after it left Dover.

She got back to her office just before 6pm that evening. She was keen to call her contacts in Hungary, but then she realised that as they were an hour ahead of Swiss time it would be 7pm and very unlikely that her contacts were there. She tried, but unsurprisingly the phone remained unanswered. Frustratingly that call would now have to wait until tomorrow, or more likely Monday.

Now to focus on what she had learned from the bug in Elias's office. How she could tell COGS about the new plans for the next consignment of arms. It was vital that COGS knew of this new development quickly, but how could she explain how she knew. She was not about to tell them about her unapproved bugging of Elias's office, but somehow she needed to alert them.

In the event she didn't have to, as just then her phone rang, and it was COGS - and they told her.

They had been monitoring telephone traffic with the Irish customer, thanks to details that Will had photographed from Elias's cupboard. They had overheard a conversation earlier that day between Seamus Devlin, their prime target, and Mikhail. They were now aware that the date of the next arms delivery had been brought forward to next Thursday, to be delivered to a location near to Newry. COGS explained to Zoe that this delivery must not take place and briefed her for a new and urgent mission that Zoe must undertake that evening. Zoe listened intently to the details of what she was required to do.

***

It was 9pm that evening when Elias heard the rap on the door. He was inclined to ignore such a call at this time of night, but curiosity got the better of him and he strode out into the hall and faced the door. Through the obscure glass he thought he detected the shape of a woman and felt a bit more secure as he opened the door – big mistake.

When Elias opened the door there was indeed a woman standing there, she looked about thirty, very fit, but she had a pistol aimed right at him! Before he could react she ushered him forcibly back inside and closed the door behind her with her foot, whilst keeping the pistol trained unwaveringly on him. Elias started to protest, but she cut him off.

'Get into the lounge Mr. Michaels and do not speak until I tell you,' the woman commanded.

'I don't plan to harm you, but please understand that I do mean business, and will take whatever action is necessary if you do not comply with my request.'

Elias knew he had no choice and despite his fear, he was curious as to why this woman was holding him at gunpoint, what could she want? He backed into the lounge not wanting to turn away from her.

'Please sit-down Mr. Michaels,' the woman commanded, a little less sternly. Elias complied, now shaking a little from the shock, and waited. There was no mistaking that the woman was Swiss, which was some kind of relief as this meant he was not dealing with Russians.

The woman sat down in a chair opposite Elias.

'I am from a Government agency,' the woman explained calmly, 'You don't need to know which one, but you do need to know that I have authority to do whatever it takes to solve a security issue that you are now part of.'

Elias did not understand until she explained what she knew and what she wanted. He then realised just how much trouble he was in.

'We have evidence that you are shipping arms and ammunition to the UK. As you know if you are prosecuted you'll spend many years in prison.'

Elias felt the blood drain from his face.

Zoe could see that what she had said, had had the desired effect. Now to give him a way out.

'I'm here to make you an offer, a deal to avoid prison. How does that sound?'

Elias did not want to go to prison. He was in his early fifties, and he knew that the law in Switzerland was strict, and he could expect at least fifteen years for his role in arms smuggling. He would be approaching seventy when he got released. But he was also concerned for his life if he was to be asked to identify the Russians. Even if Mikhail and Sergei were prosecuted, their reach was far and their desire for retribution was unending.

But then the woman explained what she wanted. The more he thought about the plan the more he was sure it would not rebound on him, quite the opposite. There were some risks of course, but weighing up the options he realised he really had little choice. He agreed to the deal and told Zoe everything he knew about the Russians and the plans for the next consignment.

***

On Saturday night at 11pm Elias went back into his yard to carry out his first task. It was heavy tiring work and he had to do it as quietly as possible, but by 4am he was finished. By 5am he was back home soaking his aching limbs in a nice hot bath, before falling into an exhausted sleep for a few hours. He awoke at 10am and despite the cold wind blowing across the lake and mountains he had a late breakfast and went out hiking until dark. Walking in the hills was therapeutic and made him feel calm after the pressures of the last two days. He reflected on how he had reached this sorry predicament, and he missed his wife's good counsel terribly.

He had not been a bad husband, but he regretted not taking more notice of his wife when she urged him to be careful. He had always seen it as nagging, but now he could see that she was right, as always, and he was too arrogant to see the obvious. Since her passing, he missed her for lots of reasons, not least her sage advice.

She was talking to him now as he hiked, telling him he had an opportunity to do the right thing. If it went well she would be proud of him, he thought. But if it did not go well he might be joining her sooner than expected.

Twenty-two

When Will got back to Southend on Sunday it was early evening. He hadn't seen much of Alison this weekend due to her shift pattern and other plans she had made. She had been on lates on Friday when he got home and earlies on Saturday. But she had arranged to go out with the girls on Saturday night, so Will was left at home with a bottle of beer and a video. He had decided to hire 'Top Gun', a film he had been planning to watch for years but never got around to. He wasn't disappointed.

Alison turned up at his house at lunchtime Sunday. She had had a late-night clubbing and had slept in. She cooked a lovely Sunday roast for them, and they snuggled up on the sofa, but all to soon it was time for Will to leave. She left for her shift, and he gathered his belongings and jumped into his car to return to Southend. Another weekend without broaching the subject, he thought.

The journey was uneventful, and he received a cheerful welcome back from Mrs. Hollis. He dumped his bags in his room and headed back out for a walk. Having eaten a full roast dinner before he left home he decided against his usual pizza. But he did fancy a pint and a packet of crisps and headed for the Spread Eagle. He greeted the owner who was polishing glasses and scanned the sparse clientele who were now nodding acquaintances. Then he did a double-take at the man sitting in the corner nursing a pint of bitter.

He wandered over to where the man was sitting. The man looked up and smiled.

'Hello again Clive, I didn't know this was your local,' Will said sarcastically, mine's a pint of London Pride.'

'Hello dear boy,' Clive chimed in his old-fashioned way, 'Of course,' he said cheerfully, 'but let us drink up quickly as I need to have a chat to you.'

He said the words, 'I need to have a chat with you', in a serious tone, and Will was immediately on his guard. Had he learnt about Zoe?

Five minutes later after chatting about the weather and the price of fish, they left the pub and headed across the road to Clive's waiting car. John was in the driving seat as usual, and nodded pleasantly as they climbed into the back seat.

'I'll cut to the chase,' Clive said, 'The situation is moving quickly, and we need your help again. But first it is time to tell you the full story. You've proved yourself worthy and you need to know just how important your role is to the security of our country.'

Clive spent the next twenty minutes outlining the whole operation. He talked through how the IRA were buying arms and ammunition from a Russian organised crime group and how COGs had managed to secure the first consignment without the criminals being aware. Will was amazed at the sophistication of that operation as Clive talked him through the intricacies. He knew that they had to secure the arms without the crime groups knowledge, but the detailed plan and its execution was nothing short of astonishing. However, what Clive explained next was on a whole new level.

They were now planning to stop the next consignment and get both the Irish and the Russians to break cover, which would allow them to arrest some very high-profile criminal figures.

'The Irish customer is a known high ranking IRA member called Seamus Devlin,' Clive explained. 'He was an IRA Brigade Commander who was suspected of coordinating the bombing of Runwood Barracks in 1985 which injured 18 soldiers, and there was good evidence that he planted the car bomb Barnham Newry courthouse, that killed an RUC Police Officer and a civilian in 1988. He managed to avoid being caught and had kept off the radar ever since.'

COGS had determined that Seamus had risen in the ranks and was now running a Brigade with a prime role of smuggling arms and ammunition, into Northern Ireland. Like all IRA members, and particularly those in high ranks, he was being very cautious. So far COGS had been unable to find direct evidence of his involvement in the smuggling of arms. They needed a breakthrough and had decided that the only way to find him and prosecute him, was to catch him in the act of receiving a shipment of arms. How to do this had taxed the minds of the COGs strategic and operational planners, but slowly and surely their plan developed and stage one was nearing completion. The next stage would be a little trickier.

'The other side of the coin is the Russian organised crime boss. He is a ruthless known murderer, but currently his whereabouts are unknown,' Clive said.

Will didn't let on that he already knew this.

Clive then described the plan to intercept the next load and flush out both of their big targets – *so Zoe had got her wish after all.* The plan was complex and ambitious, but Will knew by now that COGs were not afraid to push the boundaries. Clive then told him how the intelligence that Will had provided on Elias and his fear of the Russians, had resulted in Elias being approached to help with the operation.

Will's next mission would be crucial to making the whole operation happen.

Instead of attending the planned course this week, Will was to travel to Lucerne again and Clive wanted him to collaborate with the contact he had met in Switzerland last year, on his first mission - *little did he know.*

'She was fully trained,' he said, 'and you will both be conducting an important phase of the operation. I won't go into detail now as Zoe has been fully briefed, but don't forget your cigarettes!'

He furnished Will with a new flight ticket for Tuesday and £200 for expenses and checked that Will still had his overnight bag in his office, containing his false passport. Zoe would meet him off the train in Lucerne on Tuesday afternoon.

'Good luck Will, we're counting on you,'

That was it. Without ceremony Will was once again ushered onto the pavement as the black Granada sped off.

He stood there for a moment, a little shell-shocked. He was left with a wealth of new information to process that was almost mind-blowing, and he was in awe of the organisation he was now part of. They had put their trust in him, and he felt incredibly humbled. But right now he was feeling like he had stepped inside the middle of a tornado, and one false step would send him spinning out of this world.

Twenty-three

Peter always enjoyed his time in Lucerne. The clubs were expensive, but he had found a couple of them that were reasonably priced, and more importantly, the girls he paid for were cheaper, and prepared to accommodate his particular needs.

He liked 'rough' sex. He never hurt the girls (well maybe a few bruises on their arms as he held them down whilst he forced sex on them). But he liked the feeling of being in control, the power of getting what he wanted, and the girls were prepared to 'play the game' with just enough resistance, to look like they were really scared. On occasion this was close to the truth.

Since he had come out of prison things had got better and better.

His last year in prison was the worst. His wife left him for an Insurance salesman, and he hated her for that. Not because he still loved her, that had gone away years before. No, it was the fact that she had left him whilst he was in prison that caused him grief. One of the inmates somehow found out, and by the end of the day everyone in the joint knew. Consequently he had the piss taken out of him almost daily.

'What was it that made her screw someone else?' they'd say, 'Was your dick not big enough for her,' or, 'When I get out next month I will go around your place and sort him out for you if you like – then I can have a go with your Missus as well.'

A couple of the inmates even offered to be his 'friend' and show him how it was really done, if he joined them in the showers. He spent the last year in prison in fear of becoming someone's bitch.

But in the final few months of his sentence he was lucky enough to share his cell with a drug smuggler called Vince, who had got eight years for smuggling heroin. They got on well and just before Peter was released, Vince put him in touch with a group on the outside who were looking for a lorry driver of his particular character – i.e. a criminal.

He saw his role as fairly low risk. They paid him well and all he had to do was drive his lorry through Customs. He had done it many of times now, almost never being stopped. On the very few times that he was pulled over they never found the illicit goods he was carrying. If they ever did, he was wise enough to cover his tracks, so they would never be able to attribute the goods to him.

Once through Customs he would simply follow the instructions he had been given and deliver the goods to the agreed location, often a farm in the countryside somewhere.

The only thing that irked him was the Russians. Most of his deliveries in recent months were for Russian customers or other Eastern Europeans, they were all the same to him. He hated that they did not talk to him in English and prattled away to each other in some stupid language. He didn't understand a word, but was convinced they were talking about him and laughing at him, so he could not wait to dump the goods and leave as soon as he could.

***

Peter picked up the lorry from Elias's yard as planned on Monday morning and prepared for his journey to Dover. An overnight stop was planned at the Aire de Service, a few miles west of Saarbrüken. He had done this route many times, so it was fairly normal, apart from the minor irritation of being tailed by four Russians in a hired black Volvo. He hated Russians.

Elias had advised him that the trip had been extended, and he was now taking the goods all the way to Northern Ireland. He didn't mind, especially as Elias confirmed he would be paid double. And Elias had another bonus for him. He was to meet a German man named Karl at the Saarbrüken service stop. The German would give him some padded envelopes to drop at an address in Luton on his way through to Liverpool. Apparently the envelopes contained some commercially sensitive documents that could not be sent through the post and had to be delivered by hand. Peter didn't believe this for a moment. But he was not about to comment when he was given 5,000 Swiss francs there and then by Elias to make the delivery - it was the easiest money he had ever made.

The only stipulation Elias had insisted on was that he would have to make sure the Russians didn't see him meeting the German contact, or see the packages. He was to place them in the cab and not the load. As the Russians were there just to keep an eye on the lorry and its load, this shouldn't be too much of a problem, thought Peter.

Armed with a very clear description of the German named Karl, (even Peter couldn't miss a very tall blond German with a three-inch scar on his cheek), he had set off.

The journey to the Saarbrüken Aire de Service, normally took about eight hours and today was no exception, but the more miles Peter covered the more irritated he became by the sight in his mirrors of the black Volvo. When he had left the yard he had waved cheerfully at his minders, but they had completely ignored him – 'ignorant bastards,' he muttered under his breath. He couldn't see why they had to be there, was he not trusted? He hoped that at some point they would get bored, or lose him or breakdown or something, but that wasn't about to happen was it.

He made his first rest stop after about five hours, just north of Colmar on the A35. He had sometimes made it all the way to Saarbrüken without stopping, but he wasn't in a rush and no reason not to rest for an hour and have a leisurely cup of tea and a plate of fries. As expected the black Volvo followed him into the service area and stationed itself about fifty metres away. Peter climbed down from his cab and waved at the occupants as he headed for the toilets, but they ignored him.

An hour later he was back on the road again with the familiar black Volvo in his wing mirrors. However, a mile up the road the car seemed to be slowing down. As he checked his mirrors again it receded into the distance until he could not see it following any more. Oh, well, he thought, not my problem, they will no doubt catch me up at some point.

He arrived at the Saarbrüken rest stop at 17:00 hours and sat in his cab for five minutes, looking out for his minders, but the Black Volvo did not appear. He decided to take the opportunity to go and find Karl. He strolled into the restaurant area and scanned the tables looking for the tall blond that Elias had described. Although it was busy, Karl was easy to spot, a lone tall blond man at a corner table reading a magazine, a half empty coffee cup in front of him. Peter walked up to him.

'My name is Peter, and you must be Karl, I believe you're expecting me,' he said.

Karl looked up and smiled, and Peter noticed the long scar down his left cheek. It wasn't fresh and Peter did wonder how Karl may have come by it, but he would not ask.

'Peter, very pleased to meet you,' Karl said with a heavy German accent. 'And you are right on time.'

Karl opened the briefcase that was sitting on an adjacent chair and handed Peter three padded envelopes.

'These are the envelopes that you must deliver, please. The address is in Luton, on an industrial park. You must hand them to the name on the envelope, no one else,' he insisted.

Peter took the envelopes and nodded. 'No problem, I can do that. Anything else?'

'That is all,' said Karl, and he stood up. 'Have a good journey Peter' He walked away.

Peter looked at the letters and the name and address on them. The name and address meant nothing to him, but he did not expect they would; all he had to do was find the address and the man and make the delivery.

When he looked up he could see Karl exiting the restaurant door and heading for the car park. He stuffed the envelopes into his half-zipped coat and headed back to his lorry. When he got outside he scanned the car park – there was still no sign of the black Volvo, so he knew he was not being watched by those pesky Russians. But he hurried to his lorry nonetheless and stowed the letters under his seat.

***

Karl got back to his car and using the rear-view mirror he carefully and slowing removed the false scar from his cheek and with some face cream and a tissue he wiped his face clean. He smiled at himself in the mirror as he then removed the blond wig to reveal his normal dark brown locks. Time to call COGs and report 'mission accomplished.'

Twenty-four

It was just after 2pm on Tuesday afternoon when Will got off the train in Lucerne. Zoe was waving to him and smiling happily as he got onto the concourse. She looked a lot perkier than when they had last met and had a spring in her step. Will was looking forward to hearing what she had been up to in the last week and particularly what the detailed plan was to be.

'Hi Will,' she greeted him with a kiss on the cheek, 'great to be working with you again - officially this time,' she said with a smirk.

'Hello again Zoe. Yes, I'm also looking forward to this and can't wait to hear the details. As usual Clive was limited in what he told me.'

At the mention of Clive's name he saw her wince a little, but she recovered her smile quickly and led him to her car. Or to be more accurate, Jan's car.

'We only run one car,' she explained, 'as our offices are close together. If either of us needs to work different hours we use public transport. I told Jan I needed the car today so he'll make his own arrangements. Let us get a coffee somewhere quiet and we can talk.'

Will felt he had got quite familiar with Lucerne by now, but Zoe drove away from the city towards the lake and into an area he didn't recognise. They chatted about his journey and the scenery, and the sunny weather, the beautiful lake made more beautiful by the mountain back-drop. They avoided any business talk for now. Ten minutes later they pulled into the car park of a small hotel overlooking Lake Lucerne.

'This will be quiet at this time of day, and they serve great coffee,' she said with glee.

She led through the entrance and into a small lounge off to the right of reception. The middle-aged lady on reception greeted Zoe and told them to take a seat and said she would organise coffee for them.

'I take it you come here often.' Will said.

'Yes, it is far enough away from the office and not somewhere my colleagues would visit, so it is ideal for Network meetings. The owner doesn't ask questions and probably thinks I'm a businesswoman. We should be quite safe to talk.'

Coffee arrived and thankfully a nice little jug of cream and some brown sugar accompanied it. Will served the coffee, black for Zoe, heaps of cream and some sugar for him, and took a sip – very nice.

'Ok Will, let me update you on what's been happening and then we can plan for tonight's excursion.'

She explained how her eavesdropping of Elias's office had revealed that the plans for the next consignment of arms had changed, and how she was faced with the dilemma of how to alert COGs of this new intelligence without admitting that she had bugged the office without approval. Then the stroke of good luck that COGs had already found out about the change from a different source. She then outlined to him the new COGs plan that had led to her and Will working together, and that she had visited Elias on Friday evening and made a deal with him.

Will processed all of this new information.

'Do you think we can trust Elias?" he questioned. 'From what you've said, he has a major role in the plan and might decide to warn Mikhail.'

'It's a risk, yes,' agreed Zoe, 'But I got the impression that he dislikes the Russians intensely, and if he plays his part correctly he would be able to deny all knowledge. He also has the promise that we would keep him out of prison.'

Will agreed, the risk was low. He could see from Zoe's face that she was keen to tell him something else. Something unrelated to Elias.

'Last week,' she continued excitedly, 'I found out that Mikhail is living in Hungary. I didn't get this from listening in to the call between Elias and Mikhail as I'd hoped, but the call got me to thinking. Was it possible Mikhail was in Hungary, as his Uncle was killed there. I called my police contacts in Hungary yesterday to check if Nico might have been living there. We had all assumed he was only visiting the country, as the car he was in had Russian number plates. They ran both Nico Brodsky and the name Mikhail through their immigration database and confirmed that Nico had been living in Hungary for several months when he was killed. They had three 'Mikhail's' from Russia who had arrived in the country between March and June, and two had returned within two weeks. But there is no record of one, Mikhail Gazenko, ever leaving. This has to be our man.'

'Ok, that's good that you know all this,' Will said, 'but how does this help you?'

'You are right, it would not help me too much, if I were to continue my solo quest,' she conceded, 'but now it seems that Clive has changed his mind. He announced that he can see an opportunity to catch the Irish leader *and* Mikhail as well,' she explained.

She was clearly very happy with this new turn of events, but got back to the business in hand.

'For this to work we need Mikhail to leave Hungary. Although I've a good relationships with the Hungarian police, generally Hungary is not a friend of Switzerland; they will not help us. We need Mikhail to come here, and if the plan works, that is exactly what he will do. With the evidence we have, and the further evidence we hope to gather, the Swiss authorities will be happy to arrest him for money laundering and if all goes to plan, arms smuggling as well.'

They discussed their mission for that night. Zoe had it all worked out and had all the necessary equipment. It would be a similar excursion to the one they made last week, but with two specific differences. This time the bugging had been approved, and this time Zoe would be working with Will legitimately.

The aim was to flush out the Principals at both ends of the chain, the Irish leader as a priority, but also Mikhail. They believed that phone tapping would be the most effective method to help track their movements and react as necessary. The only phone number they had that would help was in Elias's offices, so it was Will and Zoe's job to pay Elias's yard another visit and place a bug into his phone.

COGs had tried to do this remotely which had worked well in the past, but for some reason the phone system in

Switzerland could not accept their normal remote attack through the exchange. The only solution was that the actual handset would need to have a bug placed into the receiver. They also needed to bug under Elias's office, COGs had decided.

Plans agreed, Zoe dropped Will at the same hotel he had stayed at the previous week and said she would be back at 11pm. Will checked in and took a shower. Refreshed, he decided that as it was only 5.30pm he would go for a stroll. After a few minutes he found himself at the same food shop as before and bought some snacks. He considered a few unknown pastries on display, but in the end he chose the same sausage pastry and apple cake as last week. An hour later he was back in the hotel sampling his snacks. He tried to sleep a little, but unsurprisingly he couldn't. He thought through how Zoe had identified Mikhail's whereabouts and how happy she seemed. Let us hope she gets what she wants, he thought.

But sometimes things do not go to plan and sometimes revenge can rear its ugly head. He still believed he did the right thing back then – justice needed to be served.

***

Will and Zoe arrived at the yard at 11.30pm and all was quiet. Will took out his lock picks and set about opening up the gate padlock. That was odd? The lock was in place, but it was unlocked. He indicated to Zoe.

'Probably the last man out forgot to clamp it down,' she whispered, 'but let's go careful.'

Will pulled the lock off and they slipped through the gate. He placed the lock back in position unlocked, just as he had found it. They stayed in the shadows where they could, and made their way slowly across to the staircase leading up to the offices. It was Zoe's turn to open the door to the offices – she was far quicker than Will and this was no time to be macho he thought.

Within one minute she had the door open, and they burst in to tackle the alarm but…silence. The alarm had not sounded. There must be someone still here. The office lights were all off and as before the only light was coming through the windows from the lorry park floodlights.

Will could see Zoe's face clearly illuminated and she mouthed 'What do we do?'

He shrugged. She then motioned for him to stay where he was, and she headed off stealthily towards Elias's office. The door was closed, and from his position he could see Zoe reach the door and slowly turn the handle – the door was unlocked.

Zoe hesitated and stood stock still for ten seconds, cocking her ear to listen for any sounds, before entering. Will could see her outline and decided he could not remain where he was anymore, and slowly followed in Zoe's footsteps, scanning the rest of the open office as he went.

As he got to Elias's office Will could see Zoe under the desk seeking to retrieve her bug – the first part of their plan. But she came out from the desk empty-handed and looked up at him from the floor.

'It is not here Will,' she hissed in a shocked tone.

'Is this what you are looking for?' came a voice from behind him.

Twenty-five

Seamus hated Russians he had decided, even more than Libyans. The problem with the Libyans was that their weapons were not of good enough quality, so new providers had been sought.

At least with the Libyans he had had good service, but this new Russian who had taken over the business had not delivered, and now Seamus's own reputation was at stake. Not least because the IRA had suffered recently from the British army who had discovered several key arms caches in recent months. The IRA Army Council were very concerned. Not only did they have a need to replenish their arms caches, but they were worried that their ranks had been infiltrated. How else had so many caches have been discovered?

Seamus ran a tight unit and the Army Council decided that he was the ideal commander to lead the procurement of new arms. But this first attempt had gone wrong, and the pressure was on him to find some more arms quickly.

Seamus was known as a hard man who did not compromise; no one would dare cross him if they knew what was good for them. He may be laying-low whilst he avoided the authorities who suspected him of two bombings, but everyone knew his reputation. He was the one who sanctioned the punishment beatings, even if he was often not present. If that Russian had been reachable, Seamus thought, he would have received a lesson in how to conduct business with the IRA. But Seamus had to accept that he would probably never see this Russian in person, and that they were both still eager for a satisfactory result.

He did not know all the details of the planning that went into that failed delivery, only the final part of the plan that involved him. They had been meticulous, with a plan designed to ensure success. But more importantly to ensure that both he and the Russians would never be implicated if things went wrong. So as much as he hated to admit it, he did respect this. The failure, on the face of it, seemed like an accident, but you did not get to his position and stay out of trouble by not being suspicious. He was keen that this next consignment was just as carefully planned so that he and his unit were not exposed should things go wrong again – the Russian would pay heavily if it did.

But for Seamus, his biggest concern was the pressure he was getting from the Army Council.

He was worried and shared his concerns with one of his trusted lieutenants, Liam McGuire. The Army Council had been alerted to the possibility that there was an informant within the Northern Command, and all Brigade commanders were asked to be on their guard. They had specifically told Seamus he needed to be sure his own unit was clean, as the new arms shipment was due any day and it could not afford to be compromised.

The Army Council were always putting out these types of messages, but they had been specific with Seamus that he must ensure the shipment was properly managed; he was responsible for a good outcome, they told him, failure was not an option.

He had already decided that he would oversee this one, but what troubled him more was that he had had some suspicions of his own. For a few weeks now, he had been concerned by one of his unit, Sean O'Malley.

It was possibly nothing, but over the last few weeks Sean had been more keen than usual to find out the details of the next arms shipment. Initially Seamus put it down to Sean's enthusiasm, but as Sean's enquiries got more regular and detailed he started to get suspicious.

'You don't need to know lad' he had said, when Sean asked where the lorry would be unloading. 'You just need to be ready, because I need you there to check that the detonators are the right ones and good quality,' he had explained, 'or those bastard Russians will not get their money.'

Sean O'Malley had grown up and was educated in Newry, and during his school years had shown a skill and ability in science. When he left school he got a job as a technician in the research department of a food processing plant. His initial job was little more that cleaning and sterilising equipment that the scientists and chemical engineers used in their research and experiments. Their task was to assess how certain materials reacted with food, such as plastic containers and tins. This was all part of determining which package gave the safest and longest shelf life to their foods. Sean enjoyed his job and took great interest in the work of the scientists, and his enthusiasm got him noticed. He would often ask some pertinent questions about why certain things were done, which sometimes prompted the scientists to re-evaluate their approach. The Head of the Research unit decided to give Sean an opportunity, and paid for his studies to become a qualified chemical engineer. Three years later Sean achieved this goal and joined their ranks.

One of his colleagues at the food processing plant was Liam Maguire who worked on the production line, and they became firm friends. They had both grown up hating the English and were open supporters of the IRA's aims. Sean did not know immediately, but he soon discovered that Liam was in fact a member of the IRA. It was through Liam that Sean got introduced to an IRA group who said they could use his science skills in a different way – making bombs.

Sean was checked out by a number of IRA intelligence officers and eventually was recruited as a bomb-maker within Seamus's unit, which suited Sean down to the ground.

But one thing that the checks on him failed to reveal was that he was gay. His boyfriend was the secret love of his life. Sean was a devout catholic and went to church every Sunday which was where he met Callum, a young aspiring priest.

Growing up Sean had always known he was different. Apart from some fumbling with some girls in his teenage years he had not had any real experience of the opposite sex. As he grew older he became increasingly aware that he was attracted to boys. He tried to put the notion out of his head. But when the new priest, Callum, had arrived at his church he knew beyond doubt that he was in love.

He did not know what to do, but slowly and sensitively Callum taught him to understand his sexuality, that it was not a sin, and that he had fallen for Sean. The relationship blossomed, but all too soon was cut tragically short.

Callum had been in the wrong place at the wrong time and had become an innocent victim of an IRA bomb outside of a Courthouse in Barnham.

Sean was devastated. Inconsolable. But worse than this he could tell no one of his grief or of their secret love affair.

Sean did not blame the IRA. He was committed to their aims and was keen to prove himself as a firm supporter. Being recruited into Seamus's unit made him proud. That was until he discovered the truth.

The truth, that the particular bomb that killed Callum a few years earlier, was organised and planted by one Seamus Devlin, the now Brigade commander of the Newry unit.

Now all Sean wanted was revenge - an opportunity to do Seamus some serious harm. He would bide his time, he would be patient – the time would come. Maybe this next arms shipment would give him the opportunity? He needed to make it look like an accident if he was to avoid losing his own life, but he would be careful. 'Look out Seamus, I'm behind you!' he pantomimed in his head. The thought of revenge coursed through his blood like a cocaine hit.

Seamus shared his concerns with Liam.

'If it turns out he is trouble then I blame myself,' Liam said. He recounted to Seamus how Sean had been recruited. 'I was the one who found him, he seemed genuine and had the perfect skills, so he did.'

'It wasn't your fault,' said Seamus. 'He was thoroughly checked out by us and the Intelligence officers, so you can't be responsible. And we've no proof of anything right now, so we just need to keep an eye on him, so we do. One thing I do know,' said Seamus earnestly, 'this next shipment cannot be compromised. I'll be taking charge, so I will. And Sean will be right there with me the entire time. I will not let him out of my sight.'

Twenty-six

'Good evening Elias,' said Zoe calmly, as Will swung around to see Elias standing there holding the bug aloft.

'Good evening to you, and to you Bill,' he said, 'if that is your real name.'

Will felt like he had been caught with his hand in the till. He didn't know what to say, but Elias continued to talk.

'I never dreamed you weren't who you said you were Bill, you played a good part. But after a visit from this young lady I got to thinking about how the authorities had caught me. First of all I thought that you had been caught as well, that you had also done a deal to protect yourself, by implicating me. But then it crossed my mind that you might be working together – seems I was right.'

By now Zoe was on her feet and Will sensed her behind him getting ready for action.

Elias noticed and said, 'Don't worry, I have made my decision to do the right thing. I'll work with you both and do whatever I can to get Mikhail and his gang put behind bars. I made a big mistake getting involved with him in the first place.'

Elias looked and sounded genuine. Will prided himself on spotting a liar, after his years of experience as a Customs Officer. He was sure that Elias was telling the truth and glancing back at Zoe he could see that she was thinking the same.

Zoe relaxed and came and stood by Will. 'How did you know about the bug?' Zoe asked.

'Actually that was an accident,' he said, 'I'd guessed that Bill must have told you everything, and it never crossed my mind that you would bug my office. Yesterday I dropped a box of staples on the floor that went everywhere, and in the process of looking for them I noticed the bug under the desk.'

He handed her the bug, and they all went into Elias's office and sat at the small conference table.

'So what happens now,' Elias enquired, 'has the plan changed?'

Zoe answered. 'No change Elias, we still need you to do as we agreed, as we hope it will flush Mikhail into the open. But we do need to know as soon as possible what his plans are. We know he will talk to you, so our plan is to bug your telephone. If he says anything incriminating on the telephone we'll have all the evidence we need to arrest him at the first opportunity.'

'And what happens if Mikhail decides to come here, have you thought of that?' Elias said, a worried expression on his face.

'That's possible,' admitted Zoe, 'which is precisely why we need to know his plans. If he does plan to come here we'll be ready for him and make an arrest. But you must stay calm and play along.'

Will had sat quietly during this exchange, but felt it was time for him to speak. Elias had trusted him once and might be more encouraged if he added to what Zoe had said.

'I'm sorry I mislead you Elias, but I'm sure you understand. Now that you have agreed to help us we'll make sure that you are safe. We just need you to take these final steps and you'll be in the clear.'

Elias nodded 'Thank you, Bill. I'll do what is necessary.' He got to his feet. 'I'll leave you to your task now.' He walked towards the door, and just before leaving the office he turned, and with a smile he said, 'Don't forget to lock up.'

Zoe and Will sat and said nothing as they heard Elias's footsteps recede across the main office and the lobby door open and close. Will got up and looked out of the window. He tracked Elias as he walked across to the gate, opened it, then replaced the opened lock into position.

'Well that was a surprise,' he said to Zoe, 'but at least we know now that Elias is firmly in our camp.'

'Yes,' agreed Zoe, 'let's hope he keeps it together until we can get to Mikhail.'

Zoe then became all business and got busy placing the two bugs whilst he looked on with interest. First she unscrewed the mouthpiece to the telephone handset and placed a small flat electronic device next to the microphone and screwed the handset back together. The bug was completely hidden, and she advised him that unless anyone had a detector, it would be untraceable. Next she pocketed her own bug and brought out the official one from her rucksack. As she had done before, she positioned it in a hidden spot below the desk. When she had finished Will checked for himself. He was assured that unless someone went right underneath the desk it would not be discovered.

With the tasks complete they left the office and locked and alarmed as they went. They hesitated at the bottom of the stairs in the yard, remembering the close call from last week, but all was quiet. They quickly made their way to the yard entrance, locking the gate behind them.

During the walk back to the hotel they reviewed events. Despite the surprise with Elias they were satisfied that things had gone to plan. With nothing more to discuss Zoe went off to collect her car, agreeing to return at 11am.

Will was now dog-tired. The adrenalin from the last hour had waned and he climbed into bed and was asleep almost immediately.

Twenty-seven

Peter had waved goodbye to his Russian minders as be boarded the ferry in Calais on Tuesday evening, but as expected they didn't wave back. He had no idea why they had stopped following him back in Colmar, but they had turned up at the Saarbrüken rest stop about three hours after he had met with Karl. All day they had been following him again, so he was glad to be shot of them.

He arrived in Dover later than planned as the ferry had reported some engine problems. It was nearly 9pm when he headed for the freight park where he would have to wait to be cleared. This normally took a couple of hours, but he knew it would probably take longer at night as the Customs Officers had fewer staff.

He decided to get his head down, but just before 1am he was roused. He assumed it was his clearance papers, but this time he was directed into the freight shed by a Customs Officer. His load had been selected for examination.

The freight shed resembled a small aircraft hangar, with high ceilings and large high roller doors at each end. If placed nose-to-tail there was enough room inside for about six big lorries. The mass of fluorescent lights suspended from the high roof, gave an impression of a floodlit arena. Along one side of the shed was a series of offices that looked a bit like a railway carriage. They were fairly small and provided some working space for Customs Officers and Port staff, when needed for the examination and unloading process. Parked on the other side were two forklifts and a few empty pallets. Peter maneuvered his wagon into the shed and steered to his directed spot, his diesel engine and air brakes loud in this covered space.

His was the only lorry being examined. Should he be worried? He thought about striking up a conversation with the Officers, a bit of banter perhaps. But he had learnt from previous encounters that Customs Officers seemed to lack a sense of humour. Or maybe they considered this a sign of nerves. He was feeling nervous now, so decided it was best to keep quiet. There was nothing he could do, he just had to let them get on with it. He had to rely on the clever concealments that he had helped to fill up with the weapons. If they were found he already had his story rehearsed and there was no way they would be able to show that he knew anything about them. 'I wasn't there when the goods were loaded', he would say, and there was no way they could prove he was.

But he was starting to panic a bit when they pulled down the first crate that had guns concealed in the base. He watched as they emptied the furniture items from the crate and found nothing of interest. They were about to start to re-pack it when one of the Officers who had been watching from the side-lines shouted 'Stop!'

He came across and took a closer look at the crate. Then he walked a few paces to the corner of the shed and grabbed a broom handle that was propped there. He slid it down the inside of the crate, using it as a measuring stick. He then measured the outside. Peter knew immediately that the Officer had noticed that there was several inches difference. Any minute now the game would be up. He felt sweat on his neck and had to force himself to appear calm, but inside his heart was hammering.

It took a few minutes, but eventually the Officer worked out how to lift the false bottom of the crate. The space beneath was empty – nothing.

Peter was gobsmacked, but quickly recovered his composure. A few moments earlier he was expecting them to find the arms and arrest him, but now he was wondering what had happened to them.

The Officers removed more crates and continued their examination, opening up more concealments with the same result. They were clearly very disappointed; they had found some excellent concealments and they had all turned out to be empty.

About thirty minutes later Peter was sitting in an interview room answering their questions. It was a very informal interview the Officers told him. He had not been arrested or cautioned as they had not found anything to arrest him for. They were 'just gathering intelligence,' they said. He denied knowing anything about the crates and their false bottoms, maintaining his story that he did not pack the lorry, merely collected it from EM Transport in Lucerne.

The questioning went on and off all night. After lots of waiting about, Officers leaving the room and then coming back again to ask similar questions, the Officers finally finished their 'chat' with him. They told him that without any illegal goods found, they had no choice but to clear the load. However, the adapted crates would be seized. This meant that the furniture items had to be re-packed loose. With the help of the port agents, they would get it loaded up securely and he would be sent on his way. It was now 7am so he was told to find himself some breakfast whilst the vehicle was re-packed. Peter worked out that it was 8am in Lucerne and he hoped that Elias would be at the office by now, as he was usually an early starter. He had a lot to discuss with him.

He entered the lorry park canteen, which was already quite full with the breakfast rush, and headed for the telephone booth in the corner, nodding to a few familiar faces, but making it clear that he wasn't going to stop and chat.

Peter made the call. But couldn't seem to get Elias to understand.

'I'm telling you Elias,' he said again in a harsh whisper, looking around to make sure no one was listening, 'the arms and ammunition were not there – they have vanished.'

Peter needed help, but Elias did not seem to believe what he was saying.

'They can't have just disappeared,' Elias said mockingly, 'You were there when they were loaded.'

Elias was enjoying hearing Peter in panic and was trying to keep the smile out of his voice as he made out that Peter must have imagined it.

'Yes I was there and even helped load them,' Peter said exasperated, 'So how did they vanish? They must have been stolen. But how, where, by who?' He was baffled but was beginning to wonder if the stopover in Saarbrüken was where they could have been stolen. Did Karl the German have anything to do with it, he wondered?

'What do I do now?' he asked Elias unhappily.

'Peter, stay right where you are – do not move and call me back in one hour, I have to make some calls.' Elias said with authority.

Elias ended the call and smiled to himself, imagining what was about to befall Peter.

Peter decided he couldn't face breakfast, so he went back to his lorry to see how they were getting on with the re-packing. As he entered the freight shed he was met head on by the three Customs Officers who had been questioning him all night, only this time they did not look quite as friendly.

'You are under arrest for conspiracy to smuggle arms and ammunition,' one of them said.

At the same time, the two other Officers moved behind him and he felt his arms being pulled behind him sharply and felt the cold of metal touching his wrists and a tight grip as handcuffs were suddenly locked in place. It wasn't the first time he had been cuffed, but it still took him by surprise, as the Officers were very quick and efficient.

The Officer who arrested him continued, 'I must caution you that you do not have to say anything unless you wish to do so, but anything you say may be written down and given in evidence. Do you understand?'

Peter nodded. He had no idea what had just happened, but he knew better that to say anything at all at this stage.

Rather than take him anywhere immediately, the two Officers who had handcuffed him started searching his lorry cab.

Five minutes later they showed him the three padded envelopes they had opened. Inside he noticed many sheets of what looked like dozens of small cardboard squares depicting cartoon characters and smiley faces. To the uninitiated they looked harmless, but they were in fact sheets of LSD dots. Each cartoon square or smiley face contained a small amount of liquid LSD, or 'microdot' soaked into it. Peter knew straightaway what they were, he had seen things like this in prison, but he said nothing,

'I am further arresting you on suspicion of smuggling prohibited goods, namely drugs,' recited the Customs Officer.

Things had just gone from bad to worse for Peter.

Twenty-eight

Mikhail sipped his Columbian coffee as he looked over the lake. The morning sun glinted on the water. He felt good. Things were now going well with the Irish business and the transaction should soon be completed. There had been that slight hiccup with the car breaking down, but they had advised him that they had quickly caught up with the lorry at Saarbrüken services. The load had appeared safe and secure, he was assured. His team had seen the lorry onto the ferry at Calais yesterday so now they were on their way back. It should be well on its way to Ireland by now, so he would soon, finally, be paid handsomely for its cargo. Yes, life was good.

That was until the phone call he had just received from Elias; suddenly life was not good. It was very, very bad.

Mikhail was furious – beyond furious.

He slammed the phone down. He simply could not believe what he had just heard from Elias. This was too much to bear – how could he lose another load?

As far as he could be, he was satisfied that the first load had been simple bad luck, but now he was wondering. Losing two loads was too much of a coincidence. Was he being ripped off by a rival gang? He pondered this thought for a moment before deciding that this was the most likely scenario.

The driver had apparently reported to Elias, that Customs at Dover had searched the load, finding the false bottomed crates empty. Elias advised that Bill had also contacted him. Bill had found out that the load had been searched and did some enquiries of his own. Because Bill had built a good relationship with the Customs Officers, they had told him about the empty concealments. They had also let slip that they had only searched the load because German Customs had tipped them off. Apparently the German Police had arrested members of a criminal gang selling arms on the black market. Under interrogation they had admitted that they had stolen the arms in Saarbrüken services from crates in an English registered lorry.

Elias had also mentioned that he had suspected that the driver, Peter, was doing a deal on the side, with a German organisation, but didn't have any proof. Apparently Peter had been bragging that he was making some sort of a deal with a German that paid well. Elias was very familiar with Peter's 'stories' so he had not thought anything of it at the time, but now...

Mikhail pondered what Elias had said. Why had the driver called Elias if he was involved? Was it a way of throwing suspicion on others and trying to cover his tracks? Would the driver be that stupid as to cross him? If he had then he was a dead man walking.

The thought of a rival gang stealing his goods and wrecking his reputation made his blood boil. This time someone would truly pay, starting with the lorry driver.

He needed more information quickly, before he had to have a very difficult conversation with the Irish customer. The load was due to be delivered on Thursday, so he had little time to find out what he needed to know before working out how to handle it. But the only way he was going to get more information that he could trust was to get it himself. He needed to meet with Elias face to face as soon as possible and get him to explain what had happened. He needed to see the whites of his eyes. He would know if Elias was lying to him, he would soon make him tell the truth if he was.

'Sergei,' he bellowed. Sergei hurried into the room as he recognised his boss was angry about something – nothing new there. But when he saw the look on Mikhail's face he knew this was something else.

Mikhail quickly described the call he had just had from Elias. Sergei was equally astounded – what was going on. When Mikhail told him that the driver, Peter, might be involved he was a little surprised.

'I've met Peter, didn't like him or trust him,' he said, 'but he is no more than a common criminal.' He didn't think Peter would have had the balls to go into business with a rival gang. But Peter *was* greedy and spent lots of money. 'If the cash incentive was high enough maybe Peter could be tempted,' he agreed.

'We're going to Lucerne today,' Mikhail stormed. 'I want to know from Elias exactly what he knows and if he is lying to me he'll wish he'd never been born.'

His telephone rang again, this time it was Zoltan, the head of the Hungarian team from the depot who were stationed in the hotel just outside the gates to Dover docks. They had been waiting to follow the lorry. What Mikhail was told reinforced the view that the driver was up to no good.

'What's happening Mikhail,' said Zoltan, clearly annoyed, 'We've been waiting for a call from the lorry driver to confirm he's been cleared and is leaving the docks, but we've heard nothing. The last message we got was at 7pm last night and he was just getting onto the ferry in Calais. He expected to be cleared at Dover during the night. It's now 8am here, we've been up all night and we've heard nothing. Should we carry on waiting?'

Mikhail could hardly believe it. Peter must have bolted.

'Zoltan, things are going wrong. I think the driver may be trying to give you the slip and has already left,' he said. 'He can't have got far, he must have left within the last hour. Catch him up, stop him, and don't let him go. Do you understand?' he commanded.

Zoltan knew when Mikhail was in a mood, although this one sounded worse that the last time that Zoltan had been at the end of Mikhail wrath, so he wasn't about to argue. Clearly the driver was in real trouble with Mikhail, which did not bother him in the slightest – he couldn't stand the English pig.

'Of course, we'll go straightaway and call you when we have him,' he said.

Mikhail thought for a moment. 'I may have to leave here quite soon, so call Elias in Lucerne if you can't reach me and I'll collect your message from him. But I say again – do not let him go, or it will be your head.' Mikhail ended the call.

***

The man wearing a suit and sporting a moustache, sat in the corner of the hotel dining room sipping his tea whilst he read his newspaper. He had seen the foreign gentleman talking on the phone in the hotel hallway and from where he sat he had heard half of the conversation. When the call ended the foreign gentleman was surrounded by three other men. An urgent conversation ensued in some Eastern European language.

Then he watched through the window with interest as the four men hurried out of the hotel, jumped into a car and raced up the dual carriageway outside of the dock gates. He stood up and continued to watch as the car sped on around the road that looped over the docks, before it disappeared up the hill. He walked over to the telephone in the hall, the same telephone that one of the men had used only minutes earlier. He dialed a number from memory.

'They've just left,' is all he said.

Twenty-nine

Will was surprised when the phone rang waking him from a deep sleep - it was Zoe.

'What do you want this early?' he enquired as he tried to come to.

'It is 10.30am Will, I'm only a little early,' she pointed out.

My goodness, he'd slept like a log. He apologised 'I'll be down in thirty minutes.' He grabbed a quick shower, dressed and shaved, then met her in the lobby. She had had the foresight to order them coffee.

'Elias called me one hour ago,' she announced, whilst pouring Will a coffee, passing him a small jug of milk as she did so. 'He confirmed he's told Mikhail the bad news, but he sounded a little worried. He thinks Mikhail might be coming to Lucerne.'

He poured some milk into his coffee, added some sugar then took a sip. 'That's what you hoped Mikhail would do wasn't it. How does Elias feel about that?' he enquired.

'He doesn't want to see him. They've never met, but Elias has spoken to him several times on the telephone and Mikhail has always sounded bad-tempered apparently. But he said he's never felt the anger that Mikhail exuded on this occasion.' Zoe sipped her own coffee and winced – too hot. 'He feels if he has to meet him it will be explosive.'

Will thought for a moment. 'Perhaps he doesn't have to, could your police colleagues arrest him before they meet?'

'That's what I expected,' said Zoe, 'but I've just found out this is not going to be possible.' She blew on her coffee this time before taking a sip and continued. 'It seems that our legal brains in the Federal Department of Justice and Police have been pondering the evidence we have, including the recording of the call Elias had with Mikhail a couple of hours ago. They feel that despite a lot of good material, there is simply not quite enough evidence to arrest under Swiss law. A good attorney would release Mikhail, before they could even interview him.'

Will knew from his own experience that you had to have enough evidence to make a charge stick. In his world they usually had a carload of drugs, which was a massive suspicion, but of course proving the driver knew about them was the harder bit.

'Ok, I get that, but how will a meeting with Elias make a difference?' Then it struck him. 'Of course!' he nearly shouted, and had to lower his voice when he spotted another guest looking up questioningly. 'They need Mikhail to say something damning that will be picked up by the bug under Elias's desk,' he said in a stage whisper.

Zoe nodded. 'Exactly, she said. 'So it is vital that Elias not only meets with Mikhail, but that he gets Mikhail to say the right words and implicate himself. We have to meet with Elias as soon as possible to explain this and to reassure him.'

Zoe stood up. 'Finish your coffee, I need to make a call and update COGs.' She headed off towards the phone booths beyond reception.

Will sat back, but then decided that he was feeling very peckish. He walked towards reception to enquire if he could get something to eat. He could see Zoe already in conversation at a telephone booth over by the lifts, as he tried at getting some food.

'Breakfast is finished now sir,' explained the young, sweetly smiling receptionist, 'but I could probably get you a slice of apple strudel if that would be acceptable?'

'That would be great, thank you. I'm sitting over there,' he indicated the cups on the lounge table.

Zoe was deep in her telephone conversation, so Will wandered back to his coffee. He diverted to a stand containing newspapers on his way. Most were unreadable to him as they were Swiss or German publications, but there was a copy of the Washington Post – better than nothing. As he sat down, the receptionist with Swiss efficiency arrived, smiled again sweetly and placed his Apple strudel on the coffee table.

He had finished his strudel and was had just finished reading an article on Ted Bundy, a serial killer who had been executed in America by electric chair, when Zoe returned.

'Did you know that Ted Bundy described himself as "the most cold-hearted son of a bitch you will ever meet",' he told Zoe.

She gave him the look that he sometimes got from Alison, as if to say, 'what planet are you on?' Then she dropped into a chair next to him and got down to business.

'COGs have confirmed they had heard the call this morning between Elias and Mikhail, and they are convinced that he is going to come here to Lucerne. I have told them that Elias is getting worried, and they suggested that we go and see him to calm him down, but I must call in again at 2pm as they are currently checking flight bookings to see if they can trace any sign that he is coming here and when.'

They arrived at Elias's yard at 1pm. Elias greeted them at reception and took them to his office. Will was very conscious of the bug under the desk, but it was unlikely they were being monitored yet. Even if they were there was nothing they were going to say that would have an impact.

Elias served up coffee without asking as they sat at his conference table. Elias looked tired, Will thought, but also older and greyer, the weight of what was happening clearly taking a toll.

Zoe added to his sombre look by confirming that they also thought Mikhail was going to visit, but made it clear that the police would be ready to arrest Mikhail at the earliest opportunity.

'We want Mikhail badly and we really appreciate you helping to achieve this, she said, 'but you must hold your nerve, we can't do this without you.'

Elias did not quite understand looking questionably at Zoe, waiting for her to explain.

'For us to make the arrest we need Mikhail to implicate himself, by confirming he is behind the arms shipment. We we'll listen in to your conversation with him.' She advised him that they had bugged his office again. 'As soon as we get the evidence, we'll strike,' she reassured.

Elias looked far from reassured. 'You told me you would arrest him when he came to Switzerland – now I have to meet him and trick him into admitting that he is organising the arms shipments. That's not what you said would happen.' He was panicking now. 'What if he guesses I'm trying to trick him, or he doesn't say the right words, what then. He's going to quiz me to find out what happened to his load, and he might think I am responsible.'

He looked like he was starting to hyper-ventilate – the last thing they wanted was him having a heart attack.

'Elias, Elias, listen to me,' Will said. 'Look at me.' Will dragged his chair around, so he was facing Elias and made Elias look him in the eye. 'We'll be close by and the police will react quickly, you have nothing to fear. Just have the conversation with Mikhail, don't try anything fancy, and as soon as the Police get to hear what they need they'll storm in and arrest him.'

He calmed a little then nodded. He was shaking, but more controlled now. A minute later he was still, looking down at the floor. 'I'm sorry,' he said 'This last few days have been a worry, I have not slept much, and just when I thought it might be almost over, I'm facing a bigger challenge. Don't worry, I can do this.' He straightened up, tried to smile, but failed. But he did seem to have some resilience back in his voice and posture. 'I can do this,' he said again, maybe to himself.

They chatted a bit more, with both Will and Zoe making encouraging noises. Elias seemed to brighten-up a bit.

'I need to make a telephone call,' Zoe said. 'Where can I do this in private?' Elias took her to a room two doors down. Zoe disappeared inside and closed the door. Elias came back, offered Will more coffee, which he readily accepted – anything to take Elias's mind off of the recent conversation.

While they waited Elias asked Will some questions. 'I guess you work for the British Security Services, but tell me, how do you know so much about Freight Forwarding, you seem so knowledgeable, I wouldn't have guessed.'

Will felt sorry for him and they had built up a kind of friendship, but he was not about to tell him anything about himself.

'I was well briefed Elias, that's all I can tell you.' He needed to change the subject. 'How did you get involved in the Transport business?'

Elias spent the next fifteen minutes telling Will his life story; from days as a clerk in a shipping office, to becoming a junior manager, then falling out with his boss and deciding to set up a rival and successful business. That had been great for a few years, he said as he reminisced. He met the love of his life and married. He and his wife moved to a house in the hills overlooking the lake so they could share his passion for the outdoor life. They would walk for hours in the hills. But his wife had passed away. Life and business got tougher, so he looked for ways to make extra money through less legitimate means. That led to working for the Russians.

Just then Zoe re-appeared. Will could tell by her face that they had some further challenges coming.

Zoe helped herself to the fresh coffee, took a deep breath and updated them.

'I've just spoken with,' she hesitated, 'my boss, who has advised me that they are almost certain that Mikhail is booked on a flight to Zurich this evening.' She let this sink in and looked for any reaction from Elias, who simply nodded resignedly.

Zoe continued. 'My organisation has confirmed that Sergei Koskov is booked on the 21.30 hours arrival into Zurich and is sat next to a man named…' she checked her notes, 'Laszlo Boros. He is travelling on a Hungarian passport. We believe that this is Mikhail using a false identity.' She looked at Elias. 'Elias, does Laszlo Boros sound familiar to you.'

Elias shook his head. 'No, I have never heard that name,' he said.

'My boss has asked us to go to the airport to see if we can secretly take a photograph of Sergei and the man we think is Mikhail, as this will help the arrest team tomorrow.' She did not pause long enough for Elias to complain. 'You don't need to come along Elias,' she said. 'We need to identify Sergei, and Bill can do that (she remembered to call him Bill) and we believe whoever he is travelling with should be Mikhail, if our guess is correct.'

Will thought for a moment, he could see some risks emerging and wanted to check something.

'Elias does Sergei know where you live?' he enquired.

'I don't think so,' Elias said, 'I might have told him I live up in the hills by the lake, but I'm sure he does not know where. Why are you asking?'

Will didn't want to say. What he was thinking might add to the angst Elias clearly felt, but if he was right then they needed to mitigate this risk.

'If I was Mikhail, as soon as I got here I would want to talk to you, I wouldn't want to wait until morning. I would go in search of you Elias,' he said sombrely to them both.

'My god, you are right!' Zoe exclaimed. 'We've been basing our plan on Mikhail waiting until morning and then arriving at the lorry yard, but Mikhail won't want to wait!'

'Elias, I think it would be a good idea if you don't stay at your home tonight, is there somewhere else you can go?' Will said.

For the second time, Elias was showing signs of panic, but this time he just gripped tightly to the arms of the chair for a few seconds before his composure returned, and with it a steely resolution that seemed to have sharpened his thinking.

'I could go to a cousin's house,' he said thoughtfully, 'but if Mikhail is looking for me, then I would place my cousin in danger too. No, I will find somewhere else, maybe a hotel, unless you have any better suggestions?'

'I agree with you Elias,' Zoe said. 'You would be placing your cousin in danger. But Mikhail has many resources, and he might also find you if you went to a hotel. Leave it with me, I will find you somewhere safe to go, that Mikhail will never find.'

Just then Elias's phone rang. He answered, said his name then listened for a minute, before saying, 'Ok I will tell Mikhail if I see him, but he hasn't told me he is coming here, are you sure he said that?' Zoe and Will's ears pricked up and they listened intently to Elias's responses. 'OK, I will pass on the message.'

'Who was that?' asked Will as the phone went down.

'They were some of Mikhail's men,' Elias informed. 'It seems that they were meant to meet Peter and the lorry in Dover and follow it to Liverpool, but there has been some sort of trouble. Mikhail had told them that Peter needed to be found and stopped. Unfortunately, they could not find Peter or the lorry despite many hours of searching. Mikhail told them to call me with any news and he would collect the message from me as he might not be available to take their call.'

Elias was smiling, as although he did not understand the full plan, it was clear that another layer of subterfuge had been instigated. Peter was now seen as Mikhail's prime suspect.

Thirty

Clive was tired. It was approaching midday on Wednesday. He had been monitoring 'Operation Harmless' on and off throughout the last forty-eight hours, snatching a few hours' sleep here and there.

The operation was going well and was approaching a climax, so he had to stay on top of it. The main hurdles had been jumped, so he thought he might be able to get some sleep this afternoon without interruption. He reflected on the operation name, Operation Harmless. He would have preferred something a little more dynamic sounding, but rules had changed, and he wasn't able to choose operation names anymore.

Issues had arisen recently in another case, when the Police had unwittingly chosen an identical operation name to one being used by MI6. It had caused some confusion when the police got involved in assisting the MI6 operation. Although the confusion was minor and hadn't caused operational difficulties on that occasion, concerns were raised, so a review was ordered.

It had resulted in the setting up of an independent unit who now monitored all law enforcement bodies, Police, Customs, Security Services and Military. They needed to ensure there were no crossovers, or 'blue on blue', in the future.

One role of the new unit was to issue unique operation names. Organisations got to choose the initial letter of the operation name, if they wished, but that was all. This helped organisations to narrow down the operation owner when needed. In the COGs organisation all operations that were led by Clive could be given an 'H' for 'Harrington'. Although Clive was disappointed in this operation name, he did smile to himself – if the 'H' was missing it would spell armless. As this was one of the aims of this particular operation, he would count this as a success.

So far just about everything had gone to plan. They had had to be flexible on occasion, but otherwise they had reached a good stage without any real incidents.

The original remit for the operation had been to arrest and prosecute Seamus Devlin to put a hole in the IRA organisation, as well as denying them the arms they desperately needed. By stopping the first shipment it planted doubts in the IRA's mind. COGs were well on the way to achieving their aims. They had stopped one shipment and now had the opportunity of getting Seamus out into the open so he could be arrested. They now also had the chance of disrupting the organised crime gang supplying the arms, by arresting the Russian crime boss. Clive had initially refused to entertain this when that bitch Zoe had suggested it. But when he later looked at the idea a bit more objectively, he could see some merits. The personal accolades he would receive from pulling off such an audacious coup were well worth the additional effort.

Zoe was clever as well as pretty, he thought. Clive had always considered himself to be successful where women were concerned. His power, charm and influence had encouraged many women into his bed. But he had mis-judged that bitch. He hadn't expected to be literally thrown out of her room. Maybe a future opportunity would present itself as he hated to be beaten, but he would be more careful next time, he thought.

Clive summarised in his head the progress of the Operation so far and re-assessed all the angles – he had a skill for visualising possible outcomes; second guessing how they might play-out.

The driver was now out of the game, courtesy of Elias removing the arms from the concealments then stashing them in his yard. *Clive made a mental note to remind the Swiss to secure them.* The drugs that had been planted on Peter were the icing on the cake. This would ensure that he was out of action for a long while. 'Karl' had played his part well - he was a German Customs Officer, real name Kurt, also recently recruited by Clive into COGs. Although not quite as natural as Will, he had the potential to develop into a great asset for the future. It was Kurt's idea to place the distinctive scar on his face; a bit theatrical perhaps, but what would a jury believe? Would they believe a story from Peter involving a tall blond German with a large scar on his face, giving him the drugs? He thought not, as it made Karl sound like a pirate.

Placing Peter in Mikhail's mind as a double-dealer had been slightly more complicated, but a series of clever moves by his team had built the level of mistrust they had hoped. Elias being turned was a key part of this deception, as Mikhail needed to hear Elias's suspicions about Peter for this to work.

When COGS discovered that some Russians would be minding the lorry, it was a set-back, but as usual the team had worked their magic.

When the lorry stopped at Colmar services, the three-man COGs team who had been following the Russians car, went to work. When the Russians parked up the COGs team vehicle stayed a couple of rows back out of sight. One of the COGs operatives hopped out, casually strolled towards Russians car ready to create a diversion. They had anticipated that not all the Russians would leave the car at the same time as they would likely want to have someone watch the lorry, so they had planned a minor distraction. But as it turned out the Russians were either lazy, or had weak bladders, as they all left the car together to go to the toilets. The distraction was therefore unnecessary so the plan to disable the car was simpler than expected.

The COGs operatives moved their car up behind the Black Volvo. Whilst one of them kept watch, the other one packed the exhaust pipe with wet leaves and twigs. This should stop the car from starting, or at least make it lose power. However, when the lorry set off the COGS team were surprised and disappointed when it appeared that the Russians car had started, and it followed the lorry from the services. They thought they had failed.

They would have to follow so they could seek another opportunity. But only a mile out of the services, the Volvo began to slow down and after another mile came to a halt at the edge of the road. The COGs team sailed past the broken-down Volvo and as soon as they were out of sight they pulled over. One of them returned along the road on foot to a place where he could see the car from a concealment in a hedgerow. He reported to his colleagues by radio that one of the Russians was walking back along the road towards the services, presumably to seek some roadside assistance.

This was a better result than expected. Whilst at Colmar services one of COGs team had arranged for a Roadside assistance van to be at the disposal in the event that the Russians car wouldn't start. The fact that it had made it one mile down the road created a greater delay which would give Peter plenty of time to meet with Karl.

It was two hours before the COGs operative, posing as a mechanic, reached the Russians Volvo in the Roadside assistance van. After twenty minutes of playing under the bonnet and looking under the car pretending to try to fix it, he covertly managed to remove the offending leaves from the exhaust and Russians were gratefully underway again.

Customs at Dover had been brought up to speed which had led to Peter's arrest. Following his arrest the lorry was now well on its way to Liverpool driven by Steve, one of Clive's best operatives. Steve was on a dangerous mission. He knew how to take care of himself, but measures were in place to protect him, mainly the SAS who would be deployed when the time came.

Mikhail's Hungarian team thought they were chasing Peter and his lorry, but they wouldn't find either Peter or the lorry.

Knowing that the Hungarians would be on the lookout, the COGS team had worked with Customs and changed the number plates and disguised the lorry by strapping on a new dark blue cover which looked nothing like the existing mustard coloured one. A different haulier name printed on the side added to the deception. They were good to go.

As soon as COGS had been told that the Hungarians had left the hotel, racing up the A2, Steve drove the disguised lorry out of the docks exit. He headed up the hill out of Dover. When Steve got close to Liverpool he planned to change the number plates back and remove the false cover, bringing the lorry back to the original visage. The crates were also back in the lorry, despite what Peter had been told. The lids to the crates had been adapted by the tech team. They were fitted with concealed magnetic electrical contacts, so as soon as they were opened they would send a radio alert signal to the tracking 'brick' attached under the lorry chassis. This would be the signal for the SAS to move in to make arrests.

Mikhail looked like he had taken the bait and was going to travel to Lucerne. There were plans to get him photographed when he arrived, to assist the Swiss Police who would conduct the arrest.

Clive thought it unlikely that Mikhail would make the call to Seamus to say that he had failed to deliver again, but just in case, a further plan had been put in place to intercept the call.

Clive had to hand it to the telecoms team and Gadget bods, they had worked overtime to solve this one.

If Mikhail called Seamus, the call would be intercepted, and COGS would cut the call, permanently. But, as part of the plan COGS would still dial Seamus's number from their office, then someone who *sounded* just like Mikhail would apologise for the unreliable telephone network. They would simply tell Seamus that the lorry had cleared Dover Customs and would arrive on Thursday as planned. The team had developed a gadget that could synthesise Mikhail's voice. It wasn't perfect, but pretty good. They had based it on a number of recent recordings that they had made of Mikhail's voice. The COGS person doing the speaking had trained himself to use the same style, tone and phrases that Mikhail used, to sound just like him. The suggestion of a lack of reliability on the telephone network would cover any slight voice differences that might be picked up by Seamus.

Clive spent another fifteen minutes going through all the angles in his head, and decided they were ready for the big showdown at both ends of the chain, so he took himself to bed for a well-earned sleep. It was going to be a long day tomorrow, he thought.

Thirty-one

Will and Zoe arrived at Zurich airport at 20:15 hours. The flight was due in just over an hour, so they needed to prepare and get themselves into a good vantage point to take their covert photos. The latest intelligence update from COGs confirmed, through the airline database, that Sergei and a man called Laszlo Boros had checked in together at Budapest airport.

During the afternoon Will and Zoe had been shopping. Will was very conscious of the fact that Sergei would be likely to recognise him, so either he would have to keep his head down, or be disguised. They decided that both were prudent. Zoe could take the photos and Will would alert Zoe when he spotted Sergei.

They started their shopping in a hair salon that sold wigs. Will had light brown hair which wasn't particularly distinctive, but he was amazed at how much his looks changed when he tried on wigs of different styles and colours. He obviously did not want to stand out, so although he rather liked the ginger wig, he avoided it. He chose instead a less noticeable dark brown one. It was longer and more wavy than his own hair, making him look older and more distinguished, he thought. Next on the list was a pair of spectacles. Will had perfect vision, but getting a pair of glasses with plain glass would be hard to find without opticians being suspicious, so they had to think again. In the end they found a general store that sold cheap plastic, lightly tinted sunglasses. The arrivals hall was bright and airy. They planned to be in the background, or in the shadows if possible, so no one would notice. Will had considered a beard would help, but dismissed this as overkill. Besides, where would they find a false beard that did not look stupid. The final purchase was a brown bomber jacket, as Sergei had previously seen Will in his blue anorak.

The mezzanine deck overlooked the arrivals hall so had a good view of the doors that opened from the Customs exit. This was the best place to park themselves. There were a few passengers and workers who strolled through this area as it was mainly airport offices up there. At this time of night it had little footfall. It was now just a waiting game for the flight to arrive and passengers to clear Customs.

Zoe had an expensive looking Nikon camera with a zoom lens. She was a competent photographer. At home Will had a cheap Zenith, Russian made ironically. He had taken a few good photos in his time, but did not consider himself to be that good, so was more than happy that Zoe was in charge of this task.

They watched a flight from New York arrive at 21:00 hours. Passengers spilled through the door into the arrivals hall, so Zoe used the opportunity to focus the camera lens onto an innocent husband and wife couple as they entered the hall. She pretended to press the shutter. As she had a thirty-six-exposure film in the camera she could probably afford to take the shot, but decided not to waste it.

At 21:35 the flight information boards announced that the Budapest flight had landed. They were ready for action. The first few passengers started to come through the doors, so they were now on high alert. Will made ready to indicate to Zoe when he spotted Sergei. As expected the passengers came through in fits and starts, some gaps, some crowds, but for ten minutes there was still no sign of Sergei. Then Will saw him. He was carrying a small blue suitcase. By his side was a slightly younger man of similar height and build, the man identified as Laszlo Boros, the man who they believed was Mikhail. They were both wearing black leather jackets.

'There!' Will said urgently, 'The two men in leather jackets. Sergei is the one with the blue suitcase.'

Zoe was clicking away before Will had finished talking, tracking them through the hall, taking frame after frame as the two men headed towards the outer door.

Will followed them with his eyes, keeping well out of sight, but then he noticed something that worried him – Sergei was the dominant man. He was clearly ordering the other man around.

'Zoe, I don't think that is Mikhail,' Will said. 'Look at Sergei, the one with the blue suitcase and how he is behaving.'

Zoe stopped taking photos to see what Will was talking about – then she understood. The man Will had identified as Sergei appeared to be in charge. Although she couldn't hear the conversation from where they were situated, the gestures he made towards the man, clearly demonstrated Sergei's dominance over him – it couldn't be Mikhail.

They decided to follow Sergei and the man, and raced down the stairs. They spotted them as they went through the swing doors and outside the terminal towards the airport road.

Through the glass windows and doors they could see them walking along the path outside towards a man standing next to a black Volvo. The third man, stocky and older than the other two, appeared to be angry at Sergei, and the man who was probably Laszlo after all.

Will and Zoe strolled slowly out of the doors to get a bit closer. They tried to mix in with the queues that had formed for the buses and taxis. As they got a little closer, still shielded by several passengers, Will overheard the third man berating Sergei and Laszlo, but as it was in Russian he did not understand a word.

They both came to the same conclusion – this was Mikhail. Somehow he had got out before Sergei. They had photographed the wrong man.

Zoe quickly whispered in Will's ear. Will nodded and took a few steps closer to the group of men, still largely concealed by the queues. He then turned and faced Zoe. She appeared to start taking photographs of Will, a bit like a couple might do if they were holidaymakers, but of course Zoe was taking photos of the three men, as gaps between the crowds of passengers allowed.

Suddenly, the driver of the black Volvo jumped out of the car. He started pointing at Zoe, saying something to the three men who all turned and looked at her. Zoe quickly lowered her camera, smiled at Will and shouted, 'Come on darling, we don't want to miss the bus,' She grabbed his hand. Will cottoned on immediately and they walked quickly back along the path, dodging the crowds of queuing passengers.

Zoe had noticed the Volvo driver starting to come after them just before they had turned to walk away, so she whispered to Will, 'Just follow me,' as she virtually dragged him along the path. They got to the arrivals hall door and quickly ducked inside. Will took the opportunity to glance over his shoulder. The driver had been hampered by groups of passengers queuing for a taxi and had not seen them return to the hall. He was looking further along the path, so Will pulled Zoe behind a pillar, where they stayed out of sight. The driver took one last look around and gave up. He turned and walked back to the car. Will and Zoe could just about see Mikhail as he climbed into the back seat next to Sergei, Laszlo got in the front. The car set off.

Zoe and Will considered themselves fortunate; it could have so easily gone badly wrong. They had nearly missed Mikhail, but were also nearly caught. A lucky escape. Now it was time to head back to Zoe's office to get the photos developed.

When they got there the Federal Department for Justice and Police the officers were actively planning the operation to arrest the Russian arms smuggling gang. They were eagerly awaiting the roll of film from Zoe to aid this plan. A photographic lab had been arranged to work on development and printing the film as soon it was available. Zoe handed over the roll of film for developing and the team got to work. She explained how they had initially mistaken one of the men for Mikhail. She then described what Mikhail looked like to aid them when the photographs were developed: a man about 175 centimeters tall, with ample proportions, severe eastern European facial features, mid-forties with greying hair.

There was nothing left for them to do now so they decided that sleep was in order. Zoe dropped Will at his hotel before heading home for a few hours. They agreed that Zoe would collect Will at 6am and they would head back to her office for the final briefing. They would then collect Elias and drop him off close to his yard.

Zoe had arranged for Elias to stay with a policewoman friend, one of Jan's colleagues. As was usual, the policewomen had not asked any questions of Zoe, but simply made Elias welcome and showed him the spare room. She happened to be working nights, so Elias would not be disturbing her, she said. Zoe wanted Elias in his office early, before Mikhail and his team arrived, so Elias was told to be ready for 07.30am

***

What Will and Zoe had not known, was that Mikhail had flown first class, travelling under a false Hungarian passport in the name of Istvan Nagy. He had got off the flight first and was waiting for Sergei and Laszlo to appear. He was frustrated at how long they had taken to arrive at the car.

Before he had left Hungary he had made a call from Budapest airport to the Lucerne hotel where the Russians were staying. These were the four Russians who had returned from Calais after tailing the lorry. Three of them were dispatched to go and find Elias; the fourth was to collect him along with the others from Zurich airport.

'I didn't find them, but I think they were just passengers, nothing to worry about,' the driver had said to Mikhail after trying to locate the couple who had been taking photos.

'Maybe,' Mikhail said, half to himself. 'Let's go and talk to Elias.'

Mikhail was booked into the Grand Hotel in Lucerne, the Penthouse suite. But right now he was not interested in checking in, he wanted to speak to Elias.

His team reported that they had managed to find Elias's home address. A member of the Freight forwarder office staff had been 'encouraged' to divulge it. They had also visited the address, but Elias was not home. One of them had decided to wait at his address for him to return; a wise move, thought Mikhail.

Where had Elias gone, he wondered? He could be visiting a friend and maybe would be home soon, or he might already be back. So instead of going to the Grand Hotel, he ordered the driver to take him to Elias's house.

The driver advised that he should collect his colleague from their hotel first, as they knew where the address was, and he didn't. Although exasperated, Mikhail could see the logic. When they got to the hotel, Mikhail ordered the man who knew the location of Elias's house, to join him in the car. The other men were to do some background checking into Elias, to see if there might be friends or relatives who lived nearby. Elias might be visiting, or possibly staying with them instead of going home. Mikhail, by his very nature, was suspicious of Elias not being at home, but he reasoned with himself that this might be normal. Maybe he was just feeling frustrated and tired.

It was gone midnight when Mikhail arrived with the others at Elias's house. It was in darkness. The man on watch had reported no movement. Mikhail told him to stay put for another hour and to call in if Elias arrived. If Elias did not appear by then, one of the team would come by and collect him. Mikhail was weary now and despite his motivation to talk to Elias he could see no alternative but to wait until morning. He ordered his driver to take him, Sergei and Laszlo to his hotel.

Thirty-two

Will and Zoe arrived at the police office to be present for the 06:30 briefing. Will was introduced to the Department Head, Frederick Hesse. To keep things simple, Zoe introduced Will him as a 'Liaison officer' from MI6. They were escorted into the large briefing room. Will estimated there must have been around thirty police officers in attendance. Most were either wearing body armour or getting prepared. Most wore sidearms, a few had guns in underarm holsters.

Zoe slipped off her jacket and Will was surprised to see that she also had an underarm holster. He wasn't sure why he should be surprised that she carried a weapon, he guessed it was a whole different set-up from the UK, where only a few police carried guns. He immediately recognised the pistol being used by the police (and Zoe).

'That's the Sig Sauer 220 isn't it,' Will said to Zoe.

Zoe looked up, enquiry written on her face. 'Yes it is Will, but how did you know?'

'Some might say I had a mis-spent youth, but before I discovered girls I was in the Army Cadets for a few years,' he replied. 'I had the chance to learn how to fire a rifle and actually became quite good at it. My Commanding Officer seemed to think I might be Officer material one day so he also gave me the opportunity to go on a course to learn about pistols. I got to fire many rounds with the UK Army pistol of choice, the Browning Hi-power, but also learnt about a range of other popular hardware, including the Sig.'

Zoe was impressed. 'Well first you proved yourself in counter-surveillance and now you are a marksmen. What other talents are you hiding?' she said with a smile. 'You'll tell me next that you have super-powers.'

Will was enjoying the banter. 'I could tell you, but then I would have to kill you,' he quipped. 'Actually, I've always thought it would be great to be invisible…'

Zoe was about to respond when Frederick Hesse called everyone to order and started the briefing with input from the Operational Commander (OC), Sven Fischer.

The plan he outlined was straightforward. The OC would be stationed in the Command vehicle parked outside of the yard. He would be listening to the conversation that was being relayed from the bug under the desk in Elias's office. Elias was to make sure that he used Mikhail's name in the early part of the conversation, to ensure that they had concrete evidence of his presence. Elias would stick to his story that he had no further information to give to Mikhail, but somehow get Mikhail to state that he was responsible for the smuggling operation. As soon as the OC had enough evidence he would call the 'strike' and armed police would move in to make the arrest of Mikhail and his team.

Will and Zoe would be with the OC listening to the radio traffic so they would know what was happening, but would not be allowed to be involved in the arrest phase.

Will noticed that Zoe looked unhappy with this decision and was unusually quiet as they left the office to collect Elias. But when they were in the car and out of earshot of the OC she couldn't contain her anger.

'I should've been allowed to be at the arrest of that murderer,' she spat. 'I did all the work to track him down and now it seems I'm not worthy of seeing it through. I'm weapons trained, it seems like they don't want a woman on the team.'

Will could see her point, but seeing her reaction convinced him that her personal feelings would be a risk to the operation and her outburst had just confirmed this.

'I know how important this is to you Zoe, but from what I seen back there, the arrest teams are experts in their field and will get the result you seek. He'll soon be behind bars.'

Zoe seemed to calm. 'You're right Will, I'm being unreasonable. Let's get Elias and do our bit.'

They pulled up outside of the policewoman's house at 7.30 as planned, to collect Elias. When he did not immediately appear Will walked up to the door and tapped on it lightly. The policewoman would likely be home from her night shift and in bed by now, so he did not want to disturb her. Still Elias did not appear. Zoe joined him at the front door; she had no qualms about rapping loudly on the door, which opened almost immediately by her tired looking friend. Thankfully, she was still dressed.

'I guess you want Elias,' she said. 'When I got home thirty minutes ago the house was in darkness and I haven't heard any noise. Perhaps he's overslept, I'll go and check – come in and wait.'

She disappeared up the stairs and they could hear her knocking on a door and shouting, 'Elias, your friends are here.' They heard a door open and a few seconds later the policewoman came down the stairs and reported that Elias was not in the room. *Where could he have gone?*

Zoe and Will rushed back to her office and alerted the OC. With Elias missing the operation could be completely compromised. However, the OC was very experienced and was not about to give up just yet. He would place his men in position outside the yard and see what developed. Mikhail was certain to appear soon, and they could monitor him and his team. It was still possible that Elias would appear.

Zoe and Will left the office and sat for a few minutes in the car trying to guess where Elias might have gone.

'We could try his house,' Zoe suggested.

'We don't have any other places to start looking,' agreed Will.

'Ok, but before we go to his house, I have another idea that might buy us some time,' Zoe said, but she didn't expand.

Instead of going straight to Elias's house, Zoe drove to the yard. The gates to the yard were wide open. They drove right in.

'What are we doing here? Will enquired.

'You'll see,' she said mysteriously. Will followed her as they headed for the stairs up to the offices.

On pushing the reception bell a young lady appeared who Will recognised from his previous visits. She had provided his coffee.

'Hello, I'm Lina, how can I help you,' she asked with a pleasant smile. 'It's Mr. Mitchell isn't it?' she said to Will.

Will nodded, 'Hello Lina, yes I'm Bill Mitchell and I hope you can help us.'

She invited them inside. She explained that she always started work early, so there were no other staff at the office yet. Zoe was glad of this as it avoided any complications. She showed her credentials as a member of the Federal Department for Justice and Police.

'In the next hour or so you will be visited by some Russian men, one of whom I believe you have seen before, named Sergei?'

'Yes I know Sergei,' Lina said, distaste apparent in her voice and showing on her face.

Zoe continued. 'They are looking for Elias, but Elias has been delayed. We would like you to tell them that Elias phoned you. He told you that he had been visiting a sick relative who lives about fifty kilometres away. He said he stayed overnight last night, so he would not be in the office until late morning. Can to do that for us?'

'Is Elias, ok?' she said with concern.

'Elias is fine,' Zoe lied, we just need to delay the Russian men until he can get here. So are you happy to tell them this? They may press you for more information, but that's all you know, ok?'

'If it is to help Elias, then of course I will help,' Lina said, a look of genuine loyalty to her boss in her eyes.

'That's great, thank you,' Zoe said, 'Can I use a phone please, I just have to make a brief call.'

Lina showed Zoe to a phone, and she dialled a familiar number and asked for the OC. She advised him what she had done and their plan to go looking for Elias, and hung up.

'As we were talking to Lina it crossed my mind that we needed to put the team in the picture,' Zoe explained to Will. 'It also crossed my mind that the surveillance teams might already be on site and I didn't want them to overreact to our presence!'

'Good call,' Will said as they headed out of the yard. He was learning a lot from Zoe, as he would not have thought of all these things. She had hopefully bought them a bit of time to try to find Elias.

They arrived at Elias's house, a fifteen-minute drive from the yard. Zoe knew the way of course. The house was situated halfway up a hill that overlooked Lake Lucerne. It was one of only a few hillside properties here, the nearest neighbours hundreds of metres away.

Will rapped on the front door. No answer. They walked around to the rear of the property, but as expected there was no sign of life. Will studied the house and surroundings - the rear of the house had the lake view with a fifty-metre garden of lawn and shrubs that sloped gently away towards the distant lake. There was a small garden shed and a water-butt near the back door, and one of those grates that people use to scrape mud off their boots. Will put his head against the glass of the back door which seems to be a kitchen, and tried to peer in. The glass was slightly opaque so he could just about see the doormat inside the door but not much else. As he strained to look further into the kitchen, he could make out some shapes that were probably chairs and a table. The doormat was covered in mud from two distinct boot prints. Will remembered that Elias said he enjoyed walking in the hills when his wife was alive. *Perhaps he still did?*

'Zoe, have a look at this.'

Zoe looked through the glass of the door. 'All I can see is a doormat,' she said.

'When I was talking to Elias yesterday,' Will said, 'he was telling me that he loved to walk in the hills. There are footprints and mud on the doormat, but no boots. Do you think he might be out walking?'

'It's a possibility I guess,' she agreed.

They went back around to the front of the house and looked up the hillside. There were one or two houses further up the hill surrounded by fields and hedges. As it was February the hills were mostly white with a light covering of snow, but they could make out a few paths across the landscape that looked recently used. With nothing to lose they headed for the paths and up the hillside. They did not meet anyone and after twenty minutes they reached the top of a hill and looked down the other side and across to mountains in the distance. The view from here was stunning and Will was captivated by it. He nearly forgot why they were there. They scanned in all directions looking for Elias, but there was no one in sight. They turned despondently back towards the house when suddenly Will saw a flash of light to his far left; a reflection from the sun on something shiny.

***

It was 8.30am in London and Clive had just received a call from Steve. The lorry had arrived in Belfast Docks on the overnight ferry from Liverpool. Steve would shortly be on his way to the agreed rendezvous, a layby about fifteen minutes from Newry. It was good to know Steve was OK, but Clive already knew where he was as the SAS had been monitoring the tracker on his vehicle. Covert officers had also been with the lorry on the ferry and were now positioned to follow the lorry to its destination. But it would have been comforting for Steve to know that the tracker was working, and he was being supported.

The gadget boys had made the call to Seamus yesterday to confirm delivery today. They had used the voice synthesiser to mimic Mikhail; it had worked perfectly. Seamus had given no indication that he did not believe it was Mikhail. The other reason for the call was to arrange a code word for the handover. Clive had decided that it would be in keeping for Mikhail to add some additional security at the rendezvous point. Seamus was told, by the Mikhail mimic, that the lorry would only be delivered to its destination if the code phrase, 'Boris sent me', was used. Within two hours from now, Clive calculated, they should have Seamus and his boys safely wrapped up.

The Swiss end of the operation was not going quite so well.

According to the latest intelligence updates from the Federal Department for Justice and Police and from his own teams, it looked like Mikhail had arrived in Lucerne. Some good work and foresight by Will had ensured that Elias had remained out of Mikhail's grip last night, but now it seemed that Elias had gone missing. Without him meeting with Mikhail in his office the evidence that the Swiss needed to make the arrests stick, would not be forthcoming. Mikhail would be arriving at the lorry yard soon, he guessed, so he hoped that Will and Zoe would be able to track Elias down soon.

Thirty-three

Mikhail was very annoyed and frustrated. He had not slept well as his mind could not process what was happening. His business and reputation felt like they were under threat. For a man who always got what he wanted, it was an uncomfortable feeling; the lack of information and lack of control was eating him up. He needed answers.

Elias had still not arrived home, as of 1am that morning. He had no choice but to try to track him down at the office. But it would be sensible, he thought, to send one of his team back to Elias's house to see if he had returned – he had nothing to lose. While he was about it he decided that he would post two of his men outside of the lorry yard; just to keep an eye open for anything suspicious. He did not know what was going on, so a bit of caution would not go amiss. He would have Laszlo and the other one, Dimitry, with him and Sergei.

With one of his men dispatched in the Volvo to Elias's house, they needed another car to transport six of them to the yard. He ordered two of his men to source another car. 'Steal it if you have to,' he told them.

They all arrived at the lorry yard just before 9am.

Mikhail, Sergei, Laszlo and Dimitry climbed out of the overcramped VW Passat. Why his men had not stolen a bigger car was beyond him. The car left two-up to take up station out of sight outside the yard.

Sergei led the way up the stairs and was recognised at reception. The four of them were escorted into the main building, and then taken to Elias's office. Elias was not there.

A young female office clerk advised them that Elias had called earlier to say that he would be in later that morning, as he was away visiting a sick relative. The girl apologised and said that Elias had not told her that he was expecting visitors. Mikhail thought she looked scared. He knew that most people appeared scared in his presence, so he didn't think much of it. He quizzed her for more information, but it was clear she had none. The frustration he was feeling was getting worse. The four men sat in the room and discussed the situation.

Not far away the OC could hear them clearly through the concealed bug under the desk in Elias's office. Unfortunately he realised too late, that he had made a grave error in his planning; they were speaking Russian and neither he nor any of the team listening-in could understand a word.

He made an urgent call. Within five minutes he had tracked down someone in the Department who spoke Russian. They were rushed to his covert Command vehicle outside of the lorry park, (a plain ordinary blue transit van). But it was thirty minutes before the Russian speaker was sat down. He started translating the conversation, but by then little of relevance was heard. The OC was kicking himself. Had the Russians said anything incriminating during the earlier period then he could have ordered the arrest. But the opportunity was now lost.

Thirty-four

Will could see a lone figure about half a mile away walking across a field, appearing and re-appearing behind some hedges. The flash of light occurred again. The sun must be reflecting off something that the man was carrying or wearing, but he was too far away to determine what. *Could it be Elias?* There was only one way to find out so they set off in that direction.

After five minutes of heading towards the distant figure they were close enough to be sure it was Elias. He was carrying a hiking pole with a metal crown that glinted in the sunlight.

Elias was walking with his head down as if deep in thought, so he hadn't seen them yet. It took another minute, when they were only about one hundred metres away, before he glanced up and recognised them. He didn't seem surprised and resignedly waved and continued to trudge towards them.

'Elias, we were worried,' Zoe said carefully.

'You are very clever to have sought me out,' he said. 'I'm OK, and before you ask, I went walking to talk with my wife.

Perhaps you think I'm crazy, but she's always given me good advice.'

Will was about to say that he thought Elias's wife was dead, but Zoe motioned to him to let Elias finish.

'She only comes to me when I'm hiking in the hills. When I explained my problem, she chastised me, but then we had a good discussion about how to deal with my problems. Despite the fear I felt, she persuaded me I must take this final step to redeem myself. I'm ready now. Shall we go?'

Yes, let's,' replied Zoe. 'We should get you to the yard as quickly as possible.' As Elias nodded and walked on, Zoe lowered her voice and said to Will, 'Who knows what Mikhail might do if there's further delay?'

They headed back towards Elias's house so that he could change. They left the track, Will led the way, joining the path towards the front of Elias's house. Suddenly Will stopped them and pulled them back behind a hedge.

'What's wrong Bill,' Elias said, worried by this sudden action.

'Both of you, have a look carefully down the road, but stay in the hedge,' Will said, 'What do you see?'

They both craned their necks around the hedge.

Zoe was first to realise. 'A black Volvo, just like the one that we saw at the airport, and it wasn't there when we arrived earlier.

Elias saw it, and was initially confused, but quickly realised, 'Mikhail's men are looking for me,' he said somberly.

Will stretched his neck around the hedge to take another look. The car was parked slightly up the hill from Elias's house, but facing downhill. It looked like it only had one occupant. If that occupant looked in his rear-view mirror he was bound to spot them.

'Is there a way to reach the back of your house and avoid being seen,' Will asked Elias. He had another worry as well, but first things first.

'Yes, I often cut through the back of my neighbours garden, we can get there by walking back up the hill a little and cross the track outside of the sight of the car.' Elias indicated and led the way as the three of them made their way around the back of the properties. They arrived safely at Elias's back door without being seen. Once safely inside, Zoe took control.

'Ok Elias, your first job is to call the office and talk to Lina. Tell her you are on your way and should be at the office shortly. She will probably tell you that you have visitors, so she can tell Mikhail that you won't be long.' Zoe had updated Elias as they had walked back to the house, so he was aware of what Lina was bravely doing for him; he felt humbled at the loyalty.

'When you have done that I need to update my team who are outside the yard,' she said. 'We can drop you close to the yard gates for your meeting with Mikhail.'

Whilst Elias was making his call to Lina, Will quietly informed Zoe of the other problem he had identified.

'How are we going to get past the Russian in the car outside, he is parked close to your car Zoe, and it is likely to be the driver who saw us at the airport?'

'Good point,' Zoe agreed. 'We need some sort of diversion to get past him.'

'I have an idea,' Elias said. He had finished his call to Lina and had just heard what Zoe had said. He understood the issue immediately. 'The Russian is looking for me, so let's tell him where he can find me.' Zoe and Will both looked mystified by this statement until Elias explained. 'I have a friend and neighbour who lives further up the hill and walks his dog past my house every day. I can call him and get him to speak to the man in the car. He can tell him that if he is waiting for me, that he was sure he had just seen me a few minutes ago walking further up the hill.'

'Ok, Elias, great idea,' said Zoe, 'Let's get the calls made and then make ready to leave. As soon as the Russian car moves we are out of here.'

Zoe updated the OC to advise that they had Elias with them, and he would be at the office soon. The OC advised that Mikhail and three others were in Elias's office waiting. He confirmed that the bug was working. But he didn't mention his mistake in not having a Russian interpreter at hand.

Then Elias called his friend who was happy to help.

They watched out of the window to see the plan work perfectly. At first the Russian appeared to not understand Elias's friend, so probably a language barrier. Some pointing at the house and then up the hill seemed to do the trick. The engine of the Black Volvo roared to life and the car headed off up the hill. They rushed out of the house as soon as the Volvo was out of sight; Elias shouted thanks to his friend as they piled into Zoe's car and headed to the lorry yard.

The lorry yard was only a fifteen-minute drive, but as Zoe drove something else was nagging at Will.

Zoe had mentioned that Mikhail was at Elias's office with three other Russians. One would be Sergei, and one other the man Sergei was travelling with, but where had the other one come from? They had just seen the Russian outside of Elias's house who Will thought the driver was probably who had spotted him and Zoe last night. So the third man with Mikhail was someone else. Will checked with Zoe, 'Are you sure that it was definitely three other Russians with Mikhail?'

Zoe confirmed, so Will shared his thoughts as they drove. They all pondered the question. It was Elias who had the answer, but what he said was more troubling:

'When the lorry left the yard on Monday Mikhail had insisted that it was followed by some of his team. He arranged for four of them to follow in a car. My guess is that they followed the lorry as far as Calais and then came back. Remember the call I had yesterday from some more of Mikhail's men who were meeting the lorry in Dover?

This all made sense to Will. The Russians following the lorry would not want to go through British Customs, who would immediately be suspicious – four Russians in one car would raise a red flag for any of his colleagues. So once the lorry was safely on the ferry they would have come back to Lucerne. If one of them was with Mikhail, and the driver was one other, then there were two other Russian men somewhere else. They were only about a mile from the yard. 'Stop the car Zoe!'

Zoe was surprised by Will's command, but she could tell it was urgent and immediately pulled over to the kerb.

'From what Elias has just said it is possible that there are two other Russians unaccounted for. I might be over-reacting, but from everything I have heard, Mikhail is very suspicious and trusts no one. If that is true then he could have placed his men near the yard to keep a watch.'

Zoe thought for a moment. 'If you are right then we must avoid being seen to drop Elias off. Elias, how do you normally travel to the office?'

'Normally by car, but sometimes by taxi.' Elias explained, 'Sometimes I have a drink with the staff or clients, so I leave the car at home.'

Without further discussion, Zoe pulled away from the kerb and u-turned back towards the town. In two minutes they pulled up at a taxi rank. Elias jumped out and Zoe parked up next to the taxi rank and found a telephone to contact the OC. She explained their slight change of plan, their suspicions that there might be 'watchers' outside the yard. The OC thanked her and advised her where the Command vehicle was parked and offered her and Will the opportunity to join him there.

Thirty-five

At about the same time in Northern Ireland, Steve pulled the lorry to a halt at the agreed rendezvous, a layby near Newry. He waited. He could see a car about eighty metres away at the far end of the layby, but it was too far away to confirm if it was occupied. It was the only car there, so he guessed it was probably his contact. Steve had no doubt the occupant was being cautious and would not immediately make himself known. Steve was confident that the SAS were following him, but they were too professional to 'show-out', and so would keep well clear at this stage.

It was fifteen minutes before Steve saw two men exit the car at the end of the layby and walk towards his cab.

One of them was six foot tall and looked forty years old. He was beefy and strong looking and wore a heavily worn black leather jacket. His face had a look that said, 'don't mess with me.' Steve could imagine him as a bare-knuckle wrestler. There was no doubt he was in charge. The other man was at least four inches shorter. He couldn't have been much older than eighteen and was thin and wiry. He tried to look tough, but seemed out of his depth in this environment. He had spikey blond hair, like a punk-rocker.

'Good day. What can I do for you?' Steve enquired as he wound down his cab door window and smiled at the men.

"Boris sent me,' came the expected reply from the 'wrestler', in a thick gruff Belfast accent.

'That's good to know,' Steve said. 'Shall I follow you?'

'I will be coming with you, so I will,' came the reply from Wrestler. It was more like a command. Wrestler looked Steve in the eye and Steve noticed he had his hand inside his jacket. This suggested he might have more than just bare-knuckles tucked in there. Whether he had a weapon or not, the implication was clear and all part of the act. So Steve gave a submissive gesture and invited him into the cab via the passenger door.

'Just keep your eyes on me lad there, and he will lead us to our destination, so he will,' Wrestler said, as Punk-rocker returned to his car and pulled out of the layby ahead of them.

They drove a few miles on the main road and then took some minor roads that headed east of Newry and into the country. The landscape was fairly flat, and Steve noticed they seemed to be approaching an industrial park close to a disused airfield near Ballyhalbert. All at once the car indicated left and drove down an open concrete track. He dutifully followed. They approached a gated and fenced concrete area, with weeds growing through in places. The gate was wide open. Ahead was an old aircraft hangar which the car aimed for, but otherwise there were no other buildings, just deserted open space. It was the remains of the disused airport, just a hangar and crumbling concrete runways.

The car drove through the large open hangar doors, and Steve and his lorry followed. The hangar was vast, with room for about ten lorries, but empty apart from three cars parked over to the left, which were now joined by the new arrival.

In his mirrors Steve could see a few men closing the big doors behind him. Up ahead a few more men were waving him into position. There must have been about a dozen men all told, but one stood out as the boss, just by his stance and the deference he seemed to be receiving. Seamus. All the other men were constantly checking in with him visually, to see if he had any orders.

Seamus strolled up to the cab and Steve did not need telling that it was time for him to climb down and meet him. His passenger was already getting out of the passenger door, and as Steve exited the driver's door he surreptitiously pressed a button under the dashboard. Not only had the 'gadget' boys placed a silent alarm on the crates, but they had provided Steve with a radio signal alert linked to the tracker under the lorry. The SAS would know where the lorry was and that it had stopped, but this was an additional safeguard to alert them that it was time for action.

'Pleased to meet you,' said Steve, holding out his hand. Seamus looked at him but didn't respond to the offer of a handshake.

'We hope you're bringing us what we want this time, so we are?'

'I'm sure you'll be satisfied,' replied Steve humbly.

'Open the doors,' is all Seamus said next. He wasn't here to pass the time of day. Steve walked to the back of the lorry and Seamus followed.

Suddenly there was a commotion at the hangar doors. Ten men dressed in black, wearing gasmasks and carrying automatic weapons burst through the hangar door and were moving quickly, forming into a small arc facing the lorry.

'Everyone stand still and put your hands up,' one of the lead men shouted, as the other men spread out further.

Initially everyone froze and some of the IRA men were starting to raise their hands, but then Steve saw several of them brandishing guns. The next few seconds were a blur.

Even though Steve expected it, the noise of several automatic weapons firing at once shocked him, but he quickly recovered and immediately rolled under the back of the lorry and stayed down as he saw smoke appearing from all corners. The SAS had launched smoke grenades. From his position under the lorry he saw the chaos unfolding.

The IRA men brandishing guns burst in all directions, firing wildly towards the assailants, as parts of the hangar filled with smoke. Steve saw several IRA men quickly fall to the ground. Each time a man came into Steve's limited view from under the lorry, they fell to the floor as a result of the efficient and accurate SAS firepower. Pools of blood formed around those nearest him, the smell of cordite hung heavy in the air. Carnage. This was meant to be a controlled arrest, not a firefight.

The heavy gunfire had abated as quickly as it started, but odd shots still echoed around the hangar. Without ceremony, and completely taken by surprise, Steve was suddenly dragged from under the lorry by a gas-masked man and thrust onto his face. His arms pulled behind him and restrained in plasticuffs.

Seamus had also been quick to react. Partially shielded by the lorry, he ran back towards the cab, past several of his men who had been stunned into inaction. Sean was still close to the cab and also reacted quickly as he saw Seamus running towards him. Seamus pointed past him as he approached and urged Sean to follow him towards the back of the hangar, away from the smoke and the action. Sean followed, but not before pulling his gun, the opportunity was upon him; he was now out of sight of the assailants.

They reached a small door at the back of the hangar and Seamus opened it to the outside world. He turned around to check on the situation, and to make sure Sean was behind him. Sean was just four metres away and pointing a gun directly at him.

'What's going on Sean?' he said in a remarkably calm, steady fatherly voice.

Sean held his gun steady and focused. This wasn't the time for a chat, he had waited too long to waste time now.

'This is for Callum,' Sean said, as he pulled the trigger. Seamus's eyes showed confusion as he had no idea what Sean had meant, but the thought was his last, replaced with a searing pain that made him grasp at his chest. He was dead before he hit from the ground.

Sean did not hesitate and ran past Seamus's corpse. He launched himself at the open door to the outside of the hangar. But before he was fully out he felt a huge punch to his back, so hard that he fell forward face-down, half in and half out of the door. He felt no pain, but he could not move; the SAS bullet had severed the vertebrae in his neck and paralysed him. Why was the blue sky outside suddenly going black he thought, someone was dimming the lights – then his eyes closed, and his own lights went out.

Thirty-six

The taxi drove through the gates into the yard. Elias paid and climbed out, waving thanks as the driver drove back out of the gates.

He walked slowly but deliberately over to the external staircase and climbed the stairs to the offices. He breathed in, took a look around the yard as if it was for the last time, and entered the building.

Once inside he scanned across the main office. Beyond his busy office workers, he could see through the open door to his office, Sergei and three others were sitting around the conference table in his room. His people said good morning to him as he passed their desks and Lina gave him a concerned smile.

'Would you like me to bring you and your guests coffee,' Lina said, she felt she had to say something encouraging as she sensed Elias was unhappy to see them there.

'That will be great, thank you Lina. And thank you for helping,' he said sincerely, without a need to expand on the comment.

As he reached his office Sergei spotted him, and he heard Sergei say something to the others and they all looked up.

'Hello Sergei, nice to see you, but unexpected, you should have let me know you were coming, and I would have tried to be here earlier. You must be Mikhail,' he said to the larger of the other three men and extended his hand. Mikhail eased his bulk out of the chair and greeted Elias with a handshake.

'Good to see you in person at last,' said Mikhail, disguising his distaste for this social nicety. But it didn't stop Mikhail using the greeting to look for the first signs of a lie. 'I trust your relative is not too sick?'

Elias had been fully briefed by Zoe and was expecting the question, so he had an answer ready which was close to the truth, as his cousin had needed his help last week.

'My Cousin is a lot better thanks, he had a minor fall on the stairs yesterday and hurt his back, but it has improved a little today and I'll go back this evening to check on him.'

Mikhail did not introduce the other two men and they did not offer to introduce themselves, so they all sat around the conference table in Elias's office and Lina arrived with the coffee.

Sergei started the conversation. 'Elias as you know we have a big problem so we need to know everything you can tell us so that we can make right choices.'

'I'm not sure what else I can tell you more that I told you yesterday Mikhail, he said shifting his attention to Mikhail.'

Mikhail stared at Elias, almost willing him to break eye contact, but Elias held the stare and kept his composure long enough to show deference to Mikhail and with no trace that he was hiding anything.

'Tell me again,' Mikhail said coldly.

Elias went through the story again, how Peter had made his panicked phone call, then the call from Bill who had found out more information from Customs at Dover, and the fact that Peter had not made contact. He explained again the suspicions he had had regarding Peter's boasts of some sort of deal with the Germans. Then he added the information he had received yesterday from the Hungarians who had not been unable to find Peter. Now was his chance to try to get Mikhail to admit he was in charge of the smuggling operation.

'I can't understand how the arms could have been removed, as you ordered your team to follow the lorry all the way to Calais. Did they not see anything?'

Mikhail looked at one of the men in the room who had not introduced themselves and said something to him in Russian in a harsh tone, his voice rising with every word he spoke. Mikhail was getting very annoyed.

The man looked embarrassed and worried by the onslaught.

'Sorry I don't speak Russian,' Elias said, 'Is there something I should know?'

Sergei answered. 'This man was one of the men following the lorry, but their car broke down and they lost sight of the lorry for a few hours. We think this might have been when the arms were removed.'

Mikhail said something in Russian to Sergei and took over the conversation.

'Elias, I'm a careful man and I plan in detail, so I can't believe that I've now lost two consignments of arms and ammunition. This is too much of a coincidence. I can only think that Peter and a rival gang are ripping me off, but I still can't see how. And I need to explain again to the Irish customer that this second consignment won't be arriving either. Do you know how that feels Elias?' His voice was getting louder. 'Do you know what this will do to my reputation?'

***

In the Command vehicle the OC had heard enough evidence of Mikhail's involvement and was ready to call the strike. Zoe and Will had arrived a few minutes earlier and had heard most of the conversation in Elias's office.

'All call-signs. This is a Go! Go! Go!'

There were a series of acknowledgements from the team leaders on the ground. All teams filed efficiently into the yard and separated towards their designated positions. Thirty seconds later a report.

'Red team approaching the building staircase.'

'Blue team in position at right side of building, covering staircase.'

'Green team in position front of building.'

Sven had studied the plans for the yard carefully before the raid. It had been agreed that troops would all be deployed at this end of the building, as there no other way out of the yard at the far end – the fences were three metres high.

***

'I think you know more Elias,' Mikhail barked. 'Tell me what you know. Are you in this with Peter? Are you working with a rival? Or are you perhaps working with the Police? I'll get to the bottom of this,' he said through gritted teeth.

He stood up and started pacing the room. As he did so he happened to glance out of the window of the building and thought he saw a helmeted man who looked military, disappear around the corner of the building carrying a weapon. Had he imagined this? It was only a brief glimpse and now they were gone, but he was getting an uneasy feeling. He walked to the office door opened it and looked out. Everything appeared normal.

'What's the matter Mikhail,' Sergei said in Russian with a concerned expression, but Mikhail waved away Sergei's concerns. He walked a few feet into the main office. Lina was passing at this point and asked him if he needed anything. He ignored her and scanned the office, but still everything seemed normal. Sergei appeared by his side and asked Mikhail again, 'What's wrong Mikhail?'

'I'm sure I just saw a policeman creeping around the yard. There is something going on Sergei, I can feel it,' he said. 'Elias is hiding something, and I'm now worried that we've been set-up by the authorities.' He called to Laszlo and Dimitry and they joined him and Sergei just outside of Elias's office. 'Go to the top of the outside staircase and have a look around,' he said. They dutifully followed their leaders orders and headed for the main office door.

Whilst his visitors were distracted outside the office door, Elias walked casually over to his cupboard and unlocked it. He took an item out of the cupboard, closed and locked the cupboard, and concealed the item in his jacket pocket.

Suddenly, over by the main door Mikhail detected some movement. One of the employees was looking in the direction of the stairs with a shocked expression on his face. Then a helmeted head appeared around the corner from the main door.

The man, dressed similar to the one that Mikhail thought he had seen from the window, came into view and was looking in his direction. Then a second and a third appeared. Laszlo and Dimitry were swiftly taken to the floor and handcuffed before they knew what was happening. 'Politsiya!' Mikhail shouted to Sergei and Mikhail turned quickly to return to the office.

Then Mikhail hesitated; he looked at a frightened Lina standing a few feet from him.

'Sergei, help me.' Mikhail grabbed hold of Lina and with Sergei's help, dragged her into Elias's office. She let out a small scream of surprise and the nearest office staff looked in that direction as the office door closed behind them

.

Thirty-seven

'Red team leader to OC. We have entered the building, apprehended two targets, but the others are now locked in the office and have a hostage, over.'

'Clear the building and yard of civilians,' the OC instructed the red team leader.

'Received and understand,' replied red leader. 'Also note, the two arrested persons were armed with handguns.'

The OC put his head in his hands to think. This was getting more dangerous, not going to plan at all. He prided himself on being good at this stuff with his years of experience, but this was starting to unravel.

The arrests should have been straightforward, the targets should have all been contained in an office and should have been taken by surprise by the Red team, with plenty of back-up from the other teams containing the outside of the building. They must have been tipped off by the two Russians that Zoe believed might by watching the yard – but how? Not by telephone.

He needed some of his men to deploy to look for them.

'Blue team leader. There are two targets outside the yard watching the building. Seek and arrest. Be careful, they could be armed.'

'Received and understood.' Replied blue leader.

On the plus side their surveillance of the yard earlier this morning had identified all four targets entering. So there was no hesitation by the red team in identifying and arresting the two that were spotted in the main office. The other positive was that they could still hear what was going on in Elias's office thanks to the bug under the desk, so it gave them a small advantage.

But now they had a hostage situation, with the strong possibility that the captors were armed.

He had to think fast. Not only was an innocent civilian in danger, but Elias would now be in very big trouble. He had no doubt that Mikhail would by now have realised that Elias had set him up.

From the bug feed he could hear Mikhail shouting at Elias, accusing him of working with the police, and Elias denying any such thing.

He picked up the phone, donned some headphones and checked the number of Elias's office on a pad next to him and dialed. A few seconds later he heard it ringing. It continued to ring.

Will and Zoe had heard it all as they had realised immediately the increased danger for Elias. But how could they assist?

'He is not answering, the OC advised Will and Zoe. I can't wait for back-up, I need you to keep trying the phone. I'm going to try to talk to Mikhail through the office door. If you get an answer on the phone try to keep them talking until I get there.'

He rushed out of the van without waiting for an answer. Zoe did not waste any time filling his seat and donning his headphones. 'Will, try the number again.'

Before Will could dial Zoe heard the phone ring through her headphones.

Zoe heard Sergei say 'hello' from the bug in the room, and immediately start talking quickly in Russian. She heard the name Mikhail and then Mikhail was speaking in Russian – he was talking on the phone now. It had to be the Russians that Will had realised were outside the yard somewhere. Of course, she thought, they would have seen the Police move on the yard and were trying to warn Mikhail. A bit late of course. Zoe could hear the whole Russian conversation though the headphones, but could not understand it. Will could hear the feed from the bug, so he heard Mikhail speaking in Russian and guessed it must be the Russians outside the yard warning him. Then behind them the other occupant of the command vehicle, tapped Zoe on the shoulder. He was wearing a headset like Zoe and listening to the call, but they had thought nothing of his presence – just a member of the team. Zoe pulled one of her headphones off to hear what he wanted, and he started translating what they were saying – he was the translator that the OC had brought in earlier.

'I know they are here you idiot,' said the translator, pointing to his headphones as he translated, 'I need you to be ready at the gate with the car. I have a hostage so the Police will have to move away. Keep yourselves out of sight until you can see us. The Police have already got Laszlo and Dimitry so nothing we can do for them now. I'll signal when I need you to come for us.'

They heard the phone go down in Elias's office and Mikhail talked again in Russian, which was quickly translated to her by the Swiss policeman.

'Sergei, we need to be ready to move. The Police will make contact soon I'm sure, but they will not try to stop us if we have a hostage. And maybe we have two hostages if Elias is involved, as I now suspect.'

Then they both heard the OC shouting from the main office.

'Mikhail, my name is Sven, and I'm the Police Commander in charge. You are surrounded so please open the door and surrender yourselves and the girl.'

Thirty-eight

'What are we going to do Mikhail,' said Sergei in panic.

Mikhail ignored him. 'Mr. Police Commander Sven.' He shouted through the closed door, 'I will only release the girl if you do exactly as I say, and you do it quickly. If not the girl will die. You will move all of your men to the end of the yard immediately. When I can see them I'll give you further instructions.'

'Mikhail, please do not harm the girl, I'll move my men.'

The OC was fast losing control, but he could see no options. The safety of the girl was his prime concern. Losing Mikhail would be a blow, but he would face a much bigger backlash from his bosses, and no doubt the press, if he allowed a hostage to die. He trusted his men, but they needed to be in no doubt of the risks.

'All call signs this is the OC. We have a hostage situation. Red and Green teams are to go to the rear of the yard immediately. There is an immediate threat to life so no heroics. We must not risk the hostage.' He said all this within earshot of

Elias's office, but now moved towards the main office door and quietly gave some further instructions. 'Blue team, please continue with your task, but remain outside of the yard out of sight.'

***

It was clear to Will that, although the Blue team were better placed to respond if Mikhail got away, they were impotent against him whilst he had a hostage. He also had no doubt that Mikhail would never let her go. He would use her as a bargaining chip until she was disposable – then he would kill both her and Elias.

Before Rachel was killed he had considered that there was some good in everyone, no matter how difficult, angry and violent they appeared to be. But now he considered that was naive. Gazza had shown no remorse for Rachel's death and laughed about it with his friends. Some people were just pure evil. And Mikhail, Will decided, was one of them. If someone didn't do something then Elias and Lina would soon be dead. He couldn't sit back and let that happen, he had to act, despite the risk to himself.

'Will, we need to get to my car,' Zoe said. 'The police won't be able to follow Mikhail if he escapes, but we can.' She picked up a portable radio, advised the translator what she was doing. They left the command vehicle and Zoe headed towards her car, parked fifty metres to the east of the gate entrance.

Will had other ideas. 'Ok Zoe, you head to the car, I'm going to try to help Elias,' he shouted as he headed off towards the yard gates.

'Will, it is too risky,' she shouted after him, but he ignored her and entered the gates into the yard.

The yard was eerily quiet as all civilians had been evacuated. He headed quickly towards the large rubbish container near to the bottom of the exterior staircase. This was where he and Zoe had hidden from the security guard last week. It would provide enough cover to observe the staircase without being seen. He could see the police units congregated at the end of the yard. Sven was taking no chances.

Sooner or later he anticipated Mikhail, Sergei and the hostages would descend the staircase. Mikhail was no doubt expecting his men to have a car waiting, but if the police outside had caught them this wasn't going to happen. *Think Will, what can you do?* Could he distract Mikhail and Sergei, maybe convince them to let Elias and the hostage go? Then the police could apprehend them. *But they are over a hundred metres away.*

***

Mikhail was thinking fast – although his temper was renown he had survived all these years by remaining in control when his anger surfaced. Right now he was working out the strategy for escape, considering back-up plans. He did not trust his men outside to do what he needed.

'Elias, we're going to leave here together in your car, where is it parked?'

'Mikhail, this is crazy,' pleaded Elias, 'we have to let Lina go and give ourselves up.'

Mikhail walked over to him and punched him hard in the face, causing his lip to split and blood to pour from the crack. Elias fell to the floor, but quickly recovered and scrambled back onto his feet, touching his tender face and looking at the blood that was now on his hands.

'I don't have my car here,' he said to Mikhail quickly, before Mikhail hit him again. He was expecting it this time, managed to ride the punch a little and stay on his feet, but the contact on his jaw was still painful.

'Please don't hurt him,' pleaded Lina, 'I have my car parked downstairs which you can use.'

'Give me the keys,' Mikhail stormed.

'They're on my desk in the office, just outside,' sobbed Lina.

Just then Sven shouted from outside the door. 'My men have all moved out to the rear of the yard as you asked. Please let the girl go now.' He knew this would not happen as she was Mikhail's ticket out, but he had to try.

Mikhail looked out of the window and could see about fifteen disgruntled looking officers loitering at the back of the yard. They were as far away from his escape route as possible, but he would need to be sure there were no others lurking elsewhere.

'Mr. Police Commander you had better not be lying or I promise I will kill the girl. We are going to come out shortly and you are going to lead us out of the building. If you or any of your men try anything I will kill the girl.'

He spoke to Sergei in Russian, 'We need to show this Policeman that we are serious. I want you to escort the girl to the door at gunpoint.'

Sergei nodded and drew his gun from his jacket pocket. Lina gasped and went white.

'Just do as you are told and you won't get hurt,' he promised her.

He had a firm hold on Lina's arm as he opened the door and dragged her out. She looked terrified. Mikhail and Elias followed.

'OK Mr. Police Commander stay exactly where you are.' Mikhail said. Sven did not look frightened, but looked sensible and experienced enough to know that he faced a serious and committed enemy. Mikhail judged that he would do anything to protect the girl.

'Place your gun on floor and move back.' Sven did as he was asked. Mikhail grabbed Lina's arm. 'Sergei, get the gun then go to the far window to see if there are other police.'

Sergei walked towards Sven, grabbed his gun from the floor and placed his own back in his jacket. Moving quickly to the opposite side of the office he scanned the back of the yard. There was no sign of any police. 'All clear,' he shouted.

Sergei re-joined the group and Lina indicated her keys on a nearby desk which Mikhail collected.

'Ok, Mr. Police Commander, you are going to walk out of the office ahead of us. Anyone tries anything and the girl dies first, followed by you. Do you understand.'

Sven nodded calmly and led them across the office and out of the main door. Sergei held him at gunpoint, Elias next with Mikhail holding tightly to Lina bringing up the rear. They filed through the lobby and reached the top of the external staircase. Mikhail called a halt whilst he scanned the scene. No sign of police. The entrance gate was clear. No sign of his men either. He wasn't surprised or disappointed. He trusted no one, but he would take pleasure in killing them for their incompetence when at last he was out of this mess.

'Where is your car?' Mikhail said. Lina pointed at a red VW Polo parked to the right of the stairs in front of the building.

'Sergei,' Mikhail handed him Lina's car keys, 'take Mr. Police Commander and get him to open the car doors.'

Sven walked slowly down the stairs, Sergei three feet behind holding his gun. He had no option but to do what he was told. He unlocked the car and opened the doors. Elias then took the stairs, Mikhail and Lina followed, Mikhail still with a firm grip of Lina's arm.

'Now Mr. Police Commander, walk towards the back of the yard and do not look back.'

Sven tried again. 'Mikhail, you don't need to take the girl now, I've kept my team back as agreed and you have my word they will not stop you leaving.'

'Mr. Police Commander, I trust no one. I'll be taking the girl until I am sure we are not followed. If anyone follows me she dies. It that clear?'

Sven had no choice, he did as he had been told and turned to walk towards the back of the yard.

***

Will knew he had to act now. If he could get close enough he might be able to disarm Sergei and disable him. If he couldn't get close then maybe he could distract them enough for Sven to help. He didn't have time to work it out, he just acted on instinct.

'Sergei,' Will shouted as he emerged from behind the rubbish bin, 'What's going on?'

Sergei turned, shocked to see Bill as he emerged from behind the container. 'Bill, what are you doing here?'

'Well, I thought I would come and see Elias to find out what was happening, but I see I'm a little late.'

This was the distraction Elias needed.

Elias calmly withdrew the pistol from his jacket, took a step back from them and pointed it as Mikhail. 'Mikhail. I can't let you take Lina. Let her go and I'll not stop you leaving,' he said calmly.

Mikhail swung around, still gripping Lina. He could not believe his eyes. First Bill arrives out of nowhere and now Elias had pulled a gun on him.

'You will pay for this,' Mikhail fumed.

Elias saw Sergei moving from behind Mikhail. 'Sergei drop your gun right now or I'll shoot.' Sergei looked Elias in the eye and saw a steely determination that he hadn't seen in Elias before – he hesitated for a split second, but knew without doubt that Elias meant what he said. He bent and placed Sven's gun on the ground and stood back up. 'Kick it over towards Bill.'

Sergei did as he was told. Will did not hesitate and retrieved the gun, pointing it towards Sergei and Mikhail. He hadn't expected this, but was relieved. Elias had saved the day.

'Lina, come and stand behind me.' Elias said. Lina didn't need telling twice and scurried away from Mikhail. 'Now leave Mikhail, before I change my mind,' he said, feeling totally confident and in control – *his wife would be proud*.

'You will pay with your life Elias.' Mikhail said with venom as he squeezed himself into the passenger seat of the Polo. Sergei considered pulling his own gun to regain the advantage, but it was clear that Elias would shoot him if he tried anything.

'Bravo Elias,' Sergei said, nodding at him approvingly, 'I didn't think you had it in you.' Sergei said. But then he looked at Will, a look of disgust. 'I'm not finished with you Bill, you'll regret this.'

Sergei climbed into the driver's seat and drove swiftly towards the lorry yard gate.

Will ran over to Elias. 'You were great Elias,' he said, handing him Sven's gun. 'Now I have to go,' Will shouted as he turned and sprinted after the car.

Sven was twenty meters away, heading for his men when Elias had pulled his gun. He had stopped and turned, watching as events unfolded. Now he was by Elias's side and retrieved his gun. He still had his radio which he grabbed quickly out of his pocket.

'Blue team, targets are leaving the yard in a red VW Polo. You are 'go' to intercept. I say again. Intercept the targets.'

'This is Blue team leader. Acknowledged.'

Thirty-nine

The Blue team leader had four of his men dealing with the arrest of the two Russians, who were not coming quietly, so he dispatched his other three men to intercept the red Polo. This meant a hundred metre dash for them to collect their car. Within a minute of the instruction they were on the road and heading for the yard to intercept the red Polo.

The Blue team were three hundred metres from the east/west road junction. They clearly saw the red Polo up ahead on the road going east so they gave chase as it headed into the built-up area of the town. They were travelling in an unmarked car so did not have the benefit of a siren or flashing lights to aid their pursuit. They would need to be careful how they intercepted the car so as not to endanger civilians. Strangely the red Polo did not seem to be trying to escape and was driving normally. It appeared to be heading for the railway station. They radioed the Operational Commander to update. The OC was surprised by the Blue team announcement. The railway station was in the opposite direction to where Sergei had driven.

'Are you sure it is them?' He queried, doubt in his voice.

By now the Blue team were also having doubts. They considered they were now in a safe position to pull right in front of the car to force it to stop, without immediate danger. They executed this manoeuvre and piled out of the car to the shock and surprise of the two innocent occupants.

Hindsight is a wonderful thing, but decisions made in the heat of battle are often criticised. However, when the police chiefs reviewed the case later it was accepted that the actions of the Operational Commander were reasonable given the circumstances. The instruction to intercept the red Polo was clear; the need for an index plate number was deemed unnecessary. No one could have foreseen that at the precise time that Sergei drove the red Polo out of the gate to the West, another red Polo would pass close by going East. Or that this car would contain two men of similar physical profile to Mikhail and Sergei (at least from a distance).

***

'Head towards the countryside, to the hills,' ordered Mikhail, 'we can lose anyone who tries to follow. Then we can head for the German border.'

'And what then Mikhail,' shouted Sergei over the scream of the engine as they raced along the road out of town at high speed. He nearly lost control on the first bend as he got used to the limitations of the car. 'We can't cross the border, our details must be known by now.'

'I'm now sure Elias was behind this,' Mikhail seethed, 'and Bill too. Don't worry Sergei, I can organise papers to get across borders, but I'm not leaving this country until Elias pays,' he said with deadly conviction.

They travelled on at speed and started ascending the hills. The roads got more twisty and snowier the higher they got.

***

Will reached Zoe's car puffing with exertion. He jumped in and Zoe raced after the Polo. She didn't want to be seen so remained some way behind. It was a difficult judgement; stay too close and they could be spotted, too far off and they would lose them. But Zoe knew the roads, the terrain, the likely turn-offs, so she had an advantage.

'That was a hell of a risk you took there Will,' Zoe said, 'You could've been killed.'

'I had to do something and thought if I could distract them, the police could react. But as it turned out Elias was a hero,' he said with pride. 'Who would have thought it?'

***

Without knowing the roads, all Sergei could do was continue to drive up into the hills as the snow on the ground became a little thicker, more slippery. There was very little traffic now, so he was able to use more of the road to drive a little faster; he was getting used to the car's abilities on this icy surface. He noticed a car a few hundred metres behind them that was keeping pace, but it wasn't getting any closer, so decided it was probably a local with a car much better suited to the conditions.

'I'm not sure,' Sergei said, 'but there seems to be a car following us.'

Mikhail craned his neck but could not see a car.

'It is a long way back,' continued Sergei, 'but seems to be keeping pace, maybe a local who knows these roads?'

Mikhail thought for a moment. 'OK, if it's the police we'll lose them.' They rounded the next left-hand bend and immediately off to the right was a track leading into the trees. 'Take that track,' Mikhail commanded. Sergei responded quickly and the car slipped and skidded onto the track and within seconds was consumed in the greenery and out of sight from the road. Sergei killed the engine. They waited. They couldn't see the road from there, but heard a car pass about thirty seconds later which continued to head up the hill.

Although he had given up Sven's gun earlier, he still had his own and he retrieved it from inside his jacket and checked its mechanism.

'If it comes to a showdown, I won't hesitate,' he said.

***

Zoe and Will had lost sight of the Polo, so Zoe had increased her speed for the next few minutes as she expertly navigated the curves.

'There were no turn offs.' Will said. 'They couldn't have got this far ahead, so they must have pulled off the road somewhere behind us. Do you suppose they saw us?'

'It's possible. What do we do now?'

Will thought for a moment. He was as sure as he could be that Sergei and Mikhail were not ahead of them, so they must have pulled over somewhere. Would they stay put or continue up the hill, or would they turn back? The police teams could do with alerting, but he had seen no telephone kiosks for many miles as they were well into the country. Then he remembered something and looked behind him. And there it was on the back seat.

'Zoe, when we left the command vehicle you picked up a radio. We can alert the Operational Commander!'

'Great idea Will,' she said, 'but we'll almost certainly be out of range up here with a handheld radio.'

Will reached over and picked it up. 'Only one way to find out, in the meantime we head back down the hill and search for where they could have turned.'

Will had used this type of radio before, working at the docks. It had a straightforward 'press to talk' button on the side, a channel selector and a volume knob. The volume had been turned down so they would not have heard any transmissions earlier. This did not strike Will as unusual. In the command vehicle it would have been a distraction, but it had also resulted in him forgetting that Zoe had picked it up. He was surprised that Zoe had not remembered they had it.

Zoe was silently cursing. She had not forgotten the radio, she had deliberately turned the volume down as part of her own agenda. She valued having Will alongside, she liked him, he had proven himself. But he was now getting in the way of her objective.

There was an opportunity to take revenge for the death of her Uncle. Although she had tried to convince herself she would be happy to see Mikhail locked up, she knew she would only be happy if he were dead. Apart from Will's presence, she could achieve this without witnesses. But now they had lost sight of Mikhail and Will was in danger of ruining her plans. She sub-consciously reached under her arm and checked her weapon, still concealed in her underarm holster.

She found a wide spot on the road and did an excellent one-eighty degree turn by turning the steering wheel hard to the left and using the handbrake. The icy road allowed the car to slew sideways and as it started to turn back the way they had come she adjusted the steering expertly straightening the car, and headed back down the hill.

'Wow,' Will said with excitement, 'that was some driving!'

Zoe just smiled, as she thought about her next steps.

'This is Will to any police units. Please acknowledge.' He let go of the 'press to talk' and waited, but all he got was static. He tried again, 'All police units, urgent message regarding Russian targets. Please respond.' Again all he got was static hiss.

'Well it was worth a try,' Will said. 'Keep your eyes open for anywhere they could have turned off.'

They continued down the winding snow covered road for five minutes when suddenly Will noticed a fresh set of tyre prints in the snow leading off to the left into some trees. As they passed Will caught a glimpse of the car tucked in about fifty metres back.

'I see them,' he said excitedly.

They drove on for another two hundred metres then Zoe pulled gently to a stop so as not to alert them.

'Ok Will, keep trying the radio, I'm going for a closer look.'

Without waiting for Will's response she quickly got out of the car and jogged back up the hill.

'All police units, Russian targets sighted five miles west of city in the hills.' Will didn't know exactly where they were as he had seen no signposts, but it was the best he could think of. He might not be able to receive a transmission, but it was possible they might be able to hear him.

What was Zoe doing? What could she achieve by getting closer, he thought? He could see she was now already close to the turn-off into the trees, then she disappeared into the undergrowth. He decided to follow her.

He could see from her snowy footprints where she had left the road and entered the trees and bushes. He followed the path she had made until he had a clear sight of the Polo tucked behind a tall pine. But Zoe was nowhere to be seen. Her tracks suggested that she had worked her way behind the car. He stealthily followed. Mikhail and Sergei were sat in the car which was facing back towards the road. Mikhail was in the passenger seat furthest from him. Then he caught a glimpse of Zoe on the other side of the car, stooping low, almost crawling.

She pulled her gun and checked there was a bullet in the breach before turning the safety off. She was a good markswoman who trained every month, so she was confident she could hit her target from here. Ideally she needed Mikhail to exit the car. She knew that a single shot through the side window might shatter the glass, but would likely deflect the bullet. She would probably need a second shot to be sure of a kill. She took a deep breath, lined up. She was about to fire when she heard a noise behind her.

'What the hell are you doing Zoe,' Will whispered hoarsely. He had seen the drawn gun and immediately guessed Zoe's intentions.

She turned, gave him an exasperated look, 'Damn you Will, keep out of this.'

'This is not the answer Zoe, murdering Mikhail makes you as bad as him.'

Just then the Polo engine started. They both looked up as it eased out of cover heading back to the road.

Zoe jumped up took aim at the rear of the car as it reached the road and fired off three shots. They all went wide. The car sped off up the hill.

Zoe was angry, but defeated. She sank to her knees dropping the gun and punched the ground repeatedly. Then all at once she broke down and sobbed. The opportunity was lost.

'Come on we have to catch them up,' said Will, as he picked up the fallen gun.

'I'm so sorry Will,' she cried, 'I miss my Uncle so much.' She was sobbing hard; inconsolable.

'Later,' said Will, taking command. He dragged her to her feet. He applied the safety to the gun and popped it into the waistband of his trousers. They ran back to the car, Will dragging her. Zoe didn't argue. She was still very emotional, resigned to being led, the fight gone out of her.

Will looked at Zoe as they reached the car; she was still in an emotional state, so he took a decision.

'I'll drive,' he commanded.

Again Zoe didn't argue, and climbed obediently into the passenger seat.

Although Will was shocked at Zoe for wanting to shoot Mikhail, he realised that her need was the same as his had been when Rachel was killed. She needed justice. Perhaps he should not have disturbed her and let her take the shot? He surprised himself at having this thought, but he also knew that if Mikhail escaped then his own life, and that of Zoe and Elias, were now in jeopardy. Not only was Mikhail angry, but he had the means to hunt down and kill those who wronged him. Mikhail must be caught.

But what would he do if he caught up with him? He had a gun so could make some sort of citizens arrest – was that a thing in Switzerland? Would even this action result in a breach of some law and Mikhail going free? He thought back to how he felt when Rachel's killer did not receive justice and the steps he took to redress that miscarriage. Now, in the present, he realised, with absolute clarity, that his moral compass had shifted. Mikhail was a ruthless killer and must die. Justice must be served, and he was ready to make that happen.

He set off quickly, soon getting used to the high-performing Audi around the slippery bends. After five minutes they could see the Polo ahead about a quarter mile distant, as it disappeared then reappeared around the bends. It was driving fast, but was no match for the speed and handling of the Audi.

***

Sergei had heard the shots as they resumed their journey and caught sight of a woman with a gun. And then he saw Bill.

Whatever was going on between him and Elias it was now obvious they were in cahoots. *Bill will pay for this.*

He was having great trouble keeping the car under control. He had now reached the summit so the downhill slope would give him the extra speed he needed, but the roads were treacherous.

If he had the time to ponder he would have been captivated by the view. The trees sweeping down into the meadows below, the snow-covered pines, the twisty road that hugged the rocky hill. It was a sight to behold. On a different day at a different time of year this would be a drivers dream. But today in the icy conditions it was a nightmare for someone in a hurry. And he was in a massive hurry.

'I can't outrun them,' Sergei said to Mikhail. 'But I might be able to slow them down or even stop them.'

Now six hundred metres ahead of his pursuer, he skidded round the next bend, but he got the car straight again before continuing to race down the hill.

'Sergei, be careful,' shouted a worried Mikhail. For a man who obsessed over being in control he was now in the control of someone else, and could do nothing about it.

On the next bend Sergei found what he was looking for – a viewpoint. He pulled over towards the barriers and stopped in the viewpoint layby.

'What are you doing Sergei,' Mikhail said in panic.

'Just keep your head down,' Sergei said as he exited the car. He crouched down at the back of the car, pulled his gun and waited. He spotted the Audi as it rounded the bend. He lined up and fired three shots. Missed.

***

Will saw Sergei a second before he fired and braked hard, the rear of the Audi slewed dangerously to the left. He straightened as he shouted at Zoe to get down. He managed to come to a controlled stop, now just one hundred metres from the stationery Polo and Sergei's shooting.

'Stay down,' Will shouted. The drivers side of the Audi was away from the Polo so he slid out of the car onto the ground and stayed prone. Then he worked his way around towards the front where he could see Sergei. It was a safe distance he decided. Sergei would have to be very lucky to hit them at this range, but he could still get lucky. *Maybe he could too.* He pulled out Zoe's pistol and lined up with the Polo, flipped off the safety. He took aim at one of the Polo tyres. It had been fifteen years since he had fired a gun, but he was pretty good then. He fired off a shot. He saw ice kick up about ten metres ahead and to the right of his intended target. His second shot was closer, as was his third.

Sergei fired three more shots in response, all wide of the mark. Then Will saw him jump back into the car and set off again.

***

'They may think twice about following now,' Sergei said, although he didn't really believe it.

Traffic both up and now down the hill had so far been non-existent. They had passed no one for miles, so Sergei was using all of the road. But as he rounded the next bend on the wrong side of the road a slow-moving truck was coming up the hill towards them. He swung the car to the right to avoid a collision and grazed the crash barrier. This stopped them careering off the steep cliff road. But hitting the barrier caused the car to skid and drift sideways back across the road towards the bank. Sergei fought to straighten the car, but he over-compensated, the car went sideways then backwards as it spun on the slippery surface. He lost all control. Mikhail gripped hard to his seat.

The Polo moved like a dancer on ice and spun a second time, closer to the barrier – but then there was no barrier – on the car's third spin it spun right over the cliff.

They say that your life flashes before your eyes before you die. But all that happened to Mikhail was a floating sensation – he could see the trees approaching very fast as the car had found air and arced downwards towards the woods two hundred metres below. *How ironic, his last thought, to be killed by a tree like my Uncle Nico.* The force and acceleration as it hit the tree was equivalent to driving into a brick wall at 140mph. He died instantly.

Unlike in the movies the car did not explode immediately on impact. It was just a tangled mess of metal, and a bloody mess of flesh. However, within a few seconds fuel leaked onto the hot engine from the burst petrol tank. The car was quickly engulfed in flames.

Will and Zoe were quickly at the point where the Polo had left the road, they jumped out and looked over the edge to see the burning wreck several hundred metres below in the trees, black smoke already rising rapidly. There was no chance whatsoever that Mikhail and Sergei could have survived that crash.

Forty

The landing was smooth as the wheels touched down at Gatwick at 9pm. Will was tired, but events of the last twelve hours were still bouncing around in his head, so he hadn't even dozed on the plane as he had so much on his mind:

When the dust had settled they had stood for a few minutes at the crash site watching the fire slowly subside, deciding what to do. The lorry driver had seen the crash, stopped and walked back to where Zoe and Will were standing. 'He was driving too fast, it was not my fault,' he had said.

Zoe showed her badge, reassuring him that it was not his fault. 'I'll alert the authorities,' she advised, 'You may need to make a statement, but I saw everything, so you're not to blame and don't need to worry,' she said with compassion.

Zoe took a note of his name and lorry number. After the lorry driver had left she looked Will straight in the eyes.

'I'm sorry for my actions earlier Will, but I needed justice for my Uncle Janos, and I knew that Mikhail would always find a way of escaping prison, so he had to die. I was prepared to sacrifice everything to achieve that. Now I don't have to.'

'It's ok Zoe, I understand.' And he did. Given the chance he would have had no hesitation in shooting Mikhail, the man was pure evil.

Zoe would have to explain the use of her firearm, the six bullets that had been fired. They agreed that it would be simpler if Zoe said she had been protecting them against shots fired by Sergei.

With nothing more to do Will had driven Zoe's car back towards the town. As they got closer Zoe was able to radio in what had happened. The OC dispatched a police car to the crash scene. They met with the OC. It was agreed that Will's entire role in the affair would be excluded from his report. Afterall, he had enough to explain, what with not having thought of a Russian speaker, and sending his men after the wrong car. He decided that it would also be best if Will went straightaway to the airport to fly back to the UK.

Will half expected to see Clive at Gatwick airport, but he didn't appear this time. He guessed that Clive had heard the news about Mikhail so was probably busy trying to explain to his bosses how things had gone so wrong with the arrest of a top crime boss.

He arrived back at the Southend B&B at 10pm, took a shower, then went to bed. He was asleep when his head touched the pillow.

***

Being back in the office on Friday morning felt alien to Will. He had to be business as normal, but his head was constantly replaying the events of the past days. He caught up with Dave and his colleagues then set about trying to deal with some paperwork during the morning, but he couldn't concentrate. Thankfully his HEO colleagues were not in the office that day so he had their shared office to himself. When Clive called him at just before noon he was able to talk freely.

'Will my boy, how are you today?'

Will was getting a little tired of Clive's fatherly tone, but he knew it was just his style; he doubted Clive could change this even if he wanted to.

'I'm fine thanks, I take it you are up to date with events in Lucerne?'

'Yes I've been briefed. A sad end to our Russian friends, but let's not discuss on the phone if you know what I mean.'

He understood. He had learnt somewhere that unless the telephone line was secure it could be tapped by anyone with the knowhow and resources, so Clive was being his usual careful self.

'Meet me at 5pm at the Top Rank Services on the M2,' Clive commanded. Without time for Will to argue or protest, he put the phone down.

Will arrived at the services just before 5pm. The black Granada was easy to spot, he climbed into the back seat like it was his second home. John nodded as usual, Clive wasting no time getting down to business.

'Yet again Will I understand you did a fine job. Zoe has briefed me on the events of yesterday, but I just need to clarify some points, for my report you understand.'

Will wondered where this was going, but apart from the Zoe gun incident, which he was sure she wouldn't have mentioned, he had nothing to hide.

'Before I get to that,' Clive continued, 'I owe it to you to update you on the UK activity and the Irish result. Not that we'd planned it the way it eventually turned out, but a good result in many ways.' He then set out the whole scenario; how the arms had been removed from the lorry by Elias, the plan to make the driver a scapegoat, and the shoot-out near Newry.

Will had learnt some of this from Zoe, but as usual he was astounded by the detail of the planning as well as the execution of operation. And from two planned arrests of top crime bosses, Clive now had two dead ones and several other corpses.

'It is a bit unfortunate that both the crime bosses were killed, as we might have gained some useful intelligence, but I always look on the bright side – they're now out of action and we've saved tax-payers money in trials and incarcerations,' he said happily.

And in Mikhail's case, taken an evil man out of circulation, Will thought.

'Now, I just need to check a couple of things regarding Lucerne, and you can be on your way,' he reminded. 'Zoe reported that you both followed the Polo after it left the yard, but didn't radio this in. Was there a reason for this?' he asked in a formal tone.

Will didn't know what Zoe might have said, but all he could do was tell it how it happened.

'We'd forgotten we had the radio until we were out of range,' he said. 'I guess the volume was turned down?' Even to him this sounded a bit lame, but he couldn't say he suspected Zoe had turned down the volume on purpose.

Clive didn't seem too concerned by his response and asked a further question. 'When you were at the airport in Zurich the previous evening, how did you know that the man travelling with Sergei was not Mikhail?'

Will explained how the man appeared subservient to Sergei which resulted in their decision to follow them. This had led to them discovering Mikhail waiting outside. He ran through how they had managed to get photographs before nearly being caught.

'That was excellent work Will, well done. OK, that's all I need.'

Will thought for a moment and then asked, 'Can you tell me what happened to the other Russians. I know that the two in the office were arrested as were the two watchers, but what about the man who was watching Elias's house?'

'Oh, we arrested him as well, after Zoe had alerted the OC that he was at the house the OC sent a team to get him. The Swiss sweated them all for any useful intelligence, but they were of no help, so were all placed on a plane back to Moscow – no sense in trying to charge them with anything as we had no real evidence of wrongdoing against them. They were only following orders. Laszlo, the man who travelled with Sergei was Hungarian, so he went back to Hungary.'

'That's interesting, I didn't know that. Surely he would have a bit more intelligence if he was working more closely with Mikhail?' Will said, his enquiring mind kicking in.

'Oh, he did, he's been most helpful and will continue to help us. You see, Laszlo works for us!'

Clive ignored Will's look of surprise and continued, 'Once again, thanks for your fine work, and you'll be hearing from me some time soon. Now that you've proved yourself we'll get you some of the training we had hoped to have given you before this mission, so for the next few months that is the plan.'

Then, as if it was an afterthought, but of course it wasn't, 'We've arranged for you, in your Customs job, to join the cadre of overseas trainers. You probably know that this is a new initiative and you fit the criteria. This will make it even easier to deploy you outside of the UK, as necessary. Have a great weekend!'

With that Will was politely kicked-out of the Granada again. He watched as the Granada disappeared from sight

Epilogue

The forensics report from the Swiss authorities was unambiguous. There was no doubt. How could this be, he thought?

...The burnt remains of only one adult were found within the wreckage of the car. A search of the crash site found no evidence of other persons who may have been thrown from the vehicle prior to impact. Forensic examination confirmed the body was that of an adult male, approximately 1.75 meters in length. Forensic anthropologists have determined that the age of the victim is over forty years old and probably less than fifty years old. Best estimations suggest a person of large stature. No fingerprints survived the incineration and positive identification of the body has not been possible.

Clive read the last paragraph again. He pushed his chair back and propped his legs on his desk. He needed to think. The facts were facts, and the forensic scientists could not be mistaken. Should he tell Will? What was the point. It would not change anything. He couldn't imagine how it would make a difference to Will either now or in the future.

He decided to file it.

Printed in Great Britain
by Amazon

43891962R00169